D1246357

WALL STREET TITAN

AN ALPHA ZONE NOVEL

ANNA ZAIRES

♠ MOZAIKA PUBLICATIONS ♠

Published by Mozaika Publications, an imprint of Mozaika LLC.
www.mozaikallc.com

Cover by Najla Qamber Designs
www.najlaqamberdesigns.com

Photography by Wander Aguiar
www.wanderbookclub.com

e-ISBN: 978-1-63142-494-6
ISBN: 978-1-63142-495-3

CHAPTER ONE

mma

"—AND THEN THE VET SAID MR. PUFFS IS NOT READY FOR
that, and I—"

"That's it." Kendall plunks down her glass of ice tea
with such force the six-dollar liquid sloshes over the
rim. Grabbing the napkin, she mops up the spill and
glares at me over her half-eaten plate of buckwheat
crepes.

"What?" I blink at my best friend.

"Do you realize you've been talking about Mr. Puffs
and Cottonball and Queen Elizabeth for the past half
hour?" Kendall leans in, hazel eyes narrowed. "It's cat
this, cat that, vet this."

"Oh." Flushing, I look at the clock on the wall of the
brunch place Kendall dragged me to. Sure enough, it's

1

been almost thirty minutes since we got here—and I haven't shut up during that time. Embarrassed, I look back at Kendall. "Sorry about that. I didn't mean to bore you."

"No, Emma." Kendall's tone is one of exaggerated patience as she leans back, flipping her sleek dark hair over her shoulder. "You didn't bore me. But you did make me realize something."

"What?"

"You, my darling, are officially a cat lady."

My mouth falls open. "What?"

"Yep. A bona fide cat lady."

"I am not!"

"No?" She arches one perfectly shaped eyebrow. "Let's review the facts, then. When was the last time you had your hair professionally styled?"

"Um…" Self-consciously, I tug at the explosion of red curls on my head. "Maybe a year or so ago?" It was, in fact, for Kendall's twenty-fifth birthday party, which means it's been at least eighteen months since anything other than a comb touched the frizzy mess.

"Right." Kendall cuts into her crepe with the daintiness of Queen Elizabeth—my cat, not the British monarch. After chewing her bite, she says, "And your last date was when?"

I have to really think about that one. "Two months ago," I say triumphantly when the recollection finally comes to me. I cut off a piece of my own crepe and fork it into my mouth, muttering, "That's not that long ago."

"No," Kendall agrees. "But I'm talking about a real date, not pity coffee with your sixty-year-old neighbor."

"Roger is not sixty. He's at most forty-nine—"

"And you're twenty-six. End of story. Now don't evade the question. When was the last time you had a real date?"

I pick up my glass of water and chug it down as I try to remember. I have to admit, Kendall stumped me on that one. "Maybe a year ago?" I venture, though I'm pretty sure that the date in question—a less-than-memorable occasion, clearly—predated Kendall's birthday party.

"A year?" Kendall drums her taupe-colored nails on the table. "Really, Emma? A year?"

"What?" Trying to ignore the flush creeping up my neck, I focus on consuming the rest of my twenty-two-dollar crepe. "I'm busy."

"With your cats," she says pointedly. "All three of them. Face it: You're a cat lady."

I look up from my plate and roll my eyes. "Fine. If you insist, then yes, I'm a cat lady."

"And you're okay with that?" She gives me an incredulous look.

"What, should I jump off the Brooklyn Bridge in despair?" I stuff the last bite of my crepe into my mouth. I'm still hungry, but I'm not about to order anything else off the overpriced menu. "Liking cats is not a crime."

"No, but spending all your free time scooping litter

boxes while living in New York City is." Kendall pushes her own empty plate away. "You're at a prime age to nab a man, and you don't date at all."

I blow out an exasperated breath. "Because I just don't have the time—and besides, who says I want to nab anyone? I'm perfectly fine on my own."

"Says she, repeating what every other cat lady tells herself. Honestly, Emma, when was the last time you had sex with anything other than your vibrator?"

Kendall doesn't bother lowering her voice as she says this, and I feel my face turn red again as a gay couple at the table next to us glance over and snicker.

Fortunately, before I can reply, Kendall's Prada purse vibrates.

"Oh." She frowns as she fishes her phone out and reads whatever her screen says. Looking up, she motions at the waiter. "I have to go," she says apologetically. "My boss just had a breakthrough with the dress design he's been struggling with, and he needs me to get some models to him, pronto."

"No worries." I'm used to Kendall's unpredictable job in the fashion industry. Plunking down my debit card, I say, "We'll catch up again soon," and pull out my phone to look at my checking account balance.

———

THE TEMPERATURE OUTSIDE IS JUST ABOVE FREEZING, and the subway station I need is about ten blocks away from the brunch place. Still, I walk because a) my hips could use the exercise and b) I can't afford to do anything else. This outing depleted my weekend budget to the point that I'm going to have to push my grocery trip to Monday. I've told Kendall to stop taking me to expensive places, but I should've known she wouldn't regard a twenty-five-dollar brunch as expensive.

In New York City, that's practically free.

To be fair, Kendall doesn't know just how strained my finances are. My student loans are not something I like to talk about. As far as she's concerned, I live in a basement studio in Brooklyn and clip coupons because I just like to save money. She herself is not exactly pulling in millions—being an assistant to an up-and-coming fashion designer doesn't pay much more than my bookstore job and editing gigs—but her parents cover most of her bills, so all her salary gets spent on clothes and various luxuries.

If she weren't such a good friend, I'd hate her.

As I enter the subway station, I almost trip over a homeless man lounging on the stairs. "Sorry," I mutter, about to scurry away, but he gives me a toothless grin and extends a brown bag toward me.

"It's okay, little lady," he slurs. "Want a sip? Seems like you could use a drink."

Startled, I step back. "No, thanks. I'm okay." How awful do I look if homeless people offer me alcohol? Maybe there *is* something to Kendall's cat-lady diagnosis.

Shrugging, the man takes a swig from the brown

bag, and I dash down the stairs before he offers to share something else with me—like the coins in the hat next to him.

I'm strapped for cash, but I'm not *that* desperate.

———

ONE LONG TRAIN RIDE LATER, I COME OUT OF THE subway in Bay Ridge, my neighborhood in Brooklyn. The second I step outside, a gust of wind hits me in the face.

A gust of wind and something wet.

Sleeting snow.

Great. Just great. Gritting my teeth, I clutch the lapels of my old woolen coat, trying to keep the two edges from separating at my neck, and start walking. I don't live that far from the subway—only five blocks—but they're long blocks, and I curse every one of them as the icy rain intensifies.

"Watch it," a heavyset woman snaps as I bump into her, and I automatically mumble an apology. It's not entirely my fault—it takes two people to bump into one another—but it's not in my nature to be rude.

My grandparents raised me better than that.

When I finally reach the brownstone where I'm renting my basement studio, I feel like I've scaled Mount Everest. My face is wet and frozen, and despite my best efforts to keep my coat closed, the sleet got inside, chilling me from within. I'm one of those people who has to have the top half of her body warm. I can tolerate icy feet—I have those too, since my sneakers are not waterproof—but I can't bear to have cold water trickling down my neck.

If I'd been mad at Mr. Puffs for tearing up my only decent-looking scarf before, it's nothing compared to how I feel now. That cat is going to get it.

"Puffs!" I roar, pushing the door open and stepping into my one-room apartment. "Come here, you evil creature!"

The cat is nowhere to be seen. Instead, Queen Elizabeth gives me a placid stare from my bed and licks her paw, then starts grooming herself, smoothing each fluffy white hair into place. Cottonball is next to her, napping on my pillow. Both felines look warm, content, and utterly carefree, and not for the first time, I feel a pang of irrational envy toward my pets.

I'd love to sleep all day and have someone feed me.

Shivering, I take off my wet coat, hang it up on the hook by the door, and toe off my sneakers. Then I go in search of Mr. Puffs.

I find him in his new favorite place: the top shelf of my closet. It's where I keep hats, gloves, scarves, and bags—not that I own many of each item, which is why it's a tragedy of epic proportions when the evil cat decides to shred one of them to make room for his furry body.

"Puffs, come here." I'm not exactly tall, so I have to stretch up on tiptoes to grab him. Grunting from the effort, I take him down from the shelf. The cat weighs a solid fifteen pounds, and with his paws windmilling in the air, he feels twice as heavy. "I told you you're not allowed to sit there."

I set him down on the floor, and he gives me a squinty-eyed stare that says it's only a matter of time before he gets the rest of my accessories. Like his siblings, Mr. Puffs is white and fluffy, the perfect embodiment of his Persian breed, but that's where the similarity ends. There's nothing calm and placid about him. I'm not sure the cat sleeps. Ever. It's possible he's a vampire who shapeshifts into a huge Persian for daytime.

He's certainly evil enough for that.

Just when I'm about to yell at him again for tearing up the scarf, he rubs his head on my wet jeans and emits a loud purr. Then he looks up at me, big green eyes blinking innocently.

I melt. Or maybe it's the icy droplets clinging to my clothes that are melting, but either way, there's now a warm and fuzzy feeling in my chest.

"All right, come here, you stinker," I mutter, kneeling down to pet the cat. He purrs louder, rubbing his head against my hand like I'm his favorite person in the world. I'm almost certain he's manipulating me on purpose—the cat is scary smart—but I can't help falling for it.

When it comes to my cats, I'm a total pushover.

The petting goes on until Mr. Puffs is certain I'm not going to yell at him. Then he strolls over to my bed and joins the other cats there, curling up on my pillow next to Cottonball.

I sigh and trudge to the bathroom to take a hot shower. As much as I hate to admit it, Kendall is right.

Somewhere along the way, I've turned into a bona fide cat lady.

———

As I shower, I try to convince myself that it's not a big deal. Okay, so my clothes are old and a little ratty, and I don't do anything with my hair except wash it and occasionally put a little gel in it. And yes, I have three cats. So what? Lots of people love animals. It's a positive character trait. I've never trusted anyone who doesn't like pets. It's unnatural, like hating chocolate or ice cream. I can see how one might have preferences when it comes to animals—some sadly misguided individuals prefer dogs to cats, for instance—but not liking pets at all? One might as well be a serial killer.

Nonetheless, something about that label—cat lady —stings a bit. Maybe it's because I'm only twenty-six. Like Kendall said, I'm supposed to be in my prime. If I come across as a hot mess now, what's going to happen when I'm fifty or sixty? Maybe my dateless stretches will widen from a year-plus to a decade, and I'll wander the streets cackling to myself while knitting hats out of cat hair.

No, that's ridiculous. Besides, I don't want a man. I really don't. Okay, fine, maybe I want one for sex—I'm a normal, healthy woman—but I don't need someone dictating my life and dominating my time. That's what happened with Janie, my other best friend from college. She got a serious boyfriend, and now I never see her. And even Kendall, who prides herself on being independent, disappears for weeks at a time when she's dating someone. My last serious boyfriend was my senior year of college, and I nearly flunked a class because he needed so much attention—and that was before I got the cats. Now that Queen Elizabeth, Mr. Puffs, and Cottonball are in my life, I can't imagine squeezing in a man as well.

Still, when I come out of the shower and grab my phone, some devil on my shoulder—a tiny, stylish one who looks suspiciously like Kendall—makes me pull up a dating app that Janie had me join months ago. It's the same one where she met her current boyfriend, the one who made her disappear from my life. Before said disappearance, she somehow strong-armed me into setting up a profile there. I played around with the app for a couple of days with some vague idea of finding a nice, laid-back guy who likes cats and long walks in the park, but after about a dozen dick pics, I gave up and stopped logging in.

"You didn't really give it a shot," Janie said in frustration when I informed her about the pics. "Yeah, there are some assholes on there, but there are also some good guys, like my Landon."

"Right," I said, nodding politely. Kendall and I are both of the opinion that Landon—he of the perpetual sneer and petty gossip—is an ass, but I didn't want to say anything to Janie. In hindsight, though, maybe I should've spoken up, because shortly after Janie made me create that profile, she got sucked into the black hole of her relationship, and Kendall and I haven't seen her since.

Placing the phone on the bed, I arrange my pillows to provide a backrest for me—a move that involves shooing Cottonball and Mr. Puffs off one pillow and moving Queen Elizabeth aside. Cottonball and Queen Elizabeth go amicably enough—Queen Elizabeth even jumps off the bed—but Mr. Puffs gives me an evil stare and swishes his tail threateningly from side to side before curling up next to my feet. I know he's going to remember this offense and seek retaliation later, but for now, I have a comfy spot to look at all the dick pics that are undoubtedly waiting for me on the app.

Plopping down among the pillows, I log into my profile and check the inbox. Sure enough, there are about three hundred messages, with at least a hundred of them containing attachments of penile nature. Just for fun, I click through a few of them—some are actually of decent size and shape—but then I get bored and start systematically erasing them. I don't know how men came up with the idea that dick pics are hot, because they're honestly not. I have nothing against penises, but they don't turn me on unless they're attached to a guy I like. Bonus points if that guy happens to come with washboard abs and nice pecs, but personality is what matters to me most.

I'd sooner date a three-hundred-pound baldie

who's kind to animals and old ladies than a super-model-perfect asshole with a giant cock.

It takes me close to an hour to get through most of the messages. It's when I'm in the home stretch—and firmly convinced I will never, ever use a dating app again—that I see it.

A simple, attachment-free email from a cartoon avatar of a round-faced man with a shy smile.

Intrigued, I click on the message, sent only three days ago.

Hi, Emma, it reads. *I'm sure you get this a lot, but I think you're really cute, and I love the cats in your photo. I myself have two Persians. They're fat and horribly spoiled, but I love them and I'm convinced that despite scratching up all my furniture, they love me back. Other than spending time with them, my hobbies include discovering quirky coffee shops in Brooklyn, reading (historical fiction, mostly), and rollerblading in the park. Oh, and I work in a bookstore while studying to be a veterinarian. Do you think you'd want to meet up for coffee or dinner one of these days? I know a nice little place in Park Slope. Please let me know if that's something you'd be interested in.*

Thank you,

Mark

My pulse racing in excitement, I read the letter again, then go to his profile. There are two actual pictures of Mark there, each showing a guy who appears to be exactly my type. Though the pictures are blurry, they resemble his cartoon avatar quite a bit. His rounded face looks kind, his crooked smile is both shy and self-deprecating, and in one picture, he's wearing glasses that give him a pleasantly intellectual vibe. According to the profile, he's twenty-seven, has brown hair and blue eyes, and lives in Carroll Gardens, Brooklyn.

He's so perfect I could've ordered him off my secret wish list.

Grinning, I reply that I'd love to meet up with him, then jump off the bed and do a happy booty dance. My hair tumbles in frizzy red curls all over my face, and my cats look at me like I'm crazy, but I don't care.

Kendall can shove her cat-lady labels up her skinny little ass.

I have an actual date.

CHAPTER TWO

arcus

"Yes, that's right," I say impatiently. "I want her to be neat and well-groomed at all times. She has to have a sense of style; it's very important. A brunette would be best, but a blonde would work too, as long as her hairstyle is conservative. She can't look like she just stepped out of *Playboy*, understand?"

"Yes, of course, Mr. Carelli." The stylish brunette in front of me crosses her long legs and gives me a polite smile. Victoria Longwood-Thierry, matchmaker for the Wall Street's elite, is exactly what I have in mind for my future wife, except she's in her fifties and married with three children. "What about hobbies and interests?" she asks in her carefully modulated voice. "What would you like her to be into?"

14

"Something intellectual," I say. "I want to be able to talk to her outside the bedroom."

"Of course." Victoria makes a note on her notepad. "How about her profession?"

"That doesn't really matter to me. She can be a lawyer or a doctor or spend all her time doing charity work for orphans in Haiti—it's all the same as far as I'm concerned. Once we marry, she can either stay home with the kids or continue her career. I'm comfortable with either option."

"That's very enlightened of you." Victoria's expression is unchanged, but I get a feeling she's secretly laughing at me. "How do you feel about pets? Do you prefer cats or dogs?"

"Neither. I don't like having animals indoors."

Victoria makes another note before asking, "What about her height? Do you have a preference?"

"Tall," I say immediately. "Or at least above average." I'm six-foot-three, and short women look like children to me.

"Okay, good." Victoria jots it down. "How about body type? Athletic or slender, I would assume?"

I nod tersely. "Yes. I'm into fitness, and I want her to be in good shape so she can keep up with me." Frowning, I glance at my Patek Philippe watch and see that I have only a half hour before the market opens. Turning my attention back to Victoria, I say, "Basically, I want a smart, elegant, stylish woman who takes care of herself."

"Got it. You won't be disappointed, I promise."

I'm skeptical, but I keep a poker face as she gets up and politely ushers me out of her office. She promises to contact me within a couple of days, shakes my hand, and heads back in, leaving behind a cloud of expensive perfume. It's not too strong—Victoria Longwood-Thierry would never be so tacky as to wear strong perfume—but I still sneeze as I head to the elevator.

I'll have to add this to the list: the wife candidate can't wear perfume, period.

By the time I get to my Park Avenue building from Victoria's West Village office, my programmers and traders are glued to their screens. Only a few of them notice as I make my way to my corner office. I'd normally stop by their desks to ask them about their weekend and get an update on our positions, but the market is already open, and I can't distract them.

With ninety-two billion of my investors' money at stake, there is no room for error.

My office is huge and has a great view of the skyscrapers on Park Avenue, but I don't stop to appreciate it. Once, this office felt like the pinnacle of achievement for a scrappy kid from Staten Island, but now I'm hungry for more. Success is my drug, and with each hit, I need a bigger dose to get the buzz. It's not about the money anymore—in addition to my personal stake in the fund, I have a couple of billion stashed away in real estate and other passive investments—it's about knowing that I can do it, that I can succeed where others have failed. The recent market volatility has resulted in record losses for hedge funds and mutual funds alike, but Carelli Capital Management is up in the high teens, outperforming the market by over forty percent. Foundations, pension funds, wealthy individuals—they're all tripping over each other in a rush to invest with me, and I still want more.

I want it all, including a wife who'd fit the life I've worked so hard to build.

On the surface, it should be easy. At thirty-five, I have enough money to keep the female population of Manhattan in Louis Vuitton bags and Louboutin shoes for the rest of their lives, I'm not bad-looking, and I work out daily to stay in shape. The latter I do more for health than vanity, but women seem to appreciate the results. I can pick up any woman in a club in a matter of minutes, but none of them are what I want.

I want high class. I want elegance.

I want a woman who's the complete opposite of the one who raised me—hence, Victoria Longwood-Thierry and her old-money connections.

It was my friend Ashton who pointed me in her direction. "You know the kind of woman you want isn't going to be hanging out at a bar, right?" he said when, after a couple of beers, I mentioned my specifications for a wife. "You're talking about American aristocracy here, Mayflower and all that shit. If you're serious about tapping high-end pussy, you need to talk to my aunt's friend. She's a professional matchmaker working with politicians and rich Wall Street dudes like you. She'll find you exactly what you need."

I laughed and changed the conversation, but the

germ of the idea had been planted, and the more I investigated Ashton's aunt's friend, the more intrigued I became. It turns out Victoria had matched at least two hedge fund managers I know—one with an Olympic gymnast, the other with a Princeton biologist who once moonlighted as a model. Upon further digging, I learned that both marriages are going strong so far, and that, more than anything, convinced me to give the matchmaker a shot.

I intend to be as successful in my personal life as I have been in business, and having the right kind of wife is a big part of that.

Sitting down at my gleaming ebony wood desk, I turn on my Bloomberg monitor and pick up a stack of research reports. I have Victoria on the case, so I put the wife hunt out of my mind and focus on what really matters: my work and making my clients money.

———

It's already eight p.m. when my phone buzzes with an incoming message. Rubbing my eyes, I look away from my computer screen and see that it's a text from Victoria.

I have the perfect candidate for you, the text says. *She can meet you at Sweet Rush Café in Park Slope tomorrow at 6 p.m. If that works for you, I will email you more details. Emmeline lives in Boston and is only in town for a couple of days.*

I frown at my phone. Six o'clock? I almost never

leave the office that early on a Tuesday. And Boston? How am I supposed to get to know this Emmeline if she doesn't live in New York?

I start texting Victoria that I can't make it, but stop at the last moment. This is what I wanted: for Victoria to introduce me to a woman I would never meet on my own. Given the matchmaker's track record, I can spare one evening to see if there's anything worth pursuing there.

Before I can change my mind, I fire off a quick text to Victoria agreeing to the date, and turn my attention back to my computer screen.

If I'm leaving the office early tomorrow, I have to work a few more hours tonight.

mma

I'M ALL BUT BOUNCING WITH EXCITEMENT AS I APPROACH Sweet Rush Café, where I'm supposed to meet Mark for dinner. This is the craziest thing I've done in a while. Between my evening shift at the bookstore and his class schedule, we haven't had a chance to do more than exchange a few text messages, so all I have to go on are those couple of blurry pictures. Still, I have a good feeling about this.

I feel like Mark and I might really connect.

I'm a few minutes early, so I stop by the door and take a moment to brush cat hair off my woolen coat. The coat is beige, which is better than black, but white hair is visible on anything that's not pure white. I figure Mark won't mind too much—he knows how much Persians shed—but I still want to look presentable for our first date. It took me about an hour, but I got my curls to semi-behave, and I'm even wearing a little makeup—something that happens with the frequency of a tsunami in a lake.

Taking a deep breath, I enter the café and look around to see if Mark might already be there.

The place is small and cozy, with booth-style seats arranged in a semicircle around a coffee bar. The smell of roasted coffee beans and baked goods is mouthwatering, making my stomach rumble with hunger. I was planning to stick to coffee only, but I decide to get a croissant too; my budget should stretch to that.

Only a few of the booths are occupied, likely because it's a Tuesday. I scan them, looking for anyone who could be Mark, and notice a man sitting by himself at the farthest table. He's facing away from me, so all I can see is the back of his head, but his hair is short and dark brown.

It could be him.

Gathering my courage, I approach the booth. "Excuse me," I say. "Are you Mark?"

The man turns to face me, and my pulse shoots into the stratosphere.

The person in front of me is nothing like the pictures on the app. His hair is brown, and his eyes are blue, but that's the only similarity. There's nothing rounded and shy about the man's hard features. From the steely jaw to the hawk-like nose, his face is boldly masculine, stamped with a self-assurance that borders on arrogance. A hint of five o'clock shadow darkens his lean cheeks, making his high cheekbones stand out even more, and his eyebrows are thick dark slashes above his piercingly pale eyes. Even sitting behind the table, he looks tall and powerfully built. His shoulders are a mile wide in his sharply tailored suit, and his hands are twice the size of my own.

There's no way this is Mark from the app, unless he's put in some serious gym time since those pictures were taken. Is it possible? Could a person change so much? He didn't indicate his height in the profile, but I'd assumed the omission meant he was vertically challenged, like me.

The man I'm looking at is not challenged in any way, and he's certainly not wearing glasses.

"I'm... I'm Emma," I stutter as the man continues staring at me, his face hard and inscrutable. I'm almost certain I have the wrong guy, but I still force myself to ask, "Are you Mark, by any chance?"

"I prefer to be called Marcus," he shocks me by answering. His voice is a deep masculine rumble that tugs at something primitively female inside me. My heart beats even faster, and my palms begin to sweat as he rises to his feet and says bluntly, "You're not what I expected."

"Me?" *What the hell?* A surge of anger crowds out all other emotions as I gape at the rude giant in front of me. The asshole is so tall I have to crane my neck to look up at him. "What about you? You look nothing like your pictures!"

"I guess we've both been misled," he says, his jaw tight. Before I can respond, he gestures toward the booth. "You might as well sit down and have a meal with me, Emmeline. I didn't come all the way here for nothing."

"It's *Emma*," I correct, fuming. "And no, thank you. I'll just be on my way."

His nostrils flare, and he steps to the right to block my path. "Sit down, *Emma*." He makes my name sound like an insult. "I'll have a talk with Victoria, but for now, I don't see why we can't share a meal like two civilized adults."

The tips of my ears burn with fury, but I slide into the booth rather than make a scene. My grandmother instilled politeness in me from an early age, and even as an adult living on my own, I find it hard to go against her teachings.

She wouldn't approve of me kneeing this jerk in the balls and telling him to fuck off.

"Thank you," he says, sliding into the seat across from me. His eyes glint icy blue as he picks up the menu. "That wasn't so hard, was it?"

"I don't know, *Marcus*," I say, putting special emphasis on the formal name. "I've only been around you for two minutes, and I'm already feeling homicidal." I deliver the insult with a ladylike, Grandma-approved smile, and dumping my purse in the corner of my booth seat, I pick up the menu without bothering to take off my coat.

The sooner we eat, the sooner I can get out of here.

A deep chuckle startles me into looking up. To my shock, the jerk is grinning, his teeth flashing white in his lightly bronzed face. No freckles for him, I note with jealousy; his skin is perfectly even-toned, without so much as an extra mole on his cheek. He's not classically handsome—his features are too bold to be described that way—but he's shockingly good-looking, in a potent, purely masculine way.

To my dismay, a curl of heat licks at my core, making my inner muscles clench.

No. No way. This asshole is *not* turning me on. I can barely stand to sit across the table from him.

Gritting my teeth, I look down at my menu, noting with relief that the prices in this place are actually reasonable. I always insist on paying for my own food on dates, and now that I've met Mark—excuse me, *Marcus*—I wouldn't put it past him to drag me to some ritzy place where a glass of tap water costs more than a shot of Patrón. How could I have been so wrong about the guy? Clearly, he'd lied about working in a bookstore and being a student. To what end, I don't know, but everything about the man in front of me screams wealth and power. His pinstriped suit hugs his broad-shouldered frame like it was tailor-made for him, his blue shirt is crisply starched, and I'm pretty sure his subtly checkered tie is some designer brand that makes Chanel seem like a Walmart label.

As all of these details register, a new suspicion occurs to me. Could someone be playing a joke on me? Kendall, perhaps? Or Janie? They both know my taste in guys. Maybe one of them decided to lure me on a date this way—though why they'd set me up with *him*, and he'd agree to it, is a huge mystery.

Frowning, I look up from the menu and study the man in front of me. He's stopped grinning and is perusing the menu, his forehead creased in a frown that makes him look older than the twenty-seven years listed on his profile.

That part must've also been a lie.

My anger intensifies. "So, *Marcus*, why did you write to me?" Dropping the menu on the table, I glare at him. "Do you even own cats?"

He looks up, his frown deepening. "Cats? No, of course not."

The derision in his tone makes me want to forget all about Grandma's disapproval and slap him straight across his lean, hard face. "Is this some kind of a prank for you? Who put you up to this?"

"Excuse me?" His thick eyebrows rise in an arrogant arch.

"Oh, stop playing innocent. You lied in your message to me, and you have the gall to say *I'm* not what you expected?" I can practically feel the steam coming out of my ears. "*You* messaged *me*, and I was entirely truthful on my profile. How old are you? Thirty-two? Thirty-three?"

"I'm thirty-five," he says slowly, his frown returning. "Emma, what are you talking—"

"That's it." Grabbing my purse by one strap, I slide out of the booth and jump to my feet. Grandma's teachings or not, I'm not going to have a meal with a jerk who's admitted to deceiving me. I have no idea what would make a guy like that want to toy with me, but I'm not going to be the butt of some joke.

"Enjoy your meal," I snarl, spinning around, and stride to the exit before he can block my way again.

I'm in such a rush to leave I almost knock over a tall, slender brunette approaching the café and the short, pudgy guy following her.

arcus

GRIPPING THE EDGE OF THE TABLE, I WATCH THE LITTLE redhead fly out of the restaurant, her curvy ass swaying from side to side. Even in the shapeless woolen coat, her small, lush figure is unmistakably feminine... and bizarrely sexy. I've never particularly liked curvy women, but the moment Emma came up to me, my hormones shot into overdrive and my cock turned rock hard.

If I hadn't been wearing a suit, it would've been downright embarrassing.

As it was, all of my social graces deserted me as soon as I laid eyes on her. With her wild red curls and Salvation Army sense of style, Emma was so unlike the images in my mind—and so strangely appealing despite that fact—that I straight up told her she wasn't what I'd expected. As soon as the words left my mouth, I wanted to take them back, but it was too late. Her clear gray eyes narrowed, her rosebud mouth tightened, and her flame-bright hair seemed to puff up, each curl quivering with indignation. Then she retorted that *I* looked different from my pictures, and things escalated from there. I don't remember the last time I've been less than polite with a woman, but with Emma, it was as if I'd turned into a caveman.

I all but ordered her to join me, going so far as to use my size to intimidate her into complying.

Why did Victoria send her to me—if she did, that is? Now that all the blood isn't rushing to my groin, the redhead's behavior strikes me as extremely odd. Her accusations and ramblings about cats make zero sense... unless there's been some kind of misunderstanding.

Shit.

I slide out of the booth to follow the woman, but before I can take two steps, a tall, elegant brunette steps into my path. "Hi, Marcus," she says with a cool, graceful smile. "I'm Emmeline Sommers. Sorry I'm late."

Even before she says her name, I know who she is—and I know I fucked up big.

This is the woman Victoria was talking about, the one whose file I didn't have a chance to download before getting called into an emergency meeting with my portfolio managers. Victoria sent Emmeline's pictures and bio to me this afternoon, and between the meeting and taking the subway to avoid rush-hour traffic, I showed up at the café completely unprepared—something I'd normally never do. I figured it wasn't a big deal—I'd just confess my unpreparedness to Emmeline, and we'd have a good time getting to know one another—but I didn't count on a similarly named woman who, by some bizarre coincidence, must've also come to the café on a blind date with a guy who shares my name. What were the fucking odds of *that*?

Staring at the brunette in front of me, I can't believe I mistook Emma for her. No two women could be more different. Emmeline is Princess Diana, Jackie Kennedy, and Gisele all rolled up into one stunning package. I can easily picture her at the social functions and political events that are increasingly a part of my life. She'd know which fork to use and how to make small talk with senators and waiters alike, while Emma... Well, I can see her bouncing on my dick, and that's about it.

Pushing the pornographic images out of my mind, I smile at the tall brunette. "No problem," I say, reaching out to shake her hand. "I only got here a few minutes ago myself. It's a pleasure meeting you."

Emmeline's fingers are long and slim, her skin cool and dry to the touch. "Same here," she says, squeezing my hand with just the right amount of pressure before gracefully lowering her arm. "Thank you for coming all the way out here to meet with me. My sister is a

29

student at the Brooklyn Conservatory of Music, so I'm staying in the area until my flight tomorrow morning."

"Of course. Thank you for taking the time to meet with me," I say as we sit down at the table.

For the next few minutes, we make small talk and get to know one another. I don't say anything about the mix-up with Emma—I don't need Emmeline thinking I'm a total idiot—but I do explain that I didn't have a chance to review the file Victoria sent me. As I'd hoped, Emmeline waves away my apologies, saying that it's just as well that we can get to know each other without preconceived notions. It's obvious, however, that she's gone through her file on me. She knows everything about me, from my Wharton MBA to my current role as the head of one of the most successful hedge funds in New York City.

After we place our order with the waiter, I learn that Emmeline is thirty-one years old and a graduate of Harvard Law. For the past three years, she's headed a nonprofit foundation providing legal services for abused women and children. She's passionate about her work and spends over eighty hours a week on the foundation; it's not just a hobby for her, though her family is wealthy enough that she could've done absolutely anything career-wise—or nothing.

"My great-great-grandfather made a fortune in railroads way back when," she says, smiling. "And my family has somehow managed to retain and grow it over the past century and a half. So yes, I'm one of those trust fund babies." Her smile holds a self-deprecating charm that softens the aristocratic lines of her face, and I find myself genuinely liking her.

Emmeline is the real deal, the woman I've been hoping to meet ever since I decided to set my sights on yet another marker of success: the ultimate trophy wife.

As the waiter brings out our food, we discuss everything from world events to the recent volatility in the market, and I find that Emmeline's views closely align with my own. She's knowledgeable and thoughtful in her opinions, her legal training evident in her well-reasoned approach to most issues. I enjoy listening to her, and she seems interested in what I have to say as well.

It also doesn't hurt that she's beautiful to look at, in a sleek, thoroughbred kind of way. Her long-sleeved sweater dress is stylish without being trendy, her accessories are expensive but understated, and her smooth dark hair is cut in flattering layers around her perfectly oval face.

She's a strikingly attractive woman, yet as I observe the graceful way she holds her fork, it suddenly dawns on me that I'm not attracted to her. I like the way she looks, but it's the same kind of appreciation I might have for a visually pleasing piece of art or sculpture—a purely intellectual pleasure that's the complete opposite of my visceral reaction to the redhead.

No. Stop. Before my mind can travel further down that path, I force all thoughts of Emma away. Emmeline is the woman I've always wanted, and I can't fuck it up by following the urgings of my suddenly unruly cock.

For a while, I succeed in focusing solely on Emmeline. She's a good conversationalist, and as we eat, we exchange amusing stories about school and work. I tell her about the trader in my fund who wears orange sneakers as a good-luck charm, and she tells me about her sister's penchant for dating long-haired hipster boys. Midway through the meal, I have to excuse myself to take an important call from work, and she doesn't bat an eye at that. Nor does she look the least bit put off when I have to fire off a few urgent emails upon returning to the table. It's obvious she understands the demands of a high-pressure job like mine. Still, I apologize, and she laughs it off, explaining that her father, a high-powered corporate attorney, hadn't gotten through a single dinner during her childhood without a work emergency of some kind. We chat about her family for a while—they're all as successful as she is—and then we return to more serious topics, like the political climate and what it means for the global economy. It's when we're in the middle of discussing the new mayor—whom Emmeline knows personally—that she glances at the corner of the booth and says, "Oh, look. Someone forgot a phone here."

My pulse leaps with inexplicable excitement. "A phone?"

Emmeline nods and holds up a smartphone in a battered pink case. "I found it in the corner of the seat. Here, let me go give it to our waiter..." She moves to slide out of her seat, but before she can get up, I reach over and snatch the phone from her hand.

"No need." I fight to keep my voice even as I pocket the device. "I know who this belongs to. There was a woman sitting here before us; it must've fallen out of her bag. I'll make sure it gets back to her."

"You will?" A frown creases Emmeline's smooth brow. She's confused by my behavior, and she's not the only one.

"I'll have my assistant take care of it," I lie. "She's good at stuff like that." That last part is true—Lynette is highly resourceful—but there's no way I'm getting her involved.

I want to return this phone personally. No, I *need* to return it. The urge is practically a compulsion. I have to see the redhead again—if only so I can confirm that my insane attraction to her was a fluke, and she's not nearly as appealing as my dick remembers.

"Okay, if you're sure..." Emmeline is still looking at me like I lost my mind, so I give her my most engaging smile and shift the conversation back to the mayor. My pulse is hammering with anticipation at the thought of tracking down Emma, but I'm not about to fuck things up with Emmeline.

Once I return this phone, Emma will be off my mind, and I'll be able to focus on what I really want: a wife who'll be as big of an achievement as the billions in my bank account.

mma

ASSHOLE. JERK. SLEAZEBALL LIAR. FUMING, I STOMP DOWN the street, barely cognizant of the pedestrians getting out of my way. I can't remember the last time I've been so mad. My blood is all but boiling in my veins.

How dare he write to me with a fake profile and then act like *I'm* a disappointment? Okay, so maybe I did put up my more flattering pictures on the dating app, but what woman doesn't? It's not like I used someone else's photos or even particularly old photos. The two pictures I uploaded were taken less than a year ago, when I was actually a few pounds heavier than I am now. So if anything, I look better now—or skinnier, at least. In any case, I don't see how he could've been disappointed by my physique—I'd even put my height and weight in the profile. And the cat thing? What the hell was that about? Why would he claim to love cats and then act like I'd confessed to having the plague?

In general, why would a man like that—good-looking and obviously successful—want to mess with a random girl from a dating app?

I'm so angry I make it to the subway and onto the train on autopilot. It's not until I'm a couple of stops away from my station that my temper cools enough for me to go over what happened without choking with fury.

Taking a calming breath, I review the facts. Key point number one: The man at the café insisted that I call him Marcus instead of Mark, though he wrote to me as Mark. Key point number two: He turned out to be thirty-five years old with no cats, and he looked nothing like the blurry pictures in his profile. As I put those facts together and analyze them without the jerk's proximity scrambling my brain, an embarrassing possibility occurs to me.

Could I have approached the wrong man after all?

Emmeline, he'd called me. Is it possible? Could he have been meeting someone by that name and mistaken me for her? The odds of Mark/Marcus and Emma/Emmeline on a blind date in the same place are slim, to say the least, but weirder things have happened. When Grandma met Gramps for the first time, he mistook her for one of his cousins and decided to prank her by dunking her in a pond—where a neighbor's secretly kept alligator promptly latched onto her foot. Grandma still has scars from that incident, and Gramps looks guilty whenever Grandma recounts that story—which is often.

So, yeah, crazy stuff happens, and just because something isn't likely doesn't mean it's impossible. Going by that logic, it's entirely possible that Marcus is not a total asshole.

He's just not Mark.

Groaning mentally, I snake my hand into my purse and rummage around for my phone. If I'm right, I probably have an email or a text from the real Mark, wondering where I am and why I stood him up.

It takes a full minute of rummaging for me to realize that I'm not finding the phone.

My heartbeat spikes, and a sick feeling twists my stomach. *No. Please, no.*

My hands shaking, I dump the contents of my bag onto an empty seat next to me and survey them in horror.

On the plastic orange seat next to me are a worn leather wallet, a few wadded-up tissues, a green scrunchie, a bottle of Tylenol, my apartment keys, a laser pointer, and an ancient pack of bubblegum—but no phone in a bright pink case.

Not even a hint of a phone.

I must've lost it somewhere.

Tears spring to my eyes, blurring my vision as I stuff everything back into my purse. I know that in the grand scheme of things, losing a phone is not a big deal. If Gramps saw me so upset over a *thing*, he'd give me a stern talking-to and remind me about what really matters: family, health, and doing what you love. And while I know all of that to be true, I simply can't afford that kind of hit to my bank account right now. A couple of my regular editing clients ran into some difficulties with their latest novels, so I haven't had a lengthy editing gig since the summer, leaving me with only my bookstore cashier's salary to live on. Normally, that would suffice—I know how to stretch a penny—but between the interest rate spike on my student loans and the vet bill for Cottonball's scratched nose two weeks ago, my account is a few dollars away from an overdraft fee.

I'm literally living paycheck to paycheck, and a new phone is not something I can afford.

Stop whining, Emma, and think. Where could you have lost the phone?

I can practically hear Gramps saying that to me, so I suck in a deep breath and push away my panic. I tend to get overemotional—it's the Irish in me, Grandma says—and I need to get a grip on myself. Freaking out won't solve anything.

Ignoring the stares from the other passengers on the train, I get down on all fours and peer under my seat on the off chance that the phone fell out at some point during the train ride.

Nothing—or at least nothing resembling my phone. There are gum wrappers and weird sticky-looking stains, but that's not what I'm after.

I get back on my seat and rub my hands together to brush off the floor cooties. The panic is bubbling up again, but I push it away and concentrate on mentally retracing my steps.

Did I have my phone with me on the ride to the café? Yes. I remember playing *Angry Birds* during the subway ride.

Did I have it when I got out of the subway? Yes. I used Google Maps to guide me from the subway to the café.

Did I check it at the restaurant? No. I was too occupied with the jerk.

Did I check it when I left the restaurant? No. I was too busy fuming about the jerk, plus I remembered where the subway was without needing to check the maps.

The mental Q&A calms me a bit, as does the realization that I must've lost the phone at some point between the café and now. Maybe if I'm really lucky, it's still in the café, and if I go back, I'll be able to find it.

Thus resolved, I get off the train at the next stop and go across the platform to get the one heading in the opposite direction. It takes a solid twenty minutes before it comes—*stupid MTA with its endless delays*—but finally, I'm on the train heading back to the café. I still haven't had dinner, so I'm both tired and hungry, but I'm determined.

If my phone is at that café, I'm getting it back.

I can't let this date from hell become a complete disaster.

CHAPTER SIX

*M*arcus

I KNOW IT'S NOT THE BEST THING FOR MY FUTURE relationship with Emmeline, but as soon as we're done eating, I order an Uber instead of inviting her out for drinks. I use her morning flight to Boston to justify the early end of our date, but in reality, I'm anxious to begin my search for the redhead.

As ridiculous as it is, I *need* to return that phone.

The Uber ride to Emmeline's hotel takes about a half hour in traffic. I come out of the car to open the door for her and walk her to the hotel entrance, where I give her a gentlemanly peck on the cheek and promise to call her. It's a promise I fully intend to keep —Emmeline is what I want, after all—but tonight, I need to get away from her.

I have to locate Emma and rid myself of this budding obsession.

The moment Emmeline disappears through the revolving hotel doors, I step to the side and pull out the pink phone. It's an older Android model, and fortunately, there is no password required to unlock the screen.

I start by pulling up the pictures to make sure that it is, in fact, Emma's phone. At first, all I find are snapshots of fluffy white cats—*how many does she have?*—but soon, I come across a smiling selfie of a redhead in a tank top and loose pajama pants.

It's Emma all right.

My heartbeat speeds up, and my suit pants suddenly feel tight. There's nothing in that picture that's meant to be seductive—she's sitting with her knees pulled up to her chest, so I can't even see the shape of her breasts —but something about the pale curves of her shoulders, the scattering of freckles across her nose, and the dimples in her cheeks makes me harder than an iron rod.

Fuck. What am I doing?

Lowering the phone, I lean back against the outside wall of the hotel and squeeze my eyes shut. There's something seriously wrong with me today. I never act impulsively or irrationally, yet I just cut short a date with the woman of my dreams and let her go back to her hotel room without so much as an attempt to kiss her—all so I could chase after a girl who is the complete opposite of what I need.

Maybe I *should* have my assistant return the phone to Emma. If I had such a strong reaction to her picture, it's probably not a good idea for me to see her in person again.

Opening my eyes, I look at the pink phone again. Emma's softly rounded face, framed by a halo of wild red curls, looks back at me, her gray eyes full of mischief.

Mischief and something so warm and seductive I can't help reacting to it.

Something I can't help wanting.

Staring at that picture, I understand for the first time how powerful the lure of temptation can be. Smoking, drugs, unhealthy foods, laziness—those have never been my vices. My self-discipline is legendary among my friends and colleagues. Once I set my mind on something, I do it, and I don't let anything stand in my way. Whether it's running a marathon in two and a half hours or graduating from college in two and a half years, I'm able to set goals and achieve them, and I've never understood people who say they want to do something but lack the willpower to make it happen.

Yet here I am, staring at a selfie of a woman I know would be bad for me. She's chocolate and lazy days on the couch, Netflix binging and a pack of cigarettes. She's everything I can't have and shouldn't want—an unhealthy temptation that can ruin everything. The smart thing to do would be to go home and hand over this phone to Lynette first thing in the morning. That way, I can get a good night's sleep and call Emmeline tomorrow to set a time for us to meet again—maybe even arrange a trip to her hometown of Boston.

That's the smart thing to do, but I don't do it. Instead, my hand seems to move of its own accord as my fingers swipe across the screen to get to the contacts icon. My heart thuds in a heavy, expectant rhythm as I scroll through the list of names until I get to H, where I find the entry called "Home."

Sure enough, there is an address there. When I pull out my own phone and type it into Google Maps, I see that it's in Bay Ridge, a neighborhood in Brooklyn that's not too far from here.

If I hurry, I'll make it there before it's late enough for my visit to be creepy.

Giving in to temptation for the first time in my adult life, I order another Uber to Emma's address in Bay Ridge. It's not so bad, I tell myself as I get in the car. Once I get rid of this phone, I'll forget the little redhead once and for all.

I won't let this strange new weakness of mine ruin what I've worked so hard to build.

CHAPTER SEVEN

Emma

"You didn't find anything? It's in a pink case..." I can't hide the disappointment in my voice, and the waiter gives me a sympathetic look.

"No, sorry," he says. "Wish I could help. The couple who were sitting there just left, and they didn't say anything about a phone."

"Do you mind if I take a look around the table?" I ask, glancing over at the booth where I'd approached Marcus—who may or may not be an asshole, depending on his true identity.

"Sure, go ahead," the waiter says.

I walk over to the booth, trying not to think about the man who'd sat there, but I'm not entirely successful. For some reason, my skin feels uncomfortably warm, and my breathing picks up as I picture his cool blue eyes and big hands. And if his hands are that size, how big is his—

No, stop. Focus on the phone.

With effort, I push away the graphic images flooding my mind and crouch to peer under the table.

Nothing.

I look all over the seats next.

Nothing.

Disappointment presses down on me, making my empty stomach roil with anxiety. I didn't see the phone on the street as I was retracing my steps, and if it's not in the restaurant, then it's well and truly lost. Maybe even stolen—in which case the phone-tracking app on my computer, which I was planning to check as the next step, would not help either.

Exhausted and dispirited, I trudge back to the subway. At this point, I'm almost light-headed from hunger, so I buy a banana from a street vendor—I can still afford *that*—and munch on it as I go down the steps to the train.

All I want is to get home, take a hot shower, and curl up with my cats.

This day is officially a disaster.

I'm never, ever using a dating app again.

CHAPTER EIGHT

*M*arcus

WHERE THE HELL IS SHE?

Standing by the side entrance of an ugly old brownstone, I ring the doorbell for the second time, with the same lack of results.

Emma Walsh is not home.

I know her last name thanks to her Facebook profile, which I accessed by tapping on the Facebook icon on her phone. According to that same profile, she's single (which I already suspected), twenty-six years old, and a graduate of Brooklyn College. She loves books and does freelance editing when she's not working at a small, family-owned bookstore. Oh, and she definitely owns cats—three of them, judging by her frequent posts about them on Facebook.

Knowing all this about a woman I met by accident makes me feel like a stalker, a feeling that's only exacerbated by my inexplicable desire to learn more. I played a bit with her phone on the way here—to make sure I had the right address, I told myself—and in the process, I've looked at everything from her photos to her email. I didn't read any of the email because that would've been *really* wrong, but I did glance at the subject lines. It seems like most of her inbox is occupied by messages related to her editing jobs, though there are a bunch of emails from someone named Kendall, too. Same goes for texts, though most of those are from "Grandma" and "Gramps," who I'm guessing are her grandparents.

Fuck, I *am* being a stalker.

Disgusted with myself, I turn to leave so I can give the phone to my assistant tomorrow and forget this madness, but at that moment, a small, shapely figure with curly hair approaches from the street... and freezes in place, her hands flying up to grab at the strap of her cheap purse.

In a flash, it dawns on me how I must look to Emma, with my features cast in shadow by the tiny light hanging over the door. If I were a young woman confronted by an unknown six-foot-three man on her doorstep in the dark, I'd probably be shitting my pants right about now.

"It's me, Marcus," I say quickly, wanting to reassure her. I might've acted like a stalker, but I don't mean her any harm. "From the café, remember?"

She takes a step back, still gripping her purse strap.

"What—what are you doing here?" She sounds breathless; I must've really scared her. "How did you find me?"

"Your phone," I explain, pulling the pink smartphone out of my pocket. "I found it in the booth after you left and wanted to return it to you."

"Oh." She approaches uncertainly. As the over-the-door light illuminates her pale face, I see that her expression is a mix of relief and confusion. Stopping a couple of feet away, she says in a slightly calmer voice, "Thank you. I was looking for that phone. I was almost home when I realized that I didn't have it, so I went back to the café, and the waiter said they didn't find anything and—" Cutting herself off, she takes a deep breath and says, "I'm really glad you found it, but you didn't have to come all the way here. I could've just met you somewhere tomorrow or—"

"It's not that far out of my way," I say. It's a lie, but I'm not about to admit the full extent of my insanity. "I figured you might worry, so I brought it."

She stares up at me, her gray eyes dark in the evening shadows. "Oh. Okay, well, thank you. That's very kind of you."

She extends her hand, and I give her the phone. She's careful to take it in such a way that our fingers don't touch—something I irrationally resent. Even worse, the moment the phone is out of my hands, I regret giving it to her so quickly. That phone was the only thing linking us together, and now I have no reason to be here—except my inexplicable desire to get to know her.

"Emma, listen," I say as she pockets the phone with evident relief. "I think I made a mistake earlier, at the café."

"You were supposed to meet someone named Emmeline?" A small smile appears on her lips, and I realize she's figured it out too.

"That's right." I grin at her. "Let me guess. You were supposed to meet Mark?"

"Yep." Her smile widens, exposing small white teeth and the same cute dimples I saw on the selfie. "What are the odds, right?"

"I can have one of my analysts look into that if you want," I say, only half-kidding. Researching the answer to her rhetorical question would give me an excuse to stay in touch—something I badly want. With that dimpled smile, the little redhead looks so fucking adorable I want to lick her like an ice cream cone. "I'm sure we can figure it out if we run some statistics on naming trends in the population," I add.

Emma blinks, her smile dimming. "One of your analysts? Do you run a think tank or something?"

"A hedge fund," I say. "We employ a multitude of strategies to stay ahead of the market, everything from traditional equity analysis to quant-driven trading."

The dimples disappear completely. "Oh, I see." She looks disappointed, a reaction that's the complete opposite from the one I get when women realize I must have some serious dough. Pasting on a new, less sincere smile, she says, "Thanks again for returning the phone, Marcus. I really appreciate you coming all the way out here. If you'll excuse me..." She gives me an expectant look, and I realize I'm still standing on her doorstep, blocking the door.

I should move—that would be the polite, gentlemanly thing to do—but I don't. Instead, I ask bluntly, "Do you hate Wall Street or something?"

I know I'm borderline harassing the girl, but I can't let her go like this. Once she gets into her apartment—a shithole place, judging by the rundown state of the door—it'll all be over. She'll go about her life, and I'll return to mine, and I'm not ready for that to happen.

"Um, no. I don't have anything against your profession. I mean, not really." She gives me a wary look. "I just—" She inhales. "Look, Marcus, I really appreciate the gesture and all, but I'm hungry and exhausted, and I still need to feed my cats and answer some emails. We can debate Wall Street ethics some other time."

Some other time? Something tense inside me relaxes. Though she undoubtedly meant her words as a polite brush-off, I'm going to take them at face value.

I'm going to see Emma again and figure out what it is that draws me to her.

Stepping aside, I say, "Sounds good. Goodnight, Emma. It was a pleasure meeting you."

"Same here. Goodbye, Marcus, and thanks again," she says, pulling her keys out of her purse as she steps around me.

I watch her open the door, making sure she gets

inside safely, and when the door closes behind her, I order another Uber and make a note on my phone about the next steps. My pulse is thrumming with excitement, and my muscles are coiled tight in antici-pation of the new challenge.

I'm acting completely unlike myself, but I no longer care. Emma might not be what I need for the long term, but she's what I want for the moment, and for the first time in my life, I'm going to live in the present.

I'm going to have the lush little redhead for dessert and worry about consequences later.

CHAPTER NINE

mma

My legs are shaking as I make it into my apartment and hang up my coat by the door. Whatever little energy I got from eating the banana is long gone, and I'm all but passing out from hunger. Despite that, I have the strange sensation that I'm floating on air, my heart racing from the aftereffects of adrenaline and dizzying excitement.

Marcus—tall, arrogant Marcus with his perfectly tailored suit and a coat that costs more than my quarterly rent—came to my apartment and returned my phone.

It seems impossible, surreal, yet it clearly happened, as I'm holding said phone in my hand. He gave it to me, and now instead of worrying about the hit to my bank account, I'm unsettled for a completely different reason. My breathing is panic-attack fast, my palms are sweating, and I feel so wired I could bounce off the walls despite my exhaustion.

Holy. Fucking. Shit. Marcus came to my apartment.

When I first saw him standing there, looking like some kind of caped villain in his unbuttoned knee-length winter coat, I thought he was a burglar and nearly had a heart attack. Because why else would someone be lurking on my doorstep so late in the evening? I was a second away from screaming my head off and sprinting away when he spoke, and then my knees went weak for a different reason.

The man who was on my mind all through the subway ride home—the man I was convinced I'd never see again—was by my door, being the complete opposite of an asshole.

Right now, I'm too tired and hyper to figure out what that whole encounter meant, so I don't even try. Instead, I focus on my cats, who are all rushing toward me, meowing loudly. Mr. Puffs, as the biggest, pushes Queen Elizabeth and Cottonball out of the way and stakes his claim on me by winding his giant furry body between my legs as I attempt to make my way to the kitchen.

"Stop it, Puffs," I order, but he ignores me, rubbing himself on my calves to mark his territory. His siblings follow in a calmer fashion; as usual, they let Mr. Puffs be the annoying one.

"Oh, come on, just give me a second," I say in exasperation, nearly tripping over his tail. "I'm getting you food, I promise."

Cottonball lets out a loud meow at the mention of food, and Queen Elizabeth joins in with her softer, more delicate voice.

Even when hungry, she sounds like a lady.

When I finally make it into my tiny kitchen, I grab three cans of cat food and open them, putting their contents on three individual plates. My cats are very particular about their food, so I'm careful to put on each plate the precise flavor and brand that cat prefers. Queen Elizabeth likes Fancy Feast Wild Salmon, Cottonball likes variety so he's getting the Chicken Feast Classic today, and Mr. Puffs has developed a taste for Purina Seafood Stew Entree. Once Puffs finishes his portion, he'll eat some of Queen Elizabeth's and Cottonball's too, but he has to start with his own plate.

I suspect it's because he feels more like the boss that way.

As soon as I put the plates on the floor, the cats dive in, and I'm free to feed myself. Fortunately, I got my bookstore paycheck on Monday, so my fridge is full. I have fruits, vegetables, bread, and some deli meats, so I slap together a quick sandwich and devour it while standing in the kitchen. Then, feeling infinitely more human, I check to see if I got any messages from the real Mark.

To my disappointment, the answer is no. He must've taken offense to being stood up and decided to forego all contact with me. Though I'm exhausted, I write him a quick email with an apology and explanation about the mix-up, and then I finally head to the shower.

I have to rinse off the city grime before I get into bed.

––––––––

BY THINKING ABOUT WAYS TO GET NEW EDITING CLIENTS, I manage to keep my mind off Marcus all through the shower. It's only when I'm lying under the covers, surrounded by my cats, that I realize I'm still far too hyper to sleep. It's as if an electric current is buzzing under my skin, keeping my heart rate elevated and my body uncomfortably warm.

Marcus was waiting by my door when I came home. He came all the way here to return my phone.

It still feels unreal, partially because it's hard to believe he went to such trouble just to be nice. Though our meeting in the café was brief, Marcus didn't strike me as much of a good Samaritan. Nor is his choice of profession indicative of a man who's particularly altruistic. I was an English major in college, but I know several finance majors who went to work on Wall Street after graduation, and all of them are highly ambitious, driven to maximize their productivity and monetize (their terminology, not mine) every hour of their time. They're Type A in the extreme, and if Marcus runs his own hedge fund, he must be that, times a hundred.

It doesn't make sense for a man like that to spend his limited free time returning a phone to a stranger—not unless he had some other agenda. Only I can't think of what that agenda might've been. Unless... Could he have been hoping I'd reward him financially?

Crap. I didn't think about it, but I should've probably offered him some money for his trouble.

For a moment, I feel awful, but then I remember his suit and coat—not to mention his Italian leather shoes—and my guilt fades. I doubt Marcus needs my twenty bucks, certainly not enough to go out of his way to get them. So why did he come? My phone doesn't require a password to unlock, so he could've just emailed me from my own email, and I would've picked up the device from wherever Marcus told me to meet him.

Hell, he could've had one of his analysts—say, the one he was planning to task with researching the odds of our meeting—return the phone on his behalf.

The only other explanation that occurs to me is so ridiculous that I dismiss it right away. There's no way he's interested in me in *that way*. I'm not particularly insecure about my looks—I got over that in college—but I *am* realistic. I know I'm nowhere near Marcus's league. He undoubtedly has gorgeous women falling all over themselves for the privilege of decorating his arm; he wouldn't need to go after a short, frizzy-haired redhead with too-wide hips. Besides, wasn't he meeting someone? This Emmeline that he mistook me for? With a fancy name like that, I bet *her* hips are in perfect proportion to her body, and her hair magically behaves at all times.

Okay, maybe that last bit is complete conjecture, but still, I'm almost certain I'm not Marcus's type.

So why did he come tonight? The question torments me as I toss and turn, trying to get comfortable enough to fall asleep. It's only when Mr. Puffs lies down on top of my head, pinning me in place, that I'm able to drift off.

My dreams that night are filled with big, hard-faced burglars in capes... and sex.

Lots and lots of steamy, dirty sex.

CHAPTER TEN

*M*arcus

"You want me to do what?" Lynette gapes at me, her round tortoise-shell glasses sliding down her long nose.

"I want you to send flowers and some cat food to the address I emailed you," I repeat, frowning at my assistant. "Is that a problem?"

"No, of course not." Lynette quickly regroups, her professional mask falling into place. "Do you have a preference when it comes to the type of flowers and the brand of the, um… cat food?"

"Roses—pink and white," I say. "At least a dozen of each. No, make that two dozen of each. As far as cat food, I don't know. What do cats like?"

"Depends on the cat, I think," Lynette says,

sounding more like her efficient self. "Some owners feed their cats only wet canned food; others do a mix of wet and dry. Do you happen to know about the cat in question?"

"Cats, plural," I correct. "And no, I don't. Why don't you do this? Get a variety of cat food brands, both wet and dry, and send them with the flowers. I'll email you the note to add."

"Okay, I'm on it." Lynette turns her attention to her monitor, her long fingers flying over her keyboard. I have no doubt she's going to send the best cat food and the freshest flowers money can buy. Lynette knows my predilection for high-quality products.

I like the best in all things, and I don't accept compromises.

Speaking of the best… I glance at my watch. No, it's still too early for Emmeline's flight to have landed. Pulling out my phone, I set a reminder to call her later this afternoon and head toward my office.

I have five meetings and two dozen research reports to get through before lunch, but all I can think about is Emma.

Fuck. I'll have to make sure I have my redheaded dessert this week, so I can forget her and move on with my life.

CHAPTER ELEVEN

mma

"Here you go, Mr. Roberts," I say, handing the wizened old man a stack of paperbacks. "You'll enjoy these, I'm sure."

"Oh, I have no doubt." He beams at me, showing two missing teeth in the front. "I love this series. So glad you recommended this author to me. I've loved all her books so far."

I grin back at him. "I'm happy to hear that. She's my favorite science fiction writer."

"Mine too now," he says, and we share a moment—that perfect moment of connection with someone who appreciates the same books you do. It's moments like these that keep me working at Smithson Books despite low pay and no chance of advancement. Well, moments like these and my love of physical books. Just being in this little bookstore, surrounded by shelves of paperbacks and hardbacks, lifts my mood. I like ebooks too, but there's nothing quite like the smell and feel of printed paper.

Each time we get a shipment in, I feel like a kid with a brand-new toy.

"All right then," Mr. Roberts says, putting his paperbacks into a canvas bag. "You take care now, dear. Say hello to those cats for me."

"I will, thank you." A few months ago, I showed Mr. Roberts my cats' pictures on the phone, and since then, he's mentioned them every time he sees me. Come to think of it, he's not the only one. Most of the regulars at the bookstore know about my fur babies and ask about them often.

Ugh. I *am* a cat lady.

"Hey, Emma. How's it going?" Edward Smithson's voice pulls me out of my thoughts, and I turn to see my boss ambling toward me. Walking next to him is a guy I've never seen before. Blond, geeky-looking, and a little on the short side, he's wearing rimless glasses and appears to be about my age.

"I'm good, Mr. Smithson. How about you?" I respond, smiling at my boss. He's one of the nicest people I know—yet another reason why I haven't quit this job.

"Oh, you know, still sticking to the diet." He pats his massive belly, and I suppress a laugh. As far as I can tell, his diet consists of cookies and donuts—eaten when his wife isn't looking, of course.

Stopping a few feet from me, Mr. Smithson says, "Emma, I'd like you to meet my nephew, Ian." He turns to the blond guy. "Ian, this is Emma, the girl I was telling you about."

"It's nice to meet you, Ian," I say, smiling at the nephew. "What brings you to our bookstore?"

"I just moved to the city," he says, his Adam's apple bobbing as his neck turns bright red. "I like books, so Uncle Ed wanted to show me his store."

"Of course." I give him my warmest smile. I know what it's like to be socially awkward, so I always try to be kind to shy people. "Would you like me to give you the tour?"

"That would be great," Mr. Smithson says, sounding far too enthusiastic, and I suddenly realize why Ian is here.

My boss is matchmaking.

Now it's my turn to blush. To hide the color spreading over my face, I crouch and pretend to tie my sneaker. I don't know how I feel about this, especially the part where Ian is the boss's nephew. It could get really awkward if anything goes wrong, and despite the crappy pay, I really like this job.

Oh, well. I'll have to do my best to be friendly and *only* friendly.

When I'm sure that I no longer resemble a beet, I rise to my feet and smile at Ian. "Ready for the tour?"

The tour, such as it is, takes less than ten minutes. The bookstore is only a little larger than my studio, with the back area dedicated to a row of armchairs where our patrons like to lounge, and the front populated by shelves stocked with all genres of popular fiction. We're not big on literary fiction or classics—the boring stuff, as Mr. Smithson calls it—but we have a huge selection of science fiction, fantasy, thrillers, mysteries, and romance novels. It's our way of making sure our customers aren't tempted to go online to get the books they actually like to read.

As I show all this to Ian, we make small talk, and I find out that he's an aspiring urban fantasy author. I discreetly slip in that I do freelance editing, and his eyes light up when I tell him my very reasonable rates.

"Are you going to self-publish or go the traditional route?" I ask as we return to the counter where Mr. Smithson is handling the customers in my stead.

"I'm leaning toward self-publishing," Ian answers. He seems much less shy now that we're discussing his passion. "Uncle Ed thinks I should query agents first, but I'm tempted to just put it out there and see how it does."

"That's probably smart," I say, smiling. "But then again, I'm biased. Most of my editing clients these days are independent authors, so I obviously want as many of you around as possible."

Ian laughs, and Mr. Smithson gives us a pleased smile as he rings up an old woman's purchase.

Oops. I hope my boss doesn't think we're hitting it off in some way other than editor and potential client.

Though Ian is the type of guy I normally go for—sweet, nerdy, and a little shy—I'm not the least bit attracted to him. As I wonder why that is, images of icy blue eyes and lean, hard jaw invade my mind, along with graphic details from my dreams last night.

No. No way. I push the images away before my face turns red again. I refuse to believe that my lack of attraction to Ian has anything to do with Marcus. I still don't know why the hedge fund manager returned my phone in person yesterday, but I'm certain he's forgotten all about me by now—and I need to forget all about him.

I'm not attracted to Ian, and that's all there is to it. It's for the best, really. I like Mr. Smithson's nephew as a person and I hope to edit his book someday, but that's as far as it should ever go.

To discourage any further matchmaking attempts by my boss, I tell Ian to ping me when he has his book ready, and then I hurry to relieve Mr. Smithson of the cashier duty.

I need to embrace my cat-lady-ness because this dating stuff is way too complex for me.

———

It's sleeting again when I exit the subway, and I curse my bad luck as I rush home. I can't recall a worse November. It's still early in the month, but it's already snowed once, with icy rain falling on at least two other occasions—almost as if we were in January. My phone vibrates in my pocket as I turn the corner, and I almost ignore it because I don't want to expose my ears, currently covered by the collar of my coat, to the sleeting rain. However, a long-ingrained habit makes me reach into my pocket and pull out the phone to glance at the screen.

Sure enough, it's a call I can't miss.

"Grandma, hi," I say, raising the phone to my ear. Without me holding up the collar, the coat falls back to my shoulders, exposing my neck to the sleeting rain, and I shudder as the icy water trickles inside. I should've worn my old, moth-eaten scarf today, but it's so ugly that I couldn't bring myself to do it, and now I'm paying for that moment of vanity.

I really need to buy myself a new scarf and keep it away from Mr. Puffs.

"Hi, sweetheart." Grandma's voice is warm and gentle, her Southern drawl noticeable despite several decades spent living in Brooklyn. "How are you?"

"I'm doing great," I say, making my voice as cheerful as I can. With the icy raindrops pelting my face and getting inside my collar, I'm perfectly miserable, but Grandma doesn't need to know that. "How are you and Gramps?"

"Oh, we're good. Your grandfather is gardening in the heat again. I told him not to go out there when it's eighty degrees, but he won't listen to me."

"Yeah, that's Gramps for you," I say, feeling jealous. I'd kill for eighty-degree weather instead of this hellish cold. My grandparents moved to Florida when I graduated from college, and now every time I speak to them, I hear all about how nice and hot it is over there. "You should lure him in with some chocolate chip cookies."

Grandma laughs. "How did you know I was making those?"

"Just a lucky guess," I say, shivering as a particularly strong gust of wind slaps my face. "How did your blood test go last week?"

"All clear. I'm healthy as a hog." Grandma's tone is upbeat. "Now tell me about you. How's life in the big city? Any luck finding new editing jobs?"

"Not yet, but I have some leads on potential clients," I say, crossing the street to my brownstone. "And before you ask, I'm fine. I don't need any help. Truly."

"Emma…" Grandma lets out a sigh. "I wish you'd just let us take care of those loans for you. I told you, we can take out a second mortgage and—"

"No. Absolutely not." My grandparents scrimped and saved their whole life so they could buy a house in Florida, and I have no intention of letting their retirement be ruined because of me. Their pensions and social security payments barely cover their bills as is, and a second mortgage payment would place an enormous strain on their finances. It's bad enough they worked an extra seven years to support me through middle school and high school; I'm not letting them take care of me in my adult years as well.

I'd sooner starve than impose on them like that.

Grandma sighs again. "Emma, sweetie… Accepting

a helping hand every now and then wouldn't make you like your mother. You know that, right?"

"Grandma, stop. Please. I'm getting by perfectly well," I say, fumbling for my keys as I approach my door. "Now, if you don't mind, I just got home, so I have to feed the cats. Give my love to Gramps, okay?"

"Will do. Take care, sweetheart, and talk soon. Can't wait 'till Thanksgiving," Grandma replies, and I hang up, dropping the phone back into my pocket.

Clutching my keys, I reach for the door, eager to get inside and escape the cold.

"Miss Walsh?" The male voice from behind me startles me so much that I spin around with a squeak, my keys dropping onto the wet ground.

Standing in front of me is a short, middle-aged man in a puffy winter jacket, his arms laden with a giant bouquet of pink and white roses.

"I'm so sorry, miss. I didn't mean to scare you," he says quickly. "I'm just here to make a delivery."

"A delivery?" I'm shaking both from the cold and the excess of adrenaline, my heart beating so fast I can barely speak. "For me?"

"Yes," he says with a smile. Approaching me, he bends down to pick up my keys and hands them to me, along with the giant bouquet. "This is for you."

"Um, okay." Awkwardly, I take both the keys and the flowers. The roses are covered in clear plastic that protects them from the elements, but even so, I can tell that the flowers are gorgeous. I'm about to ask who sent them when something else occurs to me. "Oh, I don't have any cash for the tip," I say, feeling like a bumbling idiot. "I'm so sorry. I meant to stop by an ATM, but—"

"Oh, no, it's all good. Everything is taken care of." A big smile splits his weathered face. "You just enjoy these, okay, miss?"

He turns and hurries away, clearly eager to get out of the rain, and it's only when he's gone that I realize I didn't have a chance to ask who ordered the delivery.

Oh, well. Hopefully, there's a note. My fingers are almost numb from the cold, but I manage to get my keys into the lock and get inside. Instantly, my three cats rush toward me, meowing like I've been gone for a week instead of just over eight hours.

"Yeah, yeah, you'll get fed," I mutter, trying not to trip over Mr. Puffs. "Just give me a second here."

The furry asshole ignores my words, and my walk to the kitchen is perilous, to say the least. Between the humongous bouquet of flowers and the giant cat winding between my legs, it's a wonder I don't trip and split my head open.

Finally, I'm in the kitchen. Putting the flowers down on the counter, I quickly prep my cats' dinner and give it to them. Then, taking a deep breath, I approach the bouquet.

Before I can pull off the protective plastic, my doorbell rings.

Cottonball looks up from his dish and gives me an inquisitive look.

"Sorry, bud. I'm as clueless as you are," I say to the

cat as I hurry toward the door. The only person who comes over unannounced is my landlady, and she has no reason to do so tonight, as I've paid my rent on time for several months straight.

When I look through the peephole, I see a man dressed in a FedEx uniform walking away.

Another delivery? What the hell?

Since I was born and raised in Brooklyn, I wait until the stranger is gone before cautiously opening the door. Sure enough, there is a big box sitting on my doorstep. I bend down to pick it up, but it's way too heavy to lift. Swearing under my breath, I wrestle it inside and close the door. Then, dying from curiosity, I grab a knife from the kitchen and open the box.

Dumbfounded, I stare at the contents.

Cat food. Lots and lots of cat food. All the best brands, in a variety of flavors, some dry and some canned, like my cats prefer.

It's enough cat food for the next several months.

I'm so confused I almost miss the small white envelope taped to the side of the box. It's only when I'm dragging the heavy box to the kitchen that I see it. Stopping, I grab it and open it, ripping the pretty paper in my eagerness. The note reads:

I hope your cats enjoy this, and you like the flowers.
-Marcus.

A wave of heat rushes through me, chasing away the lingering chill from the cold outside. The images from the sex dreams I've been trying not to think about flood my mind, and my breathing speeds up.

The deliveries are from *Marcus*.

I all but run into the kitchen, hoping there's another note with an explanation as to why, but there's nothing attached to the bouquet. Queen Elizabeth looks up from her dish and gives me a look that suggests I'm crazy, but I ignore her.

Marcus sent me roses and *cat food*.

This is far beyond any kind of good Samaritan act. I remember the ridiculous thought that had occurred to me last night—that he might be interested in me—and all of a sudden, it doesn't seem quite so ridiculous anymore. Because what other explanation is there when a man sends a woman flowers?

Well, flowers and cat food.

"Do you think he likes me that way?" I ask Queen Elizabeth, and the cat gives me a look that suggests I'm acting like I'm twelve.

Okay, fine. Maybe I'm reading too much into my cat's looks, but I swear she's able to communicate with me. She tilts her head this way and that way when I talk to her, and sometimes she even meows in response —which is exactly what she does now.

"You do think he likes me?" I ask, irrationally excited, and Queen Elizabeth meows again before returning her attention to her food.

"I'll take that as a yes," I say, and go hunting for a vase big enough to hold the enormous bouquet. As I bounce around the kitchen, I realize I feel giddy, almost high at the idea that Marcus might like me. He's the polar opposite of my type, but something about him draws me—which explains those dreams last night.

His big hands all over my body, his hard-muscled chest pressing down on my breasts as he moves inside me...

Whoa. A hot flush crawls along my hairline. Despite my lengthy dry spell, I have a healthy libido and enjoy sex, but this is something else entirely. My heart seems to have taken up drumming lessons in my chest, and my panties feel damp from the mere recollection of those dreams.

This is attraction like I've never felt before—base, primal, and having nothing to do with logic or intellectual connection. I know next to nothing about Marcus, and what little I do know suggests we don't have anything in common, yet the mere thought of him turns me on more than an hour of foreplay by my college boyfriend.

"Do you think I'm in heat?" I ask Queen Elizabeth as I grab a big pot—the closest thing I have to a vase of needed size. "I mean, I'm human and all, but this is kind of extreme, don't you think?"

Queen Elizabeth looks up and daintily runs her tongue over her face, cleaning off any remnants of her food.

"Yeah, you're right. I'm being ridiculous. Human females don't go into heat." I fill the pot with water, remove the plastic wrap from the roses, add the flower food to the water, and put the roses in. They end up listing to one side, but they still look beautiful—and very expensive.

If my grandmother knew about this, she'd say Marcus is courting me.

"Do you think he's courting me?" I ask the cat, but Queen Elizabeth just sits gracefully and starts licking her paw. She's clearly had her fill of interaction with a human, and I don't blame her.

I should be calling Kendall with this, not bugging the cat.

As soon as the thought occurs to me, I run to my phone and eagerly swipe across the screen. Before I can select Kendall's number, though, a message notification pops up, and my pulse jumps further.

It's a text message from an unknown number.

Hi, Emma, it reads. *This is Marcus. I hope the flowers and the gift for your cats got to you safely. Are you free this Thursday evening? I'd love to take you out to dinner. We can debate Wall Street ethics if you wish.*

I stare at the text, feeling like I'm hyperventilating. It shouldn't have come as a surprise—after all, I did think, just moments ago, that Marcus might be courting me—but somehow, I still feel caught off-guard.

Dinner? On Thursday? That's *tomorrow*.

Something soft taps my calf, and I glance down to see Cottonball swishing his tail back and forth as he stares up at me.

"He wants to have dinner with me tomorrow," I tell the cat, and even to my own ears, I sound shell-shocked. "Can you believe that?"

Unlike Queen Elizabeth, Cottonball is not a female

of any species, so he doesn't care about my dating issues. He just lifts his paw and swats my calf again. Sighing, I put down my phone and pick him up, knowing he won't leave me alone otherwise. Thankfully, he's not as heavy as Mr. Puffs, so I can hold him with one arm, which leaves my hand free to pick up the phone again.

Chewing on my lip, I read the text again and wonder what to do. If this were any other man—Mark from the dating app, for instance—it would be easy. I'd thank him for the thoughtful gift, suggest a pizza place next to my apartment, and see how things go. But this is Marcus—he of the tailored suits and sex-dream-inducing hands. He makes me uneasy, and not just because of my physical reaction to him.

As bizarre as it is, there's something almost... dangerous about him, something not quite civilized.

Cottonball emits a loud purr, bringing my attention back to him, and I put the phone down to stroke his soft, fluffy fur. He's the cuddliest of my cats, demanding a thorough petting session at least once a day, and I'm normally happy to oblige him. Right now, though, I'm too overwhelmed to deal with a needy cat.

Marcus asked me out on a date, and I have no idea what to say.

CHAPTER TWELVE

arcus

Why isn't she answering?

Frustrated, I glare at the phone, where a tiny notification at the bottom informs me that my text message was received and read ten minutes ago. I know my frustration is not rational—ten minutes is not *that* long—but I can't control the impatience consuming me.

Why the hell isn't she answering?

I'm still in my office, and I have a million and one things to do before I can leave tonight, but all I can focus on is Emma and the lack of response to my text. Instead of working, I've spent the past ten minutes staring at my phone—ten minutes that, at my current hourly rate of earnings, equate to several thousand dollars.

Finally, after what seems like an eternity, three dots appear.

Emma is typing something.

I find myself holding my breath like some teenager with a crush, so I force myself to look at my computer screen instead of at the phone. It's useless, though. The spreadsheets dance in front of my eyes, the numbers refusing to make sense.

This is fucking insane.

Earlier today, I called Emmeline to thank her for the dinner and inquire about her flight, and I didn't feel even a fraction of this bizarre excitement. Our conversation was calm and polite, and when I hung up the phone, I was more convinced than ever that Emmeline is exactly the kind of woman I've been looking for: beautiful, intelligent, steady, and well-mannered. She wouldn't scream, curse, or throw a fit when something didn't go her way; she wouldn't stumble home drunk with two equally drunk assholes in tow; and she certainly wouldn't fuck said assholes in front of her five-year-old son.

My mood darkens at that childhood recollection, and I glance back at the phone, where the three dots are still going strong. What is Emma doing for so long? Writing a text message essay?

The very fact of my impatience adds to my frustration. Over the decade and a half of running my fund, I've developed nerves of steel. I've had to—because as the fund's assets under management have grown, so has the amount of capital we risk on each trade. Just in the past five years, our biggest positions have gone from several million dollars to just over a billion. If I hadn't taught myself patience—if I hadn't learned to stop watching every tick of the market and focus on what needs to be done—I would've stressed myself into an early heart attack.

So if I can put a billion-dollar trade out of my mind, why can't I tear my eyes away from those three fucking dots?

Come on, I will the screen. *Just spit it out already.* If I could reach through the phone and shake the little redhead, I would do so, because this is ridiculous. How long does it take to type out a yes or a no? Preferably a yes, but even a rejection would be better than this endless waiting. I wouldn't accept it, of course, but it would give me something to go on, a starting point for the rest of my slake-hunger-for-Emma campaign. I would be able to strategize and come up with the next move—

The three dots disappear and are replaced by text.

Thank you for the flowers and the food. My cats are very pleased :). How about Papa Mario's Pizza at 7 p.m. for our ethics discussion?

My first reaction—relief—transforms into confusion as I look up the suggested restaurant. A quick search reveals a dingy website and Yelp reviews talking about a "hole in the wall with the cheapest pizza in Brooklyn." It's about two blocks from Emma's apartment, but as far as I can tell, that's the only thing the place has going for it.

Why the fuck does Emma want to go there?

I drum my fingers on the table, thinking, then text: *If you're in the mood for Italian, I know an excellent family restaurant in Bensonhurst. They have the best pizza in the five boroughs, and it's not far from where you live. Pick you up at 6:45?*

The three dots appear almost instantly this time, followed by: *What is the place called?*

I frown at the phone. In my experience, when I offer to take a woman out, she lets me pick the place and doesn't question my suggestions, especially when that particular suggestion happens to be the same type of food she seems to be in the mood for.

Emma is either a control freak or *really* particular about her pizza.

My frown deepening, I text back the name of the place and wait.

Three minutes later, I get the response: *Okay. I'll be ready.*

The surge of satisfaction is as intense as when I made my first million. Grinning savagely, I put away the phone and turn my attention back to my computer screen, where the numbers are finally making sense again.

The first big battle of the Emma campaign is won, and I can't wait for the rest of the war.

CHAPTER THIRTEEN

mma

When I tell Kendall about my upcoming date, she all but chokes on her coffee. "You what?"

"I'm meeting a hedge fund manager for dinner tonight," I say, pouring a liberal amount of milk into my own cup of java. "So you see, I'm a cat lady no more."

"Okay, whoa. Back up a step." She leans forward, her hazel eyes gleaming with the intensity of a shark smelling blood. "When and how did this happen?"

Grinning, I tell her the whole story, beginning with the mix-up in identity. "So yeah," I conclude, "I have a date tonight."

"With Marcus the hedge fund manager," she says incredulously. "Who pretty much stalked you to your apartment and sent you cat food. And gave you sex dreams."

"Yep." My grin widens. "The one and only."

Kendall and I rarely get to see each other during the weekdays, but I have this Thursday off, so I decided to come up to Manhattan to grab coffee with her.

I had to see her reaction in person.

She doesn't disappoint. "Emma!" My name comes out on a high-pitched squeal. "Holy shit, I'm so proud of you! Bagging Mr. Hedge Fund!"

The other customers in the café look our way, but I'm too excited to feel embarrassed. Ever since Marcus's text, I've been trying to come off this strange high, but I can't. I'm so hyper I barely slept last night, but I don't feel the least bit tired.

I have *a date* with Marcus.

"Do you know what his fund is called, or how big it is?" Kendall asks, bringing me out of a feverish day dream that involves Marcus's hands and other body parts. "Or what his last name is? In general, have you looked him up? Do you know if he's married, single, or divorced?"

"No and no," I say, fighting the urge to blush at Kendall's innocent mention of "big." "I'll ask all this tonight. I'm sure he's not married, though. This Emmeline sounded like a blind date, and he wouldn't be doing that if he already had someone."

"Oh, please." Kendall snorts into her coffee. "Don't be naive. Men do all sorts of things for pussy. Besides, you've just met the guy. For all you know, he could be a serial adulterer."

"True, but I don't think so." I could be totally off base, but Marcus didn't come across as someone who would cheat—not once he was in a committed relationship, at least. For a moment, I wonder what happened that day with Emmeline, but then I dismiss the thought.

If he'd clicked with her, I doubt he would've asked me out.

"All right," Kendall says, flicking her long dark hair back over her shoulder. "Just remember: do your due diligence, because men are dogs. Or if the feline analogy works better for you, tomcats. You've always dated schmucks who couldn't get two women if they tried, so you don't have a lot of experience with this—"

"Gee, thanks. Glad to hear you have such a high opinion of my charms."

Kendall has the grace to look embarrassed. "Look, I'm not saying you're not attractive—you just tend to gravitate toward guys who don't make you feel threatened in any way."

"What?" This conversation has definitely taken a turn for the weird.

Kendall sighs. "Emma... Don't take this the wrong way, but you're just not a risk taker, okay? You like to play it safe, to have everything be comfortable and routine. That's why you're still in Brooklyn instead of sunny Florida, why you're working at that little bookstore instead of trying for something better, and why you hide behind your cats and your ratty clothes and your books—and men who are the way you perceive yourself, instead of the way you really are."

"Wait, what?" There's so much bizarre psychobabble there that I don't know what to tackle first. I can't believe Kendall has these opinions of me. "You yourself said that I've turned into a cat lady, so how exactly am I misperceiving myself? And I am *so* a risk taker—I freelance, remember?" My voice rises with indignation. "As to why I haven't moved to Florida with my grandparents, you know full well that the majority of the publishing industry is here, and if I want a career in it—"

"But you don't." Kendall gives me a steady look. "A career in publishing might've been your goal once, but you've told me yourself that the industry landscape is shifting, and the big publishers aren't what they used to be. That's why you're able to get all those freelance editing jobs—which, by the way, is something you've been content to do halfheartedly on the side instead of trying to make a real go of it." She crosses her arms. "Face it, Emma: You're in Brooklyn working at your very first job because you don't like change."

"That's not true—"

"Yes, it is." She uncrosses her arms and picks up her coffee cup. "That's why you wear your clothes until they literally fall apart on you, and why you only date guys who stand no chance with another girl as pretty as you. As to the cat lady thing, I just said that because you've been neglecting yourself, and I wanted you to do something about it—which you clearly did."

She grins, obviously hoping to bring the topic back to Marcus, but I'm too upset to smile back. The worst part of Kendall's unflattering assessment of me is that she's right about one thing: the career I planned for might never come to pass, yet I haven't changed course to adjust for that, choosing to hide my head in the sand instead. When I started working at Smithson Books, I was a junior in college, and I regarded the job as a temporary part-time opportunity, a way to make a little money while being loosely connected to the industry I wanted to be in. But when I couldn't find a job with a major publishing company upon graduation because all of them were shrinking and restructuring, I stayed at the bookstore, all the while telling myself that I was just biding time until my real career began.

Weeks turned into months, then into years, and here I am, still biding time.

Self-disgust is a thick knot in my throat as I confront another unpleasant fact: Kendall is right about my freelance editing too. I *have been* half-assing it, treating it more like a hobby than a business. I haven't even built a website, though I know the importance of that in a largely online book community.

No wonder I'm drowning in student loans and stressing over every meal out: I'm living in one of the most expensive cities in the world on a cashier's salary —all so I can cling to the idea of a career that I *know* no longer makes sense.

"Why didn't you say something earlier?" I try—and fail—not to sound bitter. Being forced to face reality is a bitch. "If you saw that I was being an idiot, why didn't you say something before this?"

Kendall's expression turns somber. "Because I didn't think you were ready to hear it—and because I didn't want you to react the way you're reacting now. I know you have reasons for wanting the comfort of the familiar, and it's not like you were doing anything dangerous or self-destructive. You just let yourself get into a rut, which is something I know you can fix if you set your mind to it. Besides, I selfishly want you here, not in Florida or wherever you might move to if you had a full-time editing business that you could do from anywhere."

"Kendall…" I don't know if I want to smack her or hug her, so I settle for doing neither. Instead, I pick up my cup of coffee and try to manage my spinning thoughts as I gulp down the hot liquid. Latching on to the one inconsistency in her spiel, I ask, "If you feel this way, why are you trying to warn me away from Marcus? Isn't he a step in the right direction? Something different… something risky?"

"Yes, of course he is, and that's why I'm so proud of you." Kendall's tense expression eases as a playful grin tugs at the corners of her lips. "You're venturing out of your comfort zone, and I couldn't be happier about that. I just don't want you to rush into anything blindly and get hurt as you take your first baby steps. Not all guys are as harmless as your pet geeks, you know."

I put down my cup. "Of course. I know that." *Harmless* is definitely not how I'd describe Marcus. Forcing a smile to my lips, I say, "I'll be careful, I promise. I'll question him about everything and make sure there's no wife lurking in the bushes. In fact, I'll drill him so good he won't know what hit him."

Kendall looks at me, owl-eyed, and I look back at her. In the next instant, we're both laughing uncontrollably, and the tension between us dissolves without a trace.

————

AFTER I RETURN HOME, I SHOWER, SHAVE MY LEGS, AND let my hair air dry to ensure that the curls don't turn too frizzy. Afterward, I spend a solid hour trying on and discarding various outfits. I finally settle on a pair of jeans, my newish pair of high-heeled boots (only a couple of seasons old and still mostly in fashion), and my dressiest blouse with a sweater wrap over it. I even add a little jewelry and a full layer of makeup, including foundation—which I promptly wash off because it makes me look like a clown. I end up with a little mascara to darken my auburn lashes, a light dusting of powder to make my freckles less visible, and a simple application of lip gloss—my usual first-date look.

In fact, everything about the way I look tonight is my usual, though I've spent double the amount of time it took me to prepare for the date with Mark. I don't know what I was hoping to achieve with all my primping, but after I'm done, I look the way I always do, just maybe a shade more polished. I'm not one of those girls who has the skills to transform herself with a few strokes of a makeup brush; whenever I try, I end up with a clown look, like I did earlier. Normally, it doesn't bother me, but tonight, I wish I knew how to shade and contour, how to make my eyes look huge and my cheekbones more prominent.

Tonight, I want to look pretty for *him*.

Stop being pathetic, Emma. Just stop it.

Even as I tell myself this, I know it's useless. The jittery high that prevented me from sleeping last night is nowhere near abating, the mixture of excitement and nervous anticipation making me unable to sit still for longer than a minute. I have to proofread a short story for a client, but whenever I sit down and try to focus on it, the words dance on the page, and all I see are his cool blue eyes staring back at me.

Great, just freaking great. This is why I should've said no. Maybe Kendall is right, and I tend to go for safe guys, but that's how I like it. This unsettled, insecure feeling—this desperate desire to please a man—is not something I enjoy. In college, when all my friends were going crazy for jocks and bad boys, I dated nice, quiet guys—like Jim, my last serious boyfriend. With him, I never had to worry about dressing up; he liked me as much in my dorky pajamas and house slippers as in skirts and high heels. In fact, he often couldn't tell the difference between the two; to him, a girl was a girl, regardless of what she was wearing. We ended up breaking up because he became too clingy, demanding my time and energy to an exhausting degree, but until then, dating him had been like being with one of my friends: easy and comfortable.

Staring at myself in the mirror, I see a pink flush on my cheeks and fever-bright gleam in my gray eyes. This dinner with Marcus is not going to be easy and comfortable, I know that much.

It also won't be cheap. The restaurant Marcus chose is at the upper limit of my budget, so I'll be skimping on groceries for the rest of the week. I should've insisted on going to Papa Mario's, but I was afraid Marcus would hate it, so I caved—something I wouldn't have done with Jim or any other guy I've dated.

For a moment, I wonder if it's too late to back out, but then I chide myself for being a coward. I can survive one dinner with a man who makes me feel like this. If what Kendall says is true, it should actually be good for me, get me out of my comfort zone and all. Besides, it's not like anything long-term would come from it. Whatever Marcus's reasons are for asking me out, I'm sure he'll realize right away that we have very little in common, and it'll end there.

I can do one date with Mr. Hedge Fund.

In fact, I'm looking forward to it.

CHAPTER FOURTEEN

*M*arcus

I'M ON EMMA'S DOORSTEP AT 6:45 P.M. SHARP DESPITE the usual rush-hour traffic. My regular driver, Wilson, is excellent like that. Through some uncanny combination of driving apps and instinct, he always manages to get me places on time—a virtual impossibility in New York City.

Taking a breath to steady myself, I ring the doorbell. Anticipation curls through me as I hear a loud meow, followed by light, rapid footsteps.

"Stop it, Puffs." Emma's irritated voice is muffled by the door. "Come on, you evil creature. Shoo!"

A second later, the door swings open, and I see her standing there, flushed and a little disheveled. Instantly, heat surges through me, centering low in my groin as images of how she'd look after I fuck her slide through my mind.

Focus, Marcus. Deep breath.

It's obvious she's made an attempt to tame her red curls, but one stubborn one is already sticking out sideways, and her well-worn beige coat is askew and covered with white cat hair—the source of which must be the three cats in the hallway behind her. One is calmly licking its paw, the other one is swishing its tail, and the third one—a giant one—is giving me what I can only interpret as a glare. In the next moment, the giant cat streaks toward me, and Emma bends down to catch him.

"Hi," she says breathlessly, straightening with the wriggling cat held tightly against her chest. "Sorry about that. Mr. Puffs gets jealous when men come over."

"Really?" My voice is tight. To my shock, I understand exactly how the white fluffy creature feels, because the thought of men coming over to Emma's apartment makes me want to strangle someone. Swallowing down the irrational surge of jealousy, I force my tone to lighten. "Possessive, is he?"

"Oh, yeah. Big time." She blows at another messy curl to get it out of her eyes. "Hold on, let me grab my bag." Straining to hold the cat with one arm, she reaches for the brown purse I saw her with before, and I help her by grabbing it off the hook by the door.

"Thanks," she says, bending down again to lower the cat to the floor. He tries to rush at me again, but

Emma expertly blocks him with her legs, snatches the bag out of my hand, and says, "Let's go."

I step outside, grateful to be out of the cat-infested hallway. When I was a boy, I used to like dogs and cats, but pets are no longer my thing. I dislike the idea of taking care of them, plus there is the whole messy and unsanitary aspect of having animals indoors.

Not your problem, I remind myself as Emma manages to step outside sans cats and turns around to lock the door. If I were actually considering Emma for a relationship, this would be a stumbling block, but I'm not.

I'm here to satisfy this odd craving and get her out of my system.

Done with the door, Emma turns around to face me and gives me a sheepish smile. "Sorry about that. My cats can be a bit of a handful."

"No problem." I politely offer her my arm, and my stomach clenches when her small hand slips through the crook of my elbow. She's tiny next to me, the top of her head barely coming up to my shoulder, but there is nothing childlike about the sensual sway of her hips as I lead her toward the car.

Emma Walsh might not be my type, but I want her too much to care.

mma

MARCUS LEADS ME TO A FANCY BLACK CAR PARKED AT the curb and opens the door for me. I climb into the back seat, my face hot despite the chilly November wind as he takes a seat next to me. The car is large and spacious, but with Marcus there, it feels stiflingly small. It's not just his large frame, either; it's everything about him. He takes up space in a way that goes beyond the physical, commanding the very air around him.

Next to him, I feel like an asteroid caught in Jupiter's orbit—small and powerless to escape the massive planet's pull.

"The restaurant, please, Wilson," Marcus says to the driver, and I see the man nodding in the rearview mirror as the car starts moving. The fact that Marcus knows his name makes me wonder if Marcus hired the car for the evening, or if Wilson is his personal or company driver. Do people even have personal drivers these days?

Before I can ask, Marcus transfers his attention to me. "So, Emma," he says, his deep voice tugging at that something in me again. "Tell me about yourself."

"What would you like to know?" I ask, hoping I sound like a confident woman instead of the nervous twelve-year-old who seems to have taken up residence in my body. I have the unsettling sensation that I'm at an interview—an impression heightened by the fact that Marcus is wearing a suit and tie under his unbuttoned winter coat. I know he probably just came from work, and his wearing a suit doesn't mean I'm horribly underdressed, but I feel that way: awkward and uncertain and out of place.

Stop it, Emma. He's just a guy. A hot and intimidating one, but still just a guy.

"Have you lived in Brooklyn long?" he asks, his pale gaze shadowed in the darkened interior of the car.

"All my life," I say, striving for a casual tone. "Born and raised. How about you?"

"I was born on Staten Island," he says. "So I'm a New Yorker like you."

"Oh. Are you from an Italian family, by any chance?" That could explain the olive tint to his skin.

"On my mother's side." His words are curt, as if I'd touched a nerve.

"I'm mostly Irish," I volunteer, hoping to smooth over whatever error I made.

"I guessed as much." Marcus's reply is wry, and as the car stops at a streetlight, I see a hint of a smile on his face.

I instinctively touch my hair. "It's pretty obvious, huh?"

"It was just a lucky guess," Marcus says, and I grin at him, some of my nervousness ebbing.

We continue to make small talk for the rest of the fifteen-minute ride, and I learn that Marcus lives in Tribeca while his office is in Midtown. I'm not surprised; if anyone could afford to live and work in Manhattan, it would be a hedge fund manager. My Wall Street salary index is fuzzy, but I'm pretty sure those guys make bank.

"What's your fund called?" I ask, remembering Kendall's question as the car comes to a stop in front of a small, cozy-looking restaurant. My friend will undoubtedly drill me on this, so I better gather all the facts.

"Carelli Capital Management," Marcus replies as he opens the door and climbs out, then holds open the door for me. As I step out, he gently clasps my elbow, making sure I don't trip, and warmth floods my cheeks again. Even through the thick wool of my winter coat, I feel the restrained strength in his grip, the power that could be devastating if unleashed.

He doesn't let go of my arm when I'm out of the car, and my heart pounds heavily as I stare up at him. The streetlights illuminate his mouth and the hard cast of his jaw, leaving his eyes in shadow, and for a brief, fanciful moment, I feel like a small animal caught in a hunter's snare. Something hot and electric arcs between us, the moment fraught with tension—then he releases my arm and turns, offering me his elbow.

"Shall we?" His tone is calm, as if he's completely unaffected by whatever just passed between us, but I see his jaw flex and know he'd felt it too.

My mouth feels dry as I slip my hand through the crook of his elbow, trying not to think about how thick and solid his arm feels. It's like holding onto a curved tree trunk—albeit one that's covered by expensive cashmere-wool.

"Do you come to this restaurant a lot?" I ask, trying not to pant audibly as we walk toward the restaurant. Marcus's legs are so long I have to take two steps for every one of his, and the exertion, combined with the heat thrumming under my skin, makes me feel like I've just run up three flights of stairs.

"I've been here a few times," he says, opening the door for me. I step inside and appreciatively inhale the rich, savory aroma of basil, roasted garlic, and fresh-baked dough. It smells like Papa Mario's, but the ambiance is infinitely better. The restaurant is small, but clean and cozy, with about a dozen tables covered by white linen tablecloths and topped with vases with real flowers. Even though it's a Thursday night, each table is occupied except the one in the far corner.

This dinner might be worth the hit to my budget.

Unbuttoning my coat, I smile up at Marcus. "This looks like a very nice place. Thanks for suggesting it."

"My pleasure. Here, let me take your coat." He reaches for it, and I have no choice but to let him help me. His fingers brush over my shoulders in the process, and despite my sweater wrap, a tingle of heat radiates from the spot where he touched me.

God, if he ever puts his hands on my bare skin... Just the thought of it makes my insides tighten.

A short, dark-haired man of indeterminate age approaches us. "Mr. Carelli, welcome." His Italian accent is strong, and his dark eyes twinkle brightly in his thin face. "Please follow me."

He leads us to the corner table. As we walk, Marcus places his hand on the small of my back, and I suck in a breath, stunned by the unexpectedly possessive gesture. My heart hammers faster, and the hot tingling spreads throughout my body, centering low in my core. Marcus's touch is light, solicitous, but there's no mistaking the purely male intent behind it. He's staking a claim, announcing to the other patrons in the restaurant that, for this evening at least, I belong to him.

It's something a man might do with a woman he's had sex with—or one he intends to have sex with very shortly.

Stop it, Emma. He's just being a gentleman. Even as I tell myself that, my pulse picks up further, and the images from my sex dream return in all their graphic glory.

"Are you okay?" Marcus asks, glancing down at me, and I realize my burning face must match my hair.

"Yes, of course," I say, trying to ignore the feel of his large palm resting on my back. "I'm just a little hungry, that's all."

"Then let's feed you," he says, dropping his hand as the waiter pulls out a chair for me. Marcus steps around the table to his side, and I sit down, grateful for the reprieve from his devastating nearness.

"What would you like to drink?" the waiter asks, hovering next to our table.

"Just regular water for me, please," I say.

"Same for me," Marcus says without missing a beat.

I smile, pleased he didn't try to force an alcoholic beverage on me. Some men like to do that, as if a woman drinking plain water somehow offends their masculinity. I'm no stranger to alcohol—I got puking-drunk in college more than once—but I don't enjoy the taste of wine and beer enough to have it with every meal.

Picking up the menu, I study it carefully. The only thing that looks to be within my price range is the pizza appetizer, so that makes my choice easy. I look up to find Marcus watching me with strange intensity.

"What is it?" I ask, feeling self-conscious.

"Nothing." One corner of his mouth turns up. "You're just really cute when you're concentrating."

Treacherous heat blooms in my cheeks again. "Um, thanks." The words come out on an awkward mumble.

Clearing my throat, I ask in a steadier tone, "What are you getting?"

"I'm thinking of the calamari for the appetizer and the squid ink risotto for the main course. You're welcome to share either or both with me," he says, closing his menu. "What about you? Anything in particular look appealing? If you'd like, I can recommend a couple of dishes, depending on what you're in the mood for."

"Oh, no, I'm good, thanks. I'm going to get the pizza appetizer."

He smiles. "Good choice. It's excellent here. What about the main course?"

"I'm not *that* hungry, so I'll just stick with the appetizer." It's not a lie, because I had a peanut butter sandwich before leaving the house. It's my way of ensuring I don't get starvation jitters while waiting for the food to arrive—and that I don't blow through my monthly food budget in one meal.

"Are you sure?"

He's frowning at my about-face, so I give him my best not-hungry smile. "Yep. The pizza appetizer is plenty for me."

"Okay, if that's what you want."

He motions for the waiter to come over, and we order our food. Then the waiter leaves, and it's just the two of us at the semi-private corner table. We stare at each other, and I feel that electric tension again, growing and expanding until it engulfs us in a strange kind of bubble. We're in a crowded restaurant, but it's as though we're completely alone. I'm cognizant of him to a degree that scares me; every movement of his hands, every breath that expands his chest—I feel it so completely it's as if an invisible string joins us together. Desperate to break the spell, I say, "So, Marcus—"

"So, Emma—" he begins at the same time, and we both burst out laughing, the tension bubble popping like an overfilled balloon.

"You go first," Marcus says, grinning, and I all but melt into a puddle on my seat. He has the best smile, all strong white teeth and sexy grooves in his lean cheeks. It softens his hard features and warms his cool blue eyes, taking him from intimidatingly good-looking to panty-wetting hot. It's not an exaggeration, either, because I actually feel my underwear getting damp. If I had my vibrator right now, it would take me less than two minutes to come. Maybe three minutes, tops.

God, Emma, get your mind out of the gutter.

Fighting a blush that threatens to color my face again, I say, "I was just going to ask if you ever ended up connecting with Emmeline. You know, the woman you were supposed to meet that night?"

Marcus's smile fades. "I did, yes."

"Oh?" My chest constricts for some reason. "And what happened?"

He shrugs. "We ended up having dinner. How about you? Did you ever meet up with Mark?"

"No, I didn't," I say, the tightness in my chest intensifying as I recall Kendall's warning. "I think he must've been upset by what happened, because he never responded to my apology email."

"I see." Marcus takes a sip of water. His gaze is inscrutable as he studies me over the rim of his glass. "Are you disappointed by that? Who was this Mark guy, anyway?"

"Just someone from a dating app," I say. Marcus is clearly trying to keep the focus on me, but with Kendall's words ringing in my ears, I'm not so easily deterred. "What about this Emmeline of yours?" I ask, keeping my tone casual. "Who was she, and how did your dinner go?"

"She was also from something like a dating app," he says, leaning back in his chair. His face is expressionless, and that, combined with his lack of reply to my second question, makes me even more curious about the topic.

"What's 'something like a dating app?'" I ask, reaching for my own water glass. I was just joking with Kendall about drilling Marcus, but some instinct is telling me to pursue this.

"A matchmaker," he says bluntly.

I choke on a sip of water. Coughing, I sputter out, "A what?"

"A matchmaker," he repeats, his blue gaze chilly again. "It's not that different from a dating site or app, just more personalized and exclusive."

"Right." I gulp down more water to hide my shock. I hadn't really thought about why Marcus was supposed to meet a woman he didn't know. I'd just sort of assumed he'd been set up on a blind date by a friend, or that he has a casual profile on a dating app, like I do. Lots of people do that these days; online dating is no longer just for losers. A matchmaker, however, is a different matter.

A matchmaker implies he wants something serious —and possibly quite particular.

"Are you, um…" Crap, how do I phrase it without freaking him out? "Are you looking to get married or something?"

"Of course." His expression cools further. "Isn't that the very definition of the service a matchmaker provides?"

"Well, yes…" I know I sound like an idiot, but I can't help it. I've never known the male of the species to seek out a relationship with the goal of marriage. From what I've seen, if a guy proposes, it's because he either wants to please his girlfriend, or he's met the right person and realizes it's the logical next step. I'm sure there are men who want marriage for the sake of marriage, but I've never come across such a creature personally. Even my super-clingy ex in college didn't think much of the institution; he just wanted us to be together all the time. Of course, my experience is with guys in their teens and twenties. Marcus is thirty-five —a man in his prime, not a boy still trying to find himself.

Before I can come up with something clever to say, the waiter brings our appetizers. He places both the pizza and the calamari in the middle of the table, likely assuming we're going to share them. Saliva pools in my mouth at the delicious smell. I wait impatiently until the waiter leaves, and then I grab a slice of the pizza, nearly burning my fingertips in the process.

"So you *are* hungry, after all?" Marcus asks, spearing a circle of calamari with his fork.

"For pizza? Always." I bite into the slice and close my eyes, almost moaning out loud as the taste of gooey melted cheese and perfectly seasoned tomato sauce fills my mouth. Swallowing the bite, I open my eyes to lick the drop of sauce from my fingers—and pause at the hungry look on Marcus's face.

"Want a slice?" I offer, realizing I'm being rude by hogging the entire pizza to myself. It's a small one, but that doesn't mean I can't share. Marcus is watching me eat so intently it's as if he wants to devour me instead of the pizza.

"No, thanks." His voice is slightly hoarse as he reaches for his glass of water. "You're welcome to the calamari, though."

"I'm good, thanks." I bite into the pizza again. The taste is just as orgasmic as before, but I manage to keep my eyes open this time—and see Marcus's jaw tighten as he watches me chew and swallow the bite.

He's not eating; he's just staring at me, and it makes me distinctly uncomfortable.

"You sure you don't want some?" I ask after I swallow my third bite. "I'm happy to share, honestly."

"No, I'm fine. Please, enjoy." He picks up his fork again and starts eating the calamari. I decide that turnabout is fair play, so I openly watch him as he consumes his food. It's amazing, but he somehow makes even the mundane act of eating seem powerfully masculine. The muscles in his jaw flex as he chews, and his throat works with each swallow, drawing my attention to the strong column of his neck. I've never thought of eating as a sexual act, but with Marcus, I find myself mesmerized by the way he brings each ring of calamari to his mouth and decimates it with his straight white teeth. My breathing speeds up, and the dampness in my underwear intensifies as I picture his mouth engaged in other, much dirtier activities.

To distract myself from the bizarre urge to lick a bread crumb off his lip, I focus on devouring my pizza. When only the crust remains, I look up.

"You never told me how your dinner with Emmeline went," I say. "Did your matchmaker do a good job?"

Marcus puts down his fork and very deliberately finishes his calamari. "She did," he says, patting his lips with a napkin.

"And?" I prompt when he doesn't elaborate.

"And nothing." His face is expressionless. "Emmeline fits certain criteria I have, that's all."

That's all? The pizza in my stomach turns into a brick. "If she's so perfect, then why—"

"Here you are. The squid ink risotto," the waiter announces, placing the dish in the middle of the table with a flourish as a busboy clears off the remnants of the appetizers. I clamp my lips shut, forcing myself to stay silent as the waiter puts clean plates in front of each of us.

As soon as he's gone, I open my mouth to resume my questioning, but Marcus shocks me by reaching across the table and covering my hand with his. His palm is dry and warm and so large I feel engulfed by the heat of it. My breath catches in my throat, and my heartbeat skyrockets further as he leans in, his blue eyes locked on my face.

"Emma, listen to me," he says quietly. "Emmeline has nothing to do with this. I've only met her once, and there are no commitments of any kind between us. As you might've guessed, I'm attracted to you—*very* attracted—and if I'm not mistaken, you're not completely indifferent to me either." His thumb brushes across the pulse in my wrist, which is hammering wildly, corroborating his words. He must feel it too, because his eyes darken and his voice deepens, turning low and seductive as he murmurs, "Why don't we just enjoy this meal and see where things go from here?"

I swallow thickly. I don't know what to say, or even to think. A part of me is bizarrely hurt that this other woman fits some predetermined criteria of his, but what he's saying makes sense too. One dinner doesn't make her his girlfriend, any more than it gives *me* any rights over him. If anything, his honesty is a point in his favor; he could've lied about meeting Emmeline, and I would've been none the wiser. At the same time,

I'm aware that I'm not thinking clearly, that his touch is heating me from within and turning my brain to mush.

"I, um…" Pulling my hand away, I fight to regain my composure. "I think you should eat your risotto. It's probably getting cold."

He regards me wryly, and I have a feeling he knows exactly how he's affecting me. "Of course, the risotto. We don't want it to get cold," he says, and I let out a relieved breath as he reaches for the dish.

Scooping up a spoonful of risotto, he reaches for my plate.

"Oh, no, I'm good, thanks." I move the plate out of his reach. "It's all yours."

"You don't want to try even a little?"

"I'm really full, thanks." It's a lie; my mouth is watering at the succulent-looking seafood in the risotto, but I don't want to muddy the waters when it comes time to pay the check. "It's all yours."

After a moment of hesitation, he puts the risotto on his plate and digs into it with evident enjoyment. "Not a seafood fan?" he asks after the first bite, and I shrug in response. I love seafood, but if I admit that, my refusal to try Marcus's dish will confuse him even more.

"I think it's okay," I say when he lifts his eyebrows, silently urging me to elaborate. "I'm pretty open to all foods, actually."

"Ah, an omnivore. I like it." He grins, showing those sexy cheek grooves, and I feel the magnetic pull again. It's unfair that the best-looking guys are often the ones who are off limits, either because they're assholes or because they're gay. Marcus is definitely not the second, but the jury is still out on the first.

"So," I say, leaning back in my chair to put a little distance between us. "What is your criteria? Do you have a list with all the qualities you want your future wife to possess?"

He raises his eyebrows. "Doesn't everyone? Isn't there something you'd want your future spouse to be? Some qualities you'd want him to have?"

"I guess," I say after considering it for a moment. "I'd definitely want him to be nice and kind to animals... especially cats. I'd want him to love cats."

"That's it? Just nice and an animal lover?"

"Well, it would be good if he shared some of my interests, too. The more we have in common, the greater the odds that it'll work out longer term."

Marcus regards me with a curious smile. "You don't believe in opposites attracting?"

"No—not in any sustainable way, at least," I say as he reaches for more risotto. "I think two incompatible people can be physically attracted to each other, but for an enduring relationship to form, you need a stronger foundation. There must be shared values and beliefs, goals and interests... If you don't have that, the relationship will be like a match: fragile and quick to burn out."

His smile fades, his expression turning unusually serious. "You're right. I couldn't agree more." He takes a sip of water before digging into his food again, and I watch in amazement as he polishes off a sizable portion of the risotto in record time.

"So you never told me what your criteria is," I say when Marcus's plate is almost clean. "Is it height, weight, eye color... education level?"

He puts down his fork, his gaze locking on my face. "Education is definitely important to me. So is intelligence, upbringing, and a certain amount of ambition. Obviously, I want to be attracted to her, but I'm also looking for a woman who'd be an asset at social functions, someone who'd be comfortable interacting with my existing and potential investors and wouldn't mind doing so. And above all else, I want a wife who'd understand that a successful career requires sacrifices, that you have to work hard to get somewhere in life."

I stare at him in fascination. His bluntness is both refreshing and off-putting. What he's describing sounds more like a business partner than a love interest. For some reason, I picture the wife from *House of Cards*—the cool, elegant Claire who's the female half of the scheming political power couple in that Netflix show. Marcus isn't a politician, but his requirements seem similar. I don't know what kinds of events he attends, but the fact that he refers to them as "social functions" implies they're not backyard barbecues in Brooklyn.

"What about her personality and interests?" I ask, pushing away my dismay. I don't know why I feel disappointed at Marcus's revelations; it's not as if I didn't know we were utterly different. When he asked me out, I knew the dinner would be a one-off affair, and it shouldn't upset me to learn that he wants a woman who's my polar opposite. I'm no longer as socially awkward as I was in my teens, but I'm enough of an introvert that a casual gathering with friends can tire me out. Just the thought of some big formal event makes me want to break out in hives, and I wouldn't know how to begin making small talk with those investors of his.

I can talk to strangers about books, but that's about it.

"Personality and interests?" Marcus appears to give it some thought as the waiter clears off the dishes and sets a dessert menu in front of each of us. "Yes, obviously, those are important too. I'd want her to be level-headed and reasonable, not a hothead. Also honest. Honesty and loyalty are very important to me."

"Me too," I say, nodding. "I think trust is key in any relationship."

Marcus smiles. "I'm glad we agree on that."

"What about interests?" I ask. "What do you like to do in your spare time?"

"I don't have a lot of that, but I suppose I like collecting things, and I'm also into fitness. I enjoy challenging myself physically, so I do a couple of marathons and triathlons every year, and I train in mixed martial arts when I can."

"Oh, wow." That explains his athletic build—and confirms my overall impression of him. Marcus is indeed an extreme Type A, the kind of man who accomplishes more in a week than most people do in a lifetime. "That's hardcore."

"What about you?" he asks as I glance down at the dessert menu, more out of habit than any real interest. "Do you have any hobbies?"

"I like books," I say sheepishly, looking up to meet his gaze. I wish I could tell him I'm into something cool and sporty, like skiing or rock climbing, but walking is my exercise of choice. The only time I run is when I have to catch the train. "When I'm not editing books, I'm usually reading them," I elaborate when he continues looking at me. "I also like TV shows and movies. You know, pretty normal stuff. Oh, and cats. I love my cats, obviously."

"Obviously," he says, one corner of his mouth lifting in a smile. "I like books too, by the way. In fact—"

"Would you like some dessert?" the waiter asks, approaching our table, and I shake my head.

"I'm good, thanks."

"None for me either, thank you," Marcus tells the waiter.

"We'll just take the check," I say before he can slip away.

The waiter nods and disappears, and I turn to find Marcus watching me with a frown.

"In a hurry to leave?"

"No, but I figured you might be," I say honestly. "Clearly, we don't have a lot in common, and you're a busy man, so…" My voice trails off as Marcus's frown deepens.

"Emma, listen to me," he begins, but before he can finish, the waiter returns and discreetly places a small black folder in the middle of the table. In a practiced move, I snatch up the folder and open it, quickly skimming the lines on the check to confirm that my portion is indeed what I expected.

"What are you doing?" Marcus asks as I reach into my wallet and take out twenty-eight dollars—the cost of my pizza appetizer, plus tax and tip.

I look up to find his blue eyes narrowed and his jaw set in a hard line.

"I always pay for myself," I explain, putting the money into the folder. "I don't think it's right for my date to pay for me when I'm perfectly capable of buying my own meal." I start to move the folder back to the middle of the table, but Marcus reaches across the table and catches my hand.

"Emma…" His grip on my fingers is gentle, but his eyes glint harshly as he says in an even tone, "I asked you to dinner, and I'm paying for it. End of story."

My breathing speeds up at his touch, and it's all I can do to say steadily, "I understand the custom, but I don't feel comfortable with it. I prefer to pay my own way."

A muscle ticks in his jaw. "Why? A dinner doesn't mean you owe me. You don't have to sleep with me just because I'm paying for your pizza."

The ache between my thighs returns as his words bring up the images from my dream. "I know that." My words come out strangled. His palm is warm and strong, keeping my hand pinned in place with no effort, and I feel like I'm burning up from the heat inside me. "It's just my dating policy, that's all."

He stares at me, his eyes boring into mine, and the rest of the restaurant fades away again. It's as if we're completely alone, the tension thrumming between us like an exposed wire. I feel caught, utterly powerless to break his spell as he leans in until his face is less than a foot from mine.

"This is not going to end here, kitten," he says softly. "You know that, right? It doesn't matter if you pay for your dinner or not, because we're still going to end up in the same place."

I can literally feel my panties getting soaked. "W-what place?"

"My bed." His eyes glitter darker. "Or your bed—or a hotel bed if you prefer. Hell, it doesn't even have to be a bed. I'd fuck you on the table or the floor, or up against a wall. Just tell me when and where, and I will make it happen."

My breath stops in my lungs. I've never been propositioned so bluntly, and certainly never in those terms. Most men try to couch their intent in terms of romance, or avoid talking about it at all. Certainly, my ex-boyfriend would've turned redder than my hair if those words had come out of his mouth. I should probably be insulted, but I'm too turned on to work up any real indignation. Something about his unapologetic crudeness intensifies the wet heat between my legs, turning my insides soft and liquid. I want exactly what he's offering: him, thrusting into me... on the bed, the table, the floor... Even up against the wall, though I can't quite picture it with the difference in our heights.

He's all wrong for me, and I want him. I want him more than I've ever wanted anything.

"I... I have to go." My voice sounds choked as I yank my hand out of his grip and stand up, nearly turning over my chair in my haste to get away. Spinning around, I rush to the coat check like the coward that I am, the scenes he evoked playing in my mind like a graphic movie.

I almost have my coat when a big hand reaches past me, grabbing it before I can. I look up, my pulse accelerating further as I meet that cool blue gaze.

"Let me take you home," Marcus says quietly, and I stare up at him, powerless to do anything else as he wraps the coat around my shoulders, his warm fingers brushing over my collarbone. My neck hurts from arching it back to hold his gaze, but I can't look away from those magnetic eyes, can't focus on anything but the dark, heated promise within them... and my own helpless response.

"I won't pressure you to do anything you don't want," he promises softly, and I believe him.

Swallowing my heart back into my chest, I let him button up my coat and lead me out to the car.

CHAPTER SIXTEEN

$\mathcal{M}$arcus

EMMA IS QUIET DURING THE SHORT RIDE TO HER PLACE, her gaze trained on the streets outside the window and her luscious little butt positioned as far away from me as the car's width allows. I let her be, though the temptation to touch her, to remind her of the scorching chemistry between us, is nearly impossible to resist. But resist it I do, because I promised not to pressure her into something she's not ready for.

It's bad enough I came on to her like a barbarian, all my hard-earned social graces decimated by a toxic mix of lust and confused anger.

I asked her on a date, and she paid for herself.

She paid for her own fucking pizza.

Even now, I can't believe she did that—or that I let

her. It's just that she caught me off-guard, grabbing the check so quickly and with so little hesitation. Normally, when a woman offers to split the bill or pay for her own portion, it's done more as a courtesy gesture, a nod to the modern times and the women's liberation movement. It's a woman's way of showing that she doesn't *really* need a man to pay for her, though, of course, she's secretly quite pleased if he doesn't accept her half-hearted offer and pays anyway.

At least that's how it was when I was a student and didn't have two nickels to rub together. Once I started earning real money, the half-hearted offers petered out, and by the time I made my first ten million, I forgot what it was like to have my dates play that game. Women now just assume that I will pay, both because I'm a man and because I'm filthy rich, and I don't mind. It's as it should be: if I'm with a woman, I take care of her.

Not with Emma, though. She didn't make that assumption—nor did it feel like a game with her. She didn't offer to pay; she simply did it, plopping down her cash before I could so much as look at the check. She was deadly earnest about it, too. It wasn't a joke; for whatever reason, it mattered to her.

I take a calming breath and try to talk myself into looking away from her delicate profile. She's still gazing out the window, her small hands clenched tightly in her lap and her curls wild and unruly around her freckled face. I don't understand her, and I don't understand my reaction to her. I want to reach over and scoop her up, to put her on my lap so I can feel the soft curve of her shapely ass against my groin. I want to tangle my fingers in that wild mane of hair and arch her head back, so I can kiss the pale white flesh of her throat, taste the pulse throbbing underneath that translucent-looking skin.

How have I not realized before how sexy petite, lushly curved women can be? When she was standing there, at the coat check, looking up at me with those startled gray eyes, it was all I could do not to bend down and grab her. To just lift her and carry her off like the delicious little prize she is. No other woman has ever elicited that urge in me—and certainly not Emmeline, with her sleek, elegant beauty.

I suck in another breath and finally succeed in dragging my gaze away from Emma. It's pointless to compare the two women, because what I want from them is so different. Emma is a whim, an anomaly in a lifetime of self-discipline and rigid planning, while Emmeline is what I've always wanted, what I've worked toward since I was a little boy.

Since I made a vow to myself to never, ever fall for a woman like my mother.

Not that Emma is like her—at least as far as I can tell from our short acquaintance. My mother was impulsive and selfish, and I see little evidence of those traits in my companion. Nor is Emma an alcoholic. All she had to drink at dinner was water—a choice I heartily approve. I have nothing against moderate social drinking, but I can't deny that when I see a woman imbibe more than a couple of glasses of wine, I get uncomfortable flashbacks to my vodka-and-vomit-soaked childhood.

To this day, I can't stand vodka, even of the upscale variety.

My phone vibrates in my pocket, and I pull it out, glancing at the screen.

Fuck.

My inbox is blowing up with urgent messages from Jarrod Lee, my Chief Investment Officer. I must've forgotten to check my phone during dinner because there are five emails in a row. An opportunity to invest in high-risk municipal bonds has fallen into our lap, and he needs to know if we should pull the trigger, given our views on interest rates. I swiftly review the bond specs and fire off a reply authorizing the $700 million investment.

Our analysts expect the municipality to have a successful capital raise before the next Fed meeting, which means our investment should double in value before the bond market tanks on the interest rate hike.

I finish with the emails just as the car pulls up to the curb in front of Emma's apartment. Getting out, I open the door on her side and help her out. Her hand lightly touches mine as she climbs out of the car, and I can't help closing my fingers around that small palm, then holding it a second too long.

Her startled gaze flies up to mine again, and I feel a tremor pass through her as she pulls her hand away.

"Marcus…" Her voice is decidedly unsteady. "I really need to—"

"Of course." I give her a smile as I walk her to the door, though the newly awakened caveman inside me howls in frustration. "You have to go. I understand."

She nods, fumbling inside her bag as we stop in front of the door. Extracting her keys, she looks up, adorably flushed. "I do. My cats need to be fed, and I have to get up early for work tomorrow, and—"

"Emma." I stop her rambling with another deceptively calm smile. "Say no more. I promised not to pressure you, and I won't."

Her flush intensifies. "Oh. Well, thank you. I had a great time."

"Me too. What are you doing tomorrow night?"

She blinks up at me. "Tomorrow?"

"Friday," I say helpfully. "You know, the day before the weekend?"

"Oh, I—" She stops and bites her lip. "You want to see me tomorrow?"

"I do." And the day after, and the one after that, I realize to my shock. This dinner was far too short to satisfy my curiosity about Emma and her effect on me. I want to fuck her, yes, but I'm also intrigued by her.

I want to understand what makes her tick, and why that matters to me.

"I guess…" She hesitates, then blurts, "I guess that would be okay."

"Excellent." It takes everything I have to conceal my savage satisfaction. "Any specific food preference?"

"I'm not picky about food, but I do have a budget preference," she says, and I sigh, realizing we're going to fight that battle all over again.

Now is not the time for it, though, so I just nod and say, "I'll be sure to keep that in mind. Pick you up at seven?"

"Okay." She smiles up at me. "Seven it is. Thanks again."

And before I can so much as kiss her cheek, she turns around, opens the door, and disappears inside to a chorus of outraged meows.

CHAPTER SEVENTEEN

mma

"Are you seriously telling me that you have a second date with Marcus Carelli of Carelli Capital Management?" Kendall's eyes look like they're about to pop through my phone screen.

"Yes, why? Do you know him?" I angle the phone slightly and look around to make sure the bookstore is still empty. My boss is off having a long lunch, and though it would've been smart to use this downtime to edit the short story I've been procrastinating on, I couldn't resist video-calling Kendall about my date instead.

"Do I know Marcus Carelli?" Her voice rises. "Are you shitting me? Are you that oblivious to the world?"

"Um..."

"Never mind." Her face grows in the phone camera as she leans in. "I should know by now. If it's not in a book or doesn't have a tail, it doesn't exist for you."

I sigh. My friend is nothing if not a drama queen. "Just tell me already. What do you know about Marcus? Because I'm seeing him again tonight, and—"

"You couldn't be bothered to google him?"

"I didn't get a chance. I got home pretty late, had to feed the cats right away and then respond to some editing clients. And today was an extra-early shift with a bunch of morning deliveries, so I'm just now catching my breath." I also spent some quality time with my vibrator last night, needing to relieve the tension from the date, but Kendall doesn't need to know that. I suppose I could've spent that time stalking Marcus online, but it honestly didn't occur to me.

I've never dated anyone who had anything interesting for me to find.

Kendall rolls her eyes, making sure the camera catches her doing so. "Yeah, okay, whatever. Listen up, Miss Oblivious." She leans in until her perfectly shaped nose dominates the screen. "Anyone who's ever glanced at *The Wall Street Journal* or turned on CNBC—as in, everyone in NYC with the possible exception of you and your cats—knows about Marcus Carelli. He's one of the biggest movers and shakers on Wall Street. His fund has some insane number of billions under management, and his presentations can make or break a stock. Don't you remember that thing with the corrupt tire company a couple of years ago, where a prominent hedge fund manager bet the stock would go to zero—and it did? It was all over the news, and they even made a documentary about it on Netflix."

"Maybe." I frown because that does ring a bell. "That was Marcus's fund?"

"Yep. He laid out the case against the company at one of those big-name investment conferences, and the stock dropped like sixty percent that day. The CEO was crying foul all over the news, but the regulators refused to do anything, and a few months later, the company filed for bankruptcy."

"Wow." I do recall the story now. It was all over the headlines, to the point that even I couldn't miss it. The tire company—an old and highly respected industry leader—had been accused by some hedge fund big-shot of everything from manufacturing defects to slave-labor conditions in its factories, and the resulting publicity tanked the company's stock, hastening its demise.

And that big-shot was Marcus.

The man who called me "kitten" and openly told me he wants to fuck me.

The man I'm going on a date with tonight.

For the second time.

"—has been all over the Forbes list of billionaires," Kendall continues, and I blink, realizing I briefly tuned her out.

"Billionaires?" My voice sounds choked, but I can't help it. I knew Marcus was wealthy, of course—everything about him spoke of money—but there's a huge difference between a run-of-the-mill asset manager and a hedge fund titan who can take down a huge public company with a few PowerPoint slides.

Marcus isn't just big leagues; he's the freaking Olympics.

"Yeah, he's made the list several years in a row," Kendall says. "I can't believe you didn't know. He must've taken you someplace nice. He did, right?" Her eyes narrow.

"Yeah, very nice." I still sound like I swallowed a frog, but I'm proud of the fact that I can speak at all. "It was this little Italian place in Bensonhurst, and—"

"In Brooklyn?" Kendall's eyebrows pull together. "Are you serious?"

"Yeah, why not?" I sound defensive, but I can't help it. Kendall is a total snob when it comes to the boroughs. Never mind that some areas of Brooklyn are now cooler and more expensive than certain parts of Manhattan; she still thinks it's the boonies.

She sighs and shakes her head. "You're hopeless. Just please tell me you didn't try to drag him to that pizza dump by your house."

I can feel my face turning red.

"You did? Oh my God, Emma!"

"I didn't know, okay?" I snap, feeling uncharacteristically embarrassed. "Obviously, I wouldn't have invited him there if I'd known. But we didn't end up going there—we went to a place *he* suggested—so it's all good."

She pinches the bridge of her nose. "Tell me you at least let him pay."

I stare at her, unblinking.

"Emma!"

"What?" My jaw tenses. "You know how I feel about mooching."

"It's not mooching—it's tradition for a man to pay when he invites a woman out—and he probably made more than your monthly salary in the time it took you to open your wallet."

I do a quick calculation in my head. She's not far off.

"I don't care how much he makes," I say. "That's not what it's about for me."

Kendall's expression softens. "I know, Ems. But letting a guy pay for dinner is not even in the same ballpark as—"

"I know. I'm not an idiot. I just can't—" I stop and take a breath, then glance up at the clock. "Look, I should go. My boss will be returning from lunch soon."

"Okay, but you have to tell me how it goes tonight, okay? Promise you'll call me as soon as you're home."

"Will do—unless it's late."

Her eyes widen. "Are you planning to—"

"No! I mean, I don't know. I mean—oh, never mind. I'll call you as soon as I can."

And I hang up before Kendall can give me the third degree about *that*.

As I sort and organize the romance novels in the back of the store, I can't help but think about what I didn't want to discuss with Kendall.

Am I planning to do it?

I know what Marcus wants, what he's after.

Sex. Me and him, sweaty bodies entangled—just like the mental images I masturbated to last night.

The question is, am I going to do it? Am I going to sleep with him, knowing it's most likely a one-time deal?

Even if there was no perfect Emmeline in the picture, a handsome, wealthy man like Marcus is bound to be inundated with women. Gorgeous, tall, slim-hipped women whose hair wouldn't dream of frizzing up—and who'd let him pay for their meal without a qualm.

Would he call them "kitten" too, in that rough velvet voice of his, or is that pet name reserved solely for me? How did he come up with it, anyway? Is it because I like cats? As with that proposition, I should probably feel insulted, but the way Marcus said it, the way he looked at me...

"Emma? Can you come here, please?"

I stop in the middle of shelving a new shifter romance and yell out, "Coming, Mr. Smithson," then hurry to the front, where my boss is ringing up a customer.

"Can you please recommend a new urban fantasy series to Mrs. Wilkins?" he says, nodding toward the customer—an old woman so tiny Mr. Puffs could carry her away. "She likes mind readers and such."

"Oh, no problem," I say, beaming at the woman. "I know just the thing."

And pushing aside all thoughts of my dilemma, I focus on my job.

CHAPTER EIGHTEEN

*M*arcus

As Friday afternoon wears on, I find myself watching the clock, to the point that I'm counting the minutes during the weekly fund performance review with my portfolio managers. It's nearly five p.m., which means that in two short hours, I will see Emma again.

I can't fucking wait.

"—and so I think this will make a great pitch for your Alpha Zone presentation next month," my telecom PM says, bringing my attention back to the meeting. "If you want, I'll have my analyst email you his research."

I have no idea which stock he's talking about, having zoned out like a schoolboy daydreaming about his crush, but there's no way I'm admitting that in front of everyone. "Yes, have him email it to me," I say coolly. "I'll take a look at it over the weekend."

Alpha Zone is an association of the most influential players on Wall Street, and the December conference is its bedrock. There, we each pitch our best idea— whether it be a currency play, a private equity investment, or something as boring as going long a particular stock—and the best-performing investment is awarded a prize at the following year's event. The prize itself is nothing major—a trip to Bora Bora or some such—but the boost to one's reputation is priceless.

The telecom PM's proposal better be something good.

Jarrod, my Chief Investment Officer, gives me a weird look—he's not used to me being less than 110-percent engaged—and I force myself to concentrate for the rest of the meeting, digging into the fund's major positions as thoroughly as I always do. Though the healthcare team had a big trade go against them yesterday, the fund overall is up another half a percent this week, putting us at nearly ninety-three billion in assets under management.

If this winning streak keeps up, we'll breach a hundred billion in no time.

Normally, the thought would fill me with great anticipation, but the only thing I'm anticipating right now is picking up Emma in two hours. I can already picture how this date will unfold: I'll ring her doorbell, and she'll jump out, all adorably flushed as she escapes her cats. I'll clasp her hand in mine, pulling her to me for a carefully controlled kiss—our first—and then we'll step into my car. There, we'll make out as Wilson drives us to my favorite Greek restaurant in the East Village—one that happens to be reasonably priced, as per her request.

By the time we get to the restaurant, food will be the last thing on both of our minds, and as soon as the meal is over, I'll take her to my Tribeca penthouse and fuck her senseless.

We'll spend the weekend in bed, and by Monday, I'll have her out of my system.

I'll be rid of this unhealthy craving for good.

CHAPTER NINETEEN

mma

I TURN OFF THE WATER AND PULL OPEN THE SHOWER curtain to find the bathroom floor looking like it's been snowed on. Some bits of paper are so small they float in the air as I step out, hollering, "Puffs!" at the top of my lungs.

That damn cat. He must've sensed that I'm about to leave him and his siblings alone for the second evening in a row, so he shredded the entire roll of toilet paper while I was in the shower.

Swearing, I hop around on one foot, trying to get sticky pieces of damp toilet paper off my other foot with a towel. It takes forever to do that, not to mention clean up the bathroom, and the doorbell rings as I'm frantically applying my mascara.

Crap. I'm still in my underwear.

"One sec!" I yell as I rush across the room to grab my clothes from the closet. Mr. Puffs hisses at me from the top shelf, and Cottonball lets out a plaintive meow, batting my leg with his paw so I'll cuddle him in front of the TV, as is our custom on Friday nights.

"Sorry, not tonight, buddy. I have a date." I bend down to scratch his head apologetically when Mr. Puffs jumps down from the top shelf—right onto my shoulders.

"Ahh!" I pitch forward with a startled cry, pushed off balance by fifteen pounds of feline slamming into me from an almost-six-foot height. Queen Elizabeth jumps off the bed and runs over, meowing in obvious concern as I land on all fours, and at the same time, the doorbell rings again, followed by a deep voice calling my name.

It's Marcus, and he sounds worried.

Mr. Puffs is still on my shoulders, somehow balancing without sinking his claws into my skin, and I throw him off as I get up, yelling, "Coming!"

Except I trip over Cottonball and go flying with a panicked cry.

I land on my stomach, the impact knocking all breath out of my lungs. Wheezing, I flop over onto my back and hear Marcus's deep voice shouting, "Emma, are you all right?" right before something slams into my door, causing it to rattle on its hinges.

Holy cow. Did he just try to break it down?

Another hard slam, and the door hinges creak, nearly giving way.

I want to yell that I'm all right, but I can't gather enough air. All I can manage is a pathetic wheeze that I'm okay, and with all three cats meowing loudly around me, even I can't hear what I'm saying.

Rolling over onto my stomach, I push up to all fours, so I can crawl over and stop him, when the next kick or body slam or whatever knocks the door completely off its hinges.

It flies in, like during a SWAT raid in an action movie, and behind it stands Marcus, dressed in a suit and another pricy-looking unbuttoned coat. His blue eyes narrow in on me with unmistakable concern, and he rushes over, crouching next to me as Queen Elizabeth and Cottonball zoom under the bed. Only Mr. Puffs remains by my side, arching his back and hissing at the intruder before also dashing away to hide under the bed.

"Are you okay? What happened?" Marcus demands, gripping my arms to steady me as I attempt to rise to my feet. With his help, I succeed, though my left knee complains loudly—I must've banged it on the floor.

"I'm okay. I'm fine," I croak as he begins to pat me down, looking for injuries. His big hands are hot on my bare skin, and with a wave of mortification, I realize that I never got a chance to put on clothes.

I'm standing in front of him in nothing but my blue lacy bra and panties—which, granted, is my nicest set, but still.

"What happened?" he demands again as I back away, cheeks flaming as I wrap my arms around my stomach—which is quite a bit softer than I'd like. He's undoubtedly used to fitness bunnies with rock-hard abs and—

Wait a minute. Why am I thinking about my lack of abs when he *broke down my door*?

"I tripped, okay? I tripped." I still sound winded, but I'm not sure how much of that is from the fall versus the way he's staring at me—with a worry that's gradually transforming into something else.

Something hotter and infinitely more dangerous.

"So you're not hurt?" he clarifies in a huskier tone, and I shake my head, my face burning as the heat in his eyes intensifies. And it's not just my face—my whole body feels like it's on fire as he takes a step toward me, his powerful hands flexing at his sides.

It doesn't seem like my lack of abs is a turn-off for him—at least judging by the dark hunger in that stare.

"The door..." My voice comes out thin and high. "You... um, broke down the door."

"The door?" He doesn't seem to know what I'm talking about as he takes another step toward me, his gaze falling to my bra—which is pushing up my heaving breasts, as if offering them up like a sacrifice.

I swallow as he reaches for me, one big hand curving tenderly around my jaw while the other lands on my naked shoulder, squeezing lightly. His touch burns through me, spiking my pulse and sending a heated shiver down my spine. Looming over me, he's so tall I have to crane my neck to hold his gaze, and it dawns on me that I've never felt so small and vulnerable before… or so wanted.

"Emma." His voice is low and thick as his fingers slide into my hair, sensuously cupping my skull. "Kitten, may I kiss you?" He's bending his head as he speaks, and the last word is murmured against my lips, his warm, faintly sweet breath mixing with my own shallow exhalations.

I never get a chance to respond because my hands reach up to clasp his broad shoulders, and my eyes close as my lips press against his—seemingly of their own accord. There's no logic in my decision, no reason whatsoever. We're utterly wrong for each other, and I'm bound to get hurt if we proceed, but for the first time in my life, I don't care about the risk I'm taking.

There's no room for fear in the blazing need consuming me.

He deepens the kiss, arching me back over his arm, and my breasts mold against the hard plane of his chest as my head falls back, supported only by the cradle of his palm. His lips are warm and soft, his tongue exploring my mouth with sensuous skill, and a small moan escapes my throat as his lips leave mine and trail over my jaw to nibble on my earlobe—where the heat of his breath sends goosebumps rippling down my arm. I can smell the clean, woodsy scent of his skin, like pine mixed with fresh autumn breeze, and my body tightens, tension spiraling through my core. I'm so turned on I'm on the verge of orgasm, and my hands tug at the lapels of his coat, desperate to get it off so I can—

A hissing meow startles me, jolting me out of my sensual haze. Eyes snapping open, I push at Marcus's chest, and he lets me go, though his gaze is heavy-lidded and his normally even-toned skin is edged with a flush of arousal.

Panting, we stare at each other as Mr. Puffs winds around my legs, alternately hissing at Marcus and meowing up at me.

"Your cat," Marcus says hoarsely. "He's not going to run away?"

I stare at him blankly, then recall the broken door. My cats are not in the habit of trying to run away, but then again, they've never had the temptation of a door-less entrance. "He shouldn't," I say, but just to be on the safe side, I bend down and pick up Mr. Puffs, cradling him against my chest.

The evil beast starts purring, and I stroke him, grateful for the shield his large, furry body provides. I still don't have my clothes on, and with the icy November air blowing in through the open doorway, it's quickly getting cold in the apartment.

Plus, there's that whole being semi-naked in front of Marcus bit.

"So," I say awkwardly, inching toward my closet with Mr. Puffs in my arms. "About the door—"

"I'll get it fixed, don't worry." His gaze tracks me with undisguised hunger as I make my way back to the closet, then put Mr. Puffs down so I can dress. "It looked like it was on its last legs, anyway."

"Can you turn around, please?" I blurt out, holding my jeans in front of me when he shows no sign of looking away. I know it's silly—he's already seen most of me—but I don't want him to watch my butt jiggle as I perform the maneuvers required to pull on my tight jeans.

There's way too much butt jiggle for my liking.

He opens his mouth to say something, then apparently thinks better of it and turns around. "Go ahead," he says thickly. "I won't look."

I quickly wriggle into the jeans, then throw on my second-nicest blouse—my nicest being the one I wore out yesterday. I finish off the outfit with my sweater wrap and newish boots, and when I glance at the hallway mirror, I realize that my outfit is identical to yesterday's, the only difference being the blouse. Even worse, with all of my recent exertions, my mascara has smeared, leaving a raccoon-like smudge under my left eye, and my hair looks like I've been wrestling with a wildcat—which, given Mr. Puffs's size, is not far from the truth.

So much for impressing a billionaire.

I'm muttering curses under my breath and trying to rub off the mascara smudge when Marcus asks, "Can I turn around now?"

Crap. I smooth my hands over my hair, sneak another look in the mirror, and say glumly, "Go ahead."

I'd need an hour to fix the mess I see in the mirror,

not a few minutes—not that it matters either way. Now that I'm not so frazzled and my brain is not clouded by lust, an obvious fact occurs to me.

With the door broken, I can't leave my apartment and the cats.

Tonight's date is not happening.

CHAPTER TWENTY

$\mathcal{M}$arcus

MY ERECTION IS STILL THREATENING TO RIP A HOLE IN my pants as I turn around and look at Emma—who, to my great disappointment, is now fully dressed. It almost doesn't matter, though. The sight of her clad in nothing but lacy underwear is permanently etched into my brain—and will star in every wet dream and fantasy of mine going forward.

"Sexy" doesn't even begin to describe her curvy little body. Every soft, feminine inch of her seems to be designed with my newly discovered preferences in mind. Her creamy skin is dotted in a few places with an appealing smattering of freckles, and her ass is the best I've ever seen: full and heart-shaped, infinitely squeezable. Or at least I imagine it is—I somehow managed to keep my hands off it as I devoured her mouth.

And then, of course, there are those luscious breasts of hers, the sensual dip in her navel, and her small, perfectly shaped feet with red-painted toenails.

Fuck, even her little toes turn me on.

"So, about the door," she starts again when I remain silent, eyeing her hungrily. "Should I call a repairman or...?" She lets the question trail off.

"I'll do it," I say huskily, and forcing myself to look away from the temptation of her, I pull out my phone.

My butler, Geoffrey, picks up on the first ring, and I inform him of the situation. "I need someone over here within the hour," I tell him, and he promises that it will be done.

I hang up and see Emma staring at me with her mouth open, the big cat back in her arms.

"Someone is going to come on a Friday night?" she asks incredulously. "As in, right away?"

"Of course. You can't not have a door overnight."

It makes perfect sense to me, but she's looking at me like I've sprouted a horn on my forehead—and so is her cat. "On a Friday night," she mutters, stroking the fluffy creature. "Yeah, okay, sure."

"We'll stay here until they're done," I say, shrugging out of my coat. Even with the cold draft coming in, it's still too hot inside the apartment for me to wear it. Draping it over the back of the only chair I see, I tell her, "It'll take them a little while to fix it, so we should probably go ahead and eat. Any preferences for delivery or takeout around here?"

She blinks. "You… want to have dinner here?"

"Of course." I frown. "Unless you're not hungry?"

"Oh, no, I'm hungry," she assures me, propping the cat higher on her chest. "I just figured that given what happened, we would, you know, reschedule or whatever."

Oh, no. There's no way I'm leaving her alone in a Brooklyn apartment with a broken door leading to the street. Granted, this is not what I envisioned for our second date, but I don't mind this development one bit —though she did almost give me a heart attack with all the falling sounds and the screaming.

I thought she'd gotten seriously hurt, and the chilling fear I'd experienced had been entirely out of proportion to the length of our acquaintance.

I don't want to analyze why that is, or why I don't have any desire to escape her cramped basement studio. It reminds me of the apartment my mother and I had lived in when I was in middle school, and I hated that place, so by all logic, I should hate this too. But I get an entirely different vibe here. Even though the only window in Emma's studio is the same tiny slit near the ceiling that we'd had, and the paint on her walls is also peeling in places, the stink of alcohol and desperation is missing.

Her apartment is rundown and tiny, but it's cozy. A home, not just a place to crash.

Of course, if there were no cats, it would be even

better. I can see two more white furry creatures poking their heads from under the bed, their big green eyes staring at me. Judging by all the meowing I'd heard when Emma fell, I have a strong suspicion they —or the huge one in her arms—were somehow responsible.

"We're not rescheduling," I tell Emma firmly. "I'm here, and you're here, and that"—I point at her tiny desk—"will work as a table. All we need is food, and if you tell me what you want, I can have it delivered or ask my driver to bring it to us."

Before she can respond, the big cat meows, fluffy tail swishing from side to side as he gives me a threatening look from his perch on Emma's chest. I glare back at him. I know he did that hissing-meowing thing while we were making out on purpose, to cockblock me.

If not for that, Emma and I might've made it all the way to her narrow bed, and I would now be balls deep inside her sweet, lush body.

"Sorry," she says, stroking the creature to calm him down. "He's just…"

"Possessive, I know." I would be too, if she petted me like that. In fact, just watching her small hand move over the cat's white fur is making me jealous.

I want her to touch *me* like that, to run her soft hands all over my body.

"So, yeah, about the food," Emma says when the cat starts purring. "I'm really flexible. There's a deli on the corner that makes great sandwiches, and there's also a gyros place I like a couple of blocks over. Neither one delivers, but—"

"Wilson will bring it; that's not a problem. So sandwiches or gyros?"

She hesitates, then says, "Let's do gyros. The place is called Gyro World."

Okay, good. We're having a meal together.

Concealing my satisfaction, I take out my phone and text Wilson the instructions. He immediately replies that he's on his way, and I put my phone away—only to see Emma regarding me with a strange expression.

"What?" I frown at her. "Did I do something wrong?"

She shakes her head, then blurts out, "Is it always so easy for you? Do you always just snap your fingers and things happen?"

"You mean, can I always get gyros delivered? Yes, usually. Is that a bad thing?"

She puts the cat down. "No, of course not. It's just... not what I'm used to, that's all."

She walks over to sit down on the bed, and the two cats come out from underneath to drape themselves over her lap. The big one that she just put down eyes me evilly for a moment, as if debating if I'd make a good meal, then stalks over to join the others on the bed, puffy tail held high.

I decide to ignore his disdain. It's a cat, after all.

Taking a seat on the chair on which I hung my coat, I study Emma, trying to understand what it is about her that I find so appealing. Her looks, for sure—I can't wait to sink my cock deep into her scrumptious little body—but her appearance is only part of the draw.

There's also something warm and tender about her, something that tugs at me in a way I don't fully understand.

"What are they called?" I ask, figuring that since the cats are such a big part of her life, I can at least try to get to know them. "You said that one is Mr. Puffs, right?" I nod at the bad-tempered giant, who's staked out a spot on her left leg by shoving away his much smaller competitor.

She smiles, her eyes lighting up and her dimples coming out in full force. "Yes, that's right. This one"—she looks down at her right leg, where a mid-sized cat is purring up a storm—"is Cottonball. And that"—she nods at the shoved-aside cat, the smallest of the bunch, who's now daintily licking its paw—"is Queen Elizabeth."

"How did you get them?" I ask. "And why three? Your apartment is... not very big." There's barely enough space for one small woman as far as I'm concerned.

She grimaces. "I know. I hate it that they're cooped up in this studio. They're used to it, having grown up here, but still, it's not good. I hope to afford a bigger apartment one day, but for now, all I can do is entertain them the best I can." She glances over her shoulder at the wall on the other side of her bed, and I realize that what I thought was a strange empty bookshelf is actually a cat maze that goes from floor to ceiling—an insane luxury in a place as space-constrained as this one.

She *is* committed to her pets.

"So you've had them from the time they were little?" I ask, and she nods, her expression darkening for some reason.

"They were barely two weeks old when I found them."

"Found them?"

"They came into my life by accident; I didn't plan on any pets when I got this place," she says. "My friend Janie and I were driving to Woodbury Common—you know, the big shopping mall upstate—and we stopped by a gas station on the way. I went around the back to use the restroom, and I heard these faint mewling sounds coming from the garbage can. When I looked inside, there was a box of kittens there—so tiny they barely had their eyes open." Her delicate jaw tightens, and a fierce look comes over her pretty face. "Some asshole threw them out, like they were trash."

Asshole, indeed. I don't consider myself an animal lover, but my hands itch with the urge to beat whoever did this shitty thing to a bloody pulp. "So you took them in?" I ask, doing my best to keep the anger out of my voice, and she nods again.

"Of course. What else could I do? Janie is allergic, and nobody at the gas station would claim them. I thought about bringing them to a shelter—the vet I took them to said they're purebred Persians and would be adopted quickly—but they were beginning to cling to me by then, and I didn't want to cause them any more trauma. As it was, because they weren't properly weaned from their mother, they kept trying to suckle everything in sight for the first two years of their lives. It's only recently that they've calmed down." She gazes down at them with a tender smile, all fierceness gone as she scratches one furry creature behind the ear, then pets the other two.

All three set up a loud purr, and I again battle a surge of jealousy that she's touching *them*, not *me*.

Fuck.

I may need to consult a shrink. This can't be healthy.

I'm about to ask her another question when I hear a knocking on the doorframe, and a spicy, savory aroma fills the apartment.

It's Wilson with our food.

I walk over to take the bags from him, and as I'm thanking him, Emma approaches.

"Here you go," she says brightly, stuffing what looks like a twenty into Wilson's hand. "That should cover my portion."

And ignoring the stunned look on my driver's face, she returns to join her cats on the bed.

CHAPTER TWENTY-ONE

Emma

MARCUS IS LOOKING AT ME LIKE HE'S NEVER SEEN A woman devour a gyro before—and maybe he hasn't. I bet all the supermodel types he dates survive on kale juice and broccoli. Then again, he's been eyeing me like this ever since I paid for my portion, so maybe it has something to do with that.

His driver certainly looked shocked when I gave him the twenty.

Of course, it's also possible that he's not used to seeing a woman eating on her bed, surrounded by cats who have no compunction about stealing pieces of meat straight out of her gyro. I try to shove them away from my plate, but it's useless.

There are three of them, and the gyro has too many

points of access.

"Are you sure you don't want to sit here?" he asks again from his seat at my desk, and I shake my head, my mouth too full to respond verbally. The desk is where I always eat, and other than the kitchen counter, it's the only table-like surface in my apartment. If I sat there, in the only chair I own, he'd have to stand or eat on my bed, and in the latter case, the cats would attack *his* food—not a good situation.

I already feel bad I'm subjecting him to the cramped mess that is my apartment.

"They'd be all over you," I explain after I swallow. "They really like gyros."

"Who wouldn't? These are great," he says and takes another big bite of the juicy pita in his hand.

I brighten a little. "Aren't they?" I was worried he'd feel this kind of food is beneath him—the hole-in-the-wall place we ordered from is just one step above a street cart—but he appears to be genuinely enjoying himself. In general, he seems much more comfortable in my apartment than I figured a billionaire would be—though his big, broad-shouldered frame looks rather ridiculous stuffed into my tiny IKEA chair.

"Yep, good choice," he says, chowing down on his gyro, and I give him a big smile.

Maybe this date isn't a total disaster after all.

He's done with his food in record time. Getting up, he takes his plate into the kitchen, and then I hear the sink turn on.

Is he actually washing it?

Before I can marvel at the phenomenon—my ex-boyfriend didn't know such a thing as dish soap existed—there's another knock by the entrance.

The repair guys have arrived.

There are two of them. One looks like Santa Claus's younger brother, complete with rosy cheeks and a nearly white beard, while the other is a good-looking Latino guy about my age. He has an infectious grin on his face, and I smile back as I get up and place my half-eaten gyro on the desk.

"Hi there," I say, walking over to greet them. "I'm Emma. Thanks so much for coming out so quickly."

I stick my hand out, and the young guy grabs it eagerly, giving it a vigorous shake. "Juan," he says, his grin widening. "Nice to meet you, Emma."

"And I'm Rodney," the Santa Claus sibling says, shaking my hand next. "This the door we need to fix?" He glances at the door on the floor, then studies the frame, where I notice sizable cracks near where the hinges were attached.

God, how strong is Marcus that he was able to do this much damage?

"That's the one," I say, trying not to wince as I picture the damage to my bank account from this repair bill. "Do you have any idea how much this will cost?"

"Oh, um…" Juan glances at Rodney in confusion.

"Nothing," Marcus says, coming out of the kitchen. His voice is hard, utterly uncompromising—as is his expression when he looks at me. "It will cost you absolutely nothing, as I'm the one who broke it."

"But you did it to save *me*—because you thought *I* was in trouble," I argue, but Marcus is not listening.

"You will send the bill to me," he orders, giving Rodney a piercing stare, and the man swiftly bobs his head.

"Yes, of course, Mr. Carelli."

Ugh. I'm tempted to fight further, but I don't have even a hundred dollars to spare right now, and I suspect their bill will run higher than that. It would be highly embarrassing if I insisted on taking care of the payment and then had to beg for an extension. Besides, Marcus does have a point: it *was* his savior complex that got us into this mess.

Still, my chest feels unpleasantly tight as I go back to my food, leaving him talking to the repairmen. I know letting Marcus pay for the door he broke doesn't make me like my mother—logically, I know it—but I can't help feeling like I'm taking advantage of him.

Like I'm using him, the way she'd always used her lovers and anyone else who cared about her.

Shaking off the memories, I sit down at the desk and shoo Mr. Puffs away from what remains of my gyro—which is not much. The cats have stolen most of the meat while I was away. Sighing, I quickly gobble down the rest and carry the dirty plate to the kitchen, where the sink is indeed clean.

Marcus not only washed his plate, he also dried it and put it away.

I do the same with mine and then put on some coffee, in case he wants a cup. I also take out my last remaining pint of salted caramel ice cream and two bowls, figuring I at least owe him dessert.

He enters the kitchen just as the hammering noises by the entrance begin.

"Ice cream?" I offer, scooping a generous portion into a bowl, and he shakes his head.

"None for me, thanks."

"You don't like it?"

He shrugs. "I don't really eat sweets."

Of course he doesn't. Ice cream is for ordinary bums like me, not super-achievers like Marcus who count "fitness" among their hobbies. I'm surprised he ate the greasy gyro; he's probably as disciplined in his diet as he seems to be in everything else.

"How about coffee?" I ask, and he agrees to that.

Black, of course—no sugar or milk for him.

I pour each of us a cup, then carry my coffee and ice cream bowl back to the room. The cats are nowhere to be seen at first, but then I notice the tip of a fluffy white tail sticking out from under the bed.

They must be hiding from the noise, which now includes both hammering and drilling.

Setting my coffee on the nightstand, I sit down on the bed to eat my ice cream, and to my surprise, Marcus joins me there with his coffee instead of taking his seat at the desk. He sits next to me, less than a foot away, and though we're both fully dressed, I feel the proximity of his big body as keenly as if we were naked. My mind flashes to the kiss we just shared, and a hot flush covers my skin, my heartbeat jumping as if I've launched into a sprint.

Oh God. That kiss.

I've been trying not to think about it, so I don't turn into a blushing, stuttering mess, but I can't avoid it any longer. Kissing Marcus had to be the single hottest experience of my life, better than any sex I've had—or fantasized about. Everything about it was so wrong, yet so incredibly right. The way he held me, like he never wanted to let me go, the way his lips felt and tasted... He didn't touch me anywhere but my back and my head, but I was on the verge of combusting, so aroused I can still feel the dampness in my underwear.

It doesn't help that as we sit on the bed, his weight is depressing my old mattress, creating a dip in the soft surface that makes it hard for me to sit upright instead of leaning toward him. It's like the illustrations of gravity, where a big celestial body creates an indentation in spacetime that prevents a smaller body from escaping its orbit.

That's Marcus for me.

I can't seem to escape his pull—nor am I sure I want to.

Our eyes meet, and the drilling noise intensifies, making any attempt at conversation impossible. Still, neither one of us looks away. With the men repairing the door, we have zero privacy, but the work might as well be happening miles away. All I'm aware of is him, his nearness and the growing heat in his gaze.

My hand is unsteady as I dip my spoon into the bowl and come up with some ice cream. Bringing it to my mouth, I close my lips around the creamy, salty-sweet coolness and let it slide down my throat as Marcus's eyes darken, his hard features tightening as he reaches over me and sets his coffee cup down next to mine. I can feel his desire for me, sense its danger-ous, potent draw, and my breathing quickens, my nipples pebbling inside the confines of my bra.

"Emma..." His voice is low and hoarse, somehow audible over the din. "I think... I want the ice cream, after all."

My throat goes dry. "Do you want me to go get you some?"

Holding my gaze, he slowly shakes his head. "Give me some of yours."

Oh God. There's no way he's just talking about the ice cream—not with that look in his eyes.

Still, I move to hand the bowl to him, but he stops me by laying a big hand on my knee.

"Feed it to me," he orders huskily.

My whole body now feels like it's on fire, tingles of electricity racing up my leg from where his palm is resting. The drilling noises stop, replaced by more hammering, but the construction noise is nothing compared to the roar of my pulse in my ears.

Feed it to him.

Right, okay.

My hand trembles as I scoop up a spoonful of ice cream and bring it to his mouth.

His hard, masculine, oh-so-skilled-at-kissing mouth.

His lips close around the spoon, cleaning off all the ice cream, and my breath catches in my throat as his tongue flicks out to lick off the creamy droplet left on the handle—less than half an inch from where my fingers are spasmodically gripping the spoon.

"Delicious," he murmurs, his gaze burning me alive, and I belatedly remember that I have to breathe.

Audibly sucking in air, I yank the spoon back, nearly tipping over the ice cream bowl.

"Whoa, careful there..." His hand covers mine, steadying the bowl in my grasp, and the glimmer of dark amusement in his eyes tells me he knows exactly how he's affecting me—and that he's enjoying every bit of it.

Asshole.

I want to be mad at him, but I can't work up sufficient outrage. I've never been this turned on. Ever. My underwear is soaking wet, and my sex is literally throbbing at the erotic movie playing in my mind. I can picture his skilled mouth closing over my nipple, then trailing burning kisses down my stomach before those warm, supple lips close around my clit and—

"Excuse me, Mr. Carelli? We're done."

Rodney's voice is like a bucket of ice water in my face.

I'd completely forgotten the workers are here.

Mortified, I jump to my feet, clutching the bowl in front of me like it can hide the burning flush covering my cheeks. What the hell was I thinking? Another couple of minutes, and Marcus and I would've been horizontal, ice cream and our audience forgotten.

Juan's thoughts must be in line with mine because he's smirking as he stands next to Rodney.

Marcus doesn't seem fazed. Walking over to the reattached door, he inspects the work, then nods brusquely. "Good job, thank you."

"Yes, thank you," I echo, fighting my embarrassment as the men gather their tools and leave with a friendly wave in my direction.

I'm relieved when the door closes behind them— that is, until it dawns on me that Marcus and I are now all alone in my apartment.

An apartment with a door that closes and locks.

arcus

MY HEART IS THRUMMING WITH DARK ANTICIPATION AS I lock the door and turn to face Emma, who's standing by the bed and watching me with huge gray eyes, the ice cream melting in the bowl she's still clutching with both hands.

This is it.

Finally, she's mine.

I know I'm assuming a lot, but the attraction goes both ways. I could feel her response when I kissed her, could see the rapid beating of the pulse in her neck when I laid my hand on her knee.

She wants me.

She needs this as much as I do.

Holding her gaze, I cross the room and stop in front

of her. My dick is painfully hard, but my movements are carefully restrained as I take the bowl from her shaking hands and set it on the nightstand next to our cups of coffee. Then I clasp her small hands and pull her toward me.

She stares up at me, her eyes wide and her breathing fast and shallow.

Beautiful.

She's so fucking beautiful.

Her lightly freckled skin is so delicate it's almost translucent, the flush of arousal painting her cheeks with a warm peachy glow. Her rosebud lips are parted, revealing small white teeth, and her curls are like spirals of fire around her pretty, softly rounded face.

Everything about her is soft and pretty, as delicious as that spoonful of ice cream I just had.

Placing one hand on her waist, I curve my other palm around the side of her face and dip my head, about to kiss her, when another loud meow interrupts the silence.

Oh, for fuck's sake... I cut my eyes to the side and glower at the big cat, who's emerged from under the bed and is sitting on his furry butt, bushy tail swishing from side to side as he stares up at me with slitted green eyes.

I turn my attention back to Emma, determined to ignore the cockblocking beast, but she's already stepping out of my hold, looking uncomfortable.

This won't do.

This won't do at all.

I catch her hands before she can back away. "Come to my place." It's an order, not a request, but I can't help it. I've never wanted a woman this much, have never felt as out of control as I do now. It's impossible to be suave and seductive with the violent hunger beating at me, demanding that I take her, that I do whatever it takes to make her mine.

If these were more primitive times, I'd have already thrown her over my shoulder and carried her off to my cave.

Her gray eyes round with shock. "To... to your place?"

"Yes." I hold her gaze, not bothering to hide the dark lust coiling within me. "To my place. Now."

There's a better way to do this, I know. I could take her out for a drink; then, once we're both pleasantly buzzed, I could offer to show her the rare book collection in my penthouse. We'd both know what would really happen once we got there, but we wouldn't need to discuss it. She could pretend that she's just going to see some books, and it would all be nice and civilized, properly romantic.

Except I'm not capable of being civilized right now. All my social graces seem to have deserted me again, the veneer of civilization disappearing. For whatever reason, I can't play these games with Emma, can't be smooth and urbane like I am with other women.

With her, I'm driven by pure instinct, and that instinct demands I get her into my bed *right fucking now*.

Her little tongue darts out to wet her lips, and I almost groan at the temptation. "What about—" She swallows visibly. "What about Emmeline?"

Fuck. "What about her?" I growl, pulling her closer. "I told you there are no commitments between us." And there won't be—not until I get Emma out of my system.

I'm not the kind of man who cheats.

"But you still... want to date her, right?" Her voice is breathless as her lower body molds against mine, and my erection presses into her soft belly. "So you could maybe marry her?"

"That's a big maybe," I mutter, and unable to resist a second longer, I grip her face between my palms and bend my head to kiss her.

Her lips are as soft as the first time I tasted them, soft and plush and so fucking sweet that all blood leaves my brain and surges directly to my cock. Distantly, I hear another meow, but I no longer give a fuck about the cat—or Emmeline and my lifelong ambitions. All my senses are filled with Emma... with the wet, heated slide of her tongue against mine and the faint smell of caramel on her breath, with the way her soft curves feel against me and how her hands clutch at my sides as I maneuver her toward her bed.

Fuck going to my place. Here will do just as well.

The backs of her legs touch the mattress, and she suddenly goes rigid. Gripping my wrists, she twists away from my kiss. "Wait!"

I freeze in place, using every ounce of my willpower

to remain still as she slithers out of my hold and backs away, not stopping until she's as far away from the bed —and me—as she can get.

"Listen, Marcus," she says shakily, pushing the curls off her face with a trembling hand. "I'm not... This isn't..." She gulps in a breath. "We're obviously attracted to each other, but this isn't going to work out."

And as I stare at her in disbelief, she picks up her cat from the floor and says quietly, "Leave, please. I want you to go."

mma

"You did *what*?" Kendall's voice jumps an octave as she stares at me, her half-eaten croissant clutched in her hand.

"I told him to leave," I repeat, rubbing my temples as the headache from hell worsens.

I barely slept after Marcus left last night—my second sleepless night this week—and though I've had enough caffeine to wake a horse this morning, my skull feels like it's being squeezed in a vise. Given that, I probably shouldn't have gone to Kendall's apartment for breakfast, but I needed someone other than my cats to talk to.

"Okay, back up." Kendall drops the croissant onto

her napkin and swivels her bar stool to face me fully. "Let's go through this again. He broke down your door to save you after you tripped over your cat, and you guys made out while you were almost naked. He then ate gyros with you while his repairmen fixed it. After that, you kissed *again*, and he invited you to his place. *And you told him it's not going to work out and he should leave?*"

"Technically, he kissed me *after* inviting me to his place, but yes, that's the gist of it."

"Emma! What the hell?"

I blink. "What? He's still planning to date Emmeline, and you're the one who told me to be careful. 'Men are dogs,' remember?"

"You dummy! That was *before* we knew he's a billionaire."

"Kendall—"

"No, listen to me." She leans on the countertop, her elbow nearly squishing the croissant. "This isn't some random Wall Street asshole—it's *Marcus freaking Carelli*. And he's interested in you enough to break down your door and eat takeout gyros in your shitty little studio."

"Right. Because he wants to get into my pants." I massage my brow ridge as if that would cause the pressure behind it to subside. I definitely shouldn't have come here, I see that now. If I'd caught a nap this afternoon, I'd be better equipped to deal with Kendall and her insane views on dating. As is—

"So what?" Kendall jumps off her stool and glares at

me, hands propped on her hips. "You want to get into *his* pants, don't you?"

"Well, yes, but—"

"No buts! He's rich, he's hot, he wants you, and you want him. *And*"—she leans in until her nose is almost touching my own—"he was totally upfront with you about this Emmeline thing. They're not married or even dating yet, so who cares that he *may* date her one day?"

Ugh. I squeeze my eyes shut and wish I were home with my cats. I don't know what I expected when I showed up at Kendall's apartment with the croissants and coffee from the street cart downstairs, but getting yelled at for not sleeping with Marcus wasn't on the list.

It's bad enough I spent all night second-guessing my decision and feeling like crap each time I recalled the expression on Marcus's face when I told him to leave. For a second, he'd looked almost hurt, but then his gaze had hardened, his face turning into a stony mask. Without a word, he turned and walked away, and it was all I could do to remain in place instead of running after him.

Instead of begging him to come back and finish what we started.

"Emma, listen to me," Kendall continues, and I reluctantly open my eyes as she climbs back onto her bar stool. "Marcus clearly likes you. So what if you don't fit his requirements for a wife? That doesn't mean you can't have fun with him. You've been having sex dreams about the man, for chrissakes. And just think about it: *Marcus Carelli*. Do you know what kind of doors would be open to you if you were on his arm? The places he could take you, the people you could meet?" When I stare at her blankly, she rolls her eyes and says pointedly, "That publishing industry job you've wanted forever? He could hook you up in a moment. Hell, his fund could probably *buy* any publisher you want with spare change."

I wince. "Kendall—"

She holds up a hand. "I know, I know. You're determined to stand on your own two feet, and that's admirable. But guess what, Ems? The ground under your feet can be a green lawn or a swamp, and we don't get to choose which—unless we're very lucky and fate hands us a way to cross over. And you, my darling, just got handed the equivalent of the Golden Gate Bridge. Marcus Carelli can lead you to the greenest pastures imaginable; all you have to do is say yes."

———

ON THE SUBWAY RIDE HOME, I DO MY BEST TO FORGET Kendall's words, but the bitter taste in my mouth lingers. I've told her about my childhood more than once, but she still doesn't get it, not really. To her, Marcus's billionaire status is a plus, whereas to me, it's a huge minus. His money and connections are the last thing I want, and that fact alone would've doomed any relationship we might've started.

Not that he even wants a relationship with me. I'm pretty sure it would've been a one- or two-night deal, at most. And while I *had* entertained the idea, when it came down to it—when he didn't deny that he might ultimately marry Emmeline—I couldn't go through with it, no matter how much my body begged me to.

I was too overwhelmed by how he made me feel—and downright terrified of what it would be like when he inevitably walked out of my life.

So it's for the best that I made it happen yesterday, before I got in any deeper. It really is. So what if I felt so shitty after rejecting him that I couldn't sleep? It was too much for me—*he* was too much for me—and it's good to know one's limitations.

Or at least that's what I've been telling myself from the moment Marcus walked out, closing the repaired door behind him. Without his presence, my studio immediately felt colder, emptier... less vital somehow.

No, that's not true. I refuse to go there. However volcanic our attraction, we're otherwise completely incompatible. I made the right choice, no matter what Kendall or anyone else thinks.

All I need to do is make myself believe that.

CHAPTER TWENTY-FOUR

*M*arcus

I SPEND THE REST OF FRIDAY EVENING TRYING TO convince myself that what happened was for the best, that I'm glad Emma pulled the plug on this insanity before it went any further. Granted, it would've been nice to fuck her and relieve the tension that's taken hold of me from the moment I laid eyes on her, but ultimately, this couldn't have gone anywhere.

Emmeline—or another woman like her—is what I need, and Emma would've just been a distraction. Had already been a distraction, in fact, messing with my focus at work and elsewhere.

In spite of that perfectly rational reasoning, I barely sleep Friday night, feeling tense and restless despite two cold showers and an encounter with my fist. Each time I close my eyes, I see Emma in her lacy under-wear, and my body burns with the need to have her, to feel her soft curves under my palms and taste the sweetness of her lips.

Finally, I give up on sleep and go for a ten-mile run. The hard pace I set is sufficiently exhausting, and by the time I sit down to eat the gourmet breakfast my butler has prepared for me, some of my frustration has eased. Still, I decide to call Emmeline to really get my mind off things.

We have another pleasant chat. I learn that she'll be coming to New York on a business trip in December, and we agree to meet for dinner the night she's free. It's all very proper and civilized, and when I hang up the phone, I don't feel the slightest urge to stalk her or drag her off to a cave.

And that's how it should be, I tell myself as I go into my home office to catch up on some work. With Emma, I was constantly on the verge of losing control and forgetting what's really important. The hunger the little redhead awakened in me was too potent, too dangerous. I want to be attracted to the woman I'm with, but not like that.

Not to the point where she's all that matters.

I work through the morning and most of the after-noon, and then, because my restlessness is returning, I call up my friend Ashton for a sparring session at our MMA gym.

He happens to be free, and we meet up an hour later. He's as good at mixed martial arts as I am, and after an hour of nonstop back-and-forth, the score is even and we're both dripping with sweat.

"Grab a beer after we get changed?" he offers as we walk to the locker room, and I gladly agree.

Anything to keep me from thinking about Emma.

———

"So, how did the matchmaker work out for you?" Ashton asks as we sit down at the bar. It's barely six o'clock, so even though it's a Saturday, the place is quiet enough to carry on a conversation. "My aunt told me you got in touch with Victoria," he continues as the bartender hands us our beers. "Did she find you a wife yet?"

I lift my beer and take a long sip in an effort not to snap at him. This is the last thing I want to talk about right now, but since he's the one who turned me onto Victoria Longwood-Thierry, I owe him an answer.

"She put me in touch with a promising candidate—a woman named Emmeline Sommers," I say, putting down my beer. "But she's in Boston, so we'll see how that goes."

"See? I told you." He grins, showing off his pearly whites. "That shit works—at least if you want it to. You couldn't pay me enough to be with one chick for the rest of my life, but if that's what you're after, might as well make sure that pussy is top notch."

He sounds like the asshole that he is, but the two women standing by the bar look dazzled by his smile.

It's always that way with him. Ashton Vancroft comes from old money—serious money—and it shows. His innate rich-boy arrogance, coupled with his athletic physique and golden surfer looks, draws women like a magnet, and it has for as long as I've known him—which is soon to be well over a decade.

We met in business school, where we were both getting our MBAs—me, so I could convince investors to trust me with their money, and Ashton, because it was expected of him. As he explained to me once, his career options were lawyer, doctor, or investment banker; anything else was deemed unacceptable for a Vancroft. He finally rebelled by dropping out of business school to become a personal trainer, but the damage was done.

He'd acquired too much business savvy to live the poor and carefree life he'd always wanted.

What started off as a few clients on the weekends quickly grew into a profitable business, thanks to word of mouth about his hardcore, no-nonsense approach to fitness and the app Ashton created to train his clients remotely during their travels. Before long, he had thousands of clients all over the world, and as their before-and-after pictures flooded Instagram, his training app exploded in popularity, rocketing to the top of all the app stores. Now he's a multimillionaire even without his parents' money—and is in denial about the whole thing.

"How's the business coming along?" I ask, because I know that will aggravate him—which is only fair, given how much his prying into my dating life has aggravated me.

Predictably, he grimaces. "Awful. Revenues grew by another twenty percent last month, and I'm getting flooded with sponsorship offers. I don't want any of that shit, but do they listen? No. They're convinced I must be dying to peddle their shitty supplements or gym equipment or whatever crap they're selling. Never mind that none of that quick-fix bullshit works. It's all about proper nutrition and challenging your body and—"

I automatically tune out as he launches into his usual rant about couch potatoes looking for magical solutions to their laziness, and my thoughts drift to Emma. I wonder what she's doing this Saturday night. Is she in her PJs cuddling with the cats, or is she out somewhere?

Maybe on a date?

My hand tightens on my beer mug as I picture her sitting in a restaurant with some asshole, smiling at him with her pretty, dimpled smile. He'd be panting over her, all but salivating as she ate her cheap slice of pizza or whatever, and then they'd amicably split the bill before going together to her place and—

Fuck, no. I'm not going there.

I'm already feeling homicidal as it is.

She's not yours, I tell myself as I drain my beer. She has every right to see whomever she wants and do whatever she pleases. We're not together anymore—not that we ever were. Two dates don't make a relationship, and neither do a couple of kisses... at least once you're out of high school.

So it makes no sense for me to feel like this is a real break-up, like I actually lost something when she said that this is over and told me to leave. At most, my pride should be wounded by her rejection, nothing more.

Yet when the two women by the bar sidle up to us, flirting and batting their long lashes, all I can think about is Emma and her dimpled smile. And when I excuse myself to go home, it's her lush curves I picture as I stand in the shower, my fist wrapped around my aching cock.

It's her face I see in my mind as I come.

CHAPTER TWENTY-FIVE

mma

THE NEXT ELEVEN DAYS DRAG BY AT A SNAIL'S PACE. I GO to work, I come home, and I work on my editing website. Financially, things are looking up: I got a couple of new clients through referrals, one of my regulars just sent me a new novel to work on, and an author who'd been having financial difficulties finally ponied up the payment he owed me for editing his thousand-page epic fantasy novel. My cats haven't had any costly trips to the vet either, so for once, my bank account balance is in the four figures. I've even paid down a small portion of my student loans, making the recent interest rate spike hurt a little less.

So there's no reason to feel like I'm trudging through a swamp with a fifty-pound pack on my back.

"Call him," Kendall urges me again on Wednesday morning, when I complain that I'm in a funk and have been having trouble sleeping. "Tell him you've changed your mind and want to see him again. Or at least text him a quick hello. Maybe he's still interested and will respond."

I wave away her suggestion, claiming my bad mood has nothing to do with *that*, but all of Wednesday, my phone taunts me, the bright pink case as aggravating as a red cape to a bull. I don't call—heroically, I resist the urge—but that night, I dream that I gave in… and that Marcus immediately came over.

I wake up slick and aching, on fire from my dirtiest dream yet. Sitting up, I turn on the bedside lamp, and the cats glare at me from my pillow, annoyed to be disturbed from sound sleep.

"Yeah, whatever, remember the vase you smashed in the middle of the night last week?" I mutter at Mr. Puffs, and he swishes his tail, acknowledging my point.

The cats promptly go back to sleep, but I get up, too agitated to lie still. The phone is on my nightstand, taunting me, calling to me. I reach for it but yank my hand back at the last moment, telling myself that this is a bad idea.

A very bad idea.

Still, I can't take my eyes off the device, and my hand reaches for it again, picking it up.

Don't do it, Emma.

I freeze, trying to heed the voice of reason, but a second later, my fingers are moving of their own accord, swiping across the screen to locate my texts with Marcus. My heart beats furiously in my chest as I type out, "Hey..."

Don't send it. Erase, erase, erase!

I chew on my lip, staring at the screen, my finger hovering over the delete button. To send or not to send?

A soft meow startles me out of my existential dilemma, and I look up to see Queen Elizabeth gracefully making her way toward me across the blanket.

"Do you think I should send it?" I ask her, and she meows again.

"Really?"

She gives me a look that says I'm being dumb by talking to a cat about this.

"Well, who else am I going to talk to in the middle of the night?"

She sits down and starts licking her paw.

"Okay, fine, be like that." Annoyed, I look down at my phone—and my stomach drops.

Somehow, as I was talking to the cat, my finger slipped and pressed "send."

CHAPTER TWENTY-SIX

arcus

MY PHONE PINGS AT 2:49 A.M. ON THURSDAY, WAKING me up less than two hours after I got home from work. Cursing, I pick it up—and see that it's a text message.

From Emma.

I'm instantly awake, my entire body buzzing with adrenaline as I jackknife to a sitting position and swipe across the screen.

Hey...

That's all the message says.

I throw off my blanket and turn on the light. I can see the three dots dancing on the screen, telling me that Emma is about to send a second message.

Hey... do you want to come over?

Hey... I've missed you.

Hey... so I realize I've made a mistake.

Hey... what are you doing tonight?

The possibilities are endless, and I'm fucking dying to see what she's going to say.

The three dots disappear, as if she's stopped typing and deleted her message. Five seconds later, they reappear.

I stare at the phone, my heart pounding with predatory anticipation. I can't wait for her to admit that she wants me, that she's changed her mind about sending me away. I have an important investor meeting first thing in the morning, but if she wants me to come over right now, I'm there.

If I could, I'd teleport myself to Brooklyn, so I could turn up on her doorstep as soon as I receive that text.

She's taking her sweet time composing it, so I get up, unable to sit still. Clutching the phone, I head to the bathroom to get ready in case this is, as I'm hoping, a booty call.

I'm almost done shaving when the phone finally pings with a new text. Setting down the razor, I swipe across the screen with one semi-dry finger.

Sorry, sent to the wrong person.

I reread the words in disbelief—and growing fury.

What the fuck?

She was texting *someone else* at three a.m.?

Fighting the urge to smash the phone against the marble countertop, I roughly wipe away the remnants of the shaving cream and throw the towel in the sink. Theoretically, this someone could be a friend or a relative, but practically, the chances of that are nil.

There's only one person you text at this hour, and it's someone you're fucking—or thinking about fucking.

And that someone isn't me.

White-hot fury sears through me as I picture the guy—probably some asshole fresh out of Peace Corps who owns a million cats. He wouldn't have a fucking clue how to please a woman, yet *he'd* get to be in Emma's bed because he's an animal lover and fucking "nice."

Well, *I* am not nice—and I have never given up on something I truly want. Over the past twelve days, I've done my best to forget her, to convince myself to move on, but every night, I've dreamed of her, and every morning, I've woken up hard and frustrated, unable to focus until I've relieved myself with my fist. Whether I like it or not, this new obsession of mine is not going away, and it's time I've accepted it.

Grimly, I open my email and compose a message to the private investigator I use to keep tabs on C-level executives at the companies we're heavily invested in. He operates just this side of the law and can sniff out a scandal years before any gossip rag gets a clue. I've never had him investigate a woman I'm interested in before, but there's always a first time.

Stalker move or not, I have to know whom Emma

might be seeing—because I'm done playing by the rules.

One way or another, the little redhead will be mine.

CHAPTER TWENTY-SEVEN

mma

THE FLOWERS ARRIVE THURSDAY AFTERNOON, JUST AS MY boss is telling me all about his new diet. The vase is so big that the delivery guy strains to lift it onto the counter, and when he finally succeeds, the enormous bouquet of pink, yellow, and red tulips nearly blocks the register.

"Is it your birthday today?" Mr. Smithson asks, eyeing the flowers in confusion as I hunt for a card in the forest of stems and leaves. "I could've sworn it was in September."

"Um... it's definitely in September." My face turns bright red as I find the card and read the one-word message. My boss is still looking at me quizzically, so I lie, "This is just something from my grandparents. I love tulips, and they do this once in a while, to let me know they're thinking of me."

"Oh." Mr. Smithson blinks. "Okay, well, enjoy."

He ambles away to restock the thrillers, and I exhale, my hand shaking with a mixture of trepidation and excitement as I lift the card and reread the message.

It's just one simple word.

Hey.

———

I'M ALMOST CALM BY THE TIME I GET HOME FROM WORK, having convinced myself that the bouquet was Marcus's payback for my dumb texts last night. It was definitely a cowardly move on my part to claim that I'd sent that "hey" to the wrong person, but I panicked and didn't know what else to do.

There was no reason for me to be texting him at nearly three in the morning, other than the obvious— and I'm not ready to go *there*.

I'm tempted to call Kendall and tell her about the texts and the tulips—which, by some odd coincidence, happen to be my favorite flowers—but I resist. She'd twist it all around, and next thing I know, I'd be thinking that Marcus is still interested in me instead of being well on his way to marrying Emmeline or some other equally perfect woman.

No, I need to forget all about Marcus and his weirdly nice payback message. It means nothing—and certainly not that he's still interested. This thing between us is over, and now that he let me know how stupid my texts were, I'm sure I won't hear from him again.

My conviction holds until the doorbell rings as I'm feeding the cats.

"One second!" I yell out, trying not to stumble over Mr. Puffs as I set down his plate and rush over to the door. I don't need a repeat of the other week.

There's no one at the door when I open it, but there *is* a package on the doormat.

My pulse jumps.

I'm not expecting a delivery.

The box is small and light, so I have no trouble lifting it. Heart pounding, I carry it into the kitchen and set it on the counter, then grab a knife to slice through the tape.

Inside is another box, a much prettier one with the Saks Fifth Avenue logo on it. Opening it, I gape at the contents inside.

A white cashmere scarf, one just like the cheap Chinese brand I put on my Amazon wish list for Christmas—except it's by some Italian designer and looks a thousand times more expensive.

What the hell?

I rummage through the box and find a note.

From your wrong person, it says.

"Okay, so let me get this straight," Kendall says on Friday morning, when I cave and call her from work after another sleepless night. "You texted him by accident at three in the morning on Thursday, and he's already sent you *two* gifts?"

"Yes!" A woman browsing through the mystery section gives me an annoyed look, and I sink down in my chair, so I'm half-hidden behind the counter. "Why would he do that?" I continue in a hushed tone. "And with those notes? Do you think he's just toying with me?"

"Why would he toy with you? Emma, pull your head out of your ass. He obviously still wants you. He sent you... what? Flowers and a scarf?"

"Yes. A huge bouquet of tulips and a white cashmere scarf, just like the one I was hoping my grandparents would get me for Christmas, but infinitely fancier. How did he know I needed a scarf? Or that I love tulips, for that matter?"

"Most people like tulips, and he must've seen you without a scarf. Either way, what does it matter?" Kendall's voice rises in exasperation. "He sent you *gifts*. That means he's still really into you. Did you at least text him a thank-you?"

I bite my lip. "I wanted to, but—"

"Okay, seriously? You need to get on that. Like, right now. Text him a thank-you and say you want to see him again."

"Kendall—"

"Don't you Kendall me. Text him and call me back when it's done."

"Excuse me." The woman who was browsing the mystery section approaches the counter, her broad face creased in a disapproving frown. "I can't find the latest James Patterson."

"Of course." Hanging up on Kendall, I jump up, glad for the interruption. "Let me show you where it is."

As I lead the woman through the bookstore, I try to forget all about Kendall's instructions—and the man who's the cause of my turmoil.

———

I STILL HAVEN'T WORKED UP THE COURAGE TO CALL OR text Marcus by the time I get home. Partially, it's because I have no idea what to say. Is he messing with me, or is this for real? Should I be mad or grateful? The gifts he sent me are outrageously expensive—I know, because I looked up the cost of that scarf online—so I should decline them, at the very least. But that would mean getting in touch with Marcus, which brings me back to my dilemma about his intentions.

What is he after?

Does he still want to date me, or is this all just a game to him?

I've fed the cats and am halfway through my own dinner when the doorbell rings again.

I jump up and rush over, but the FedEx guy who left

the package on my doorstep is already getting into his truck.

The box is heavy for its size. I bring it into the kitchen and slice through the tape, my hands shaking.

Inside are books, each in a hermetically sealed plastic pouch.

Gulliver's Travels, Gone with the Wind, and *The Count of Monte Cristo.*

My three favorite stories of all time—and each of them a signed first edition.

———

FOR THE FIRST TIME, I UNDERSTAND PEOPLE WHO GO FOR a run when they're stressed.

I can't sit still—and I haven't been able to for the past hour. Same goes for finishing my dinner. I'm pacing around my tiny apartment, going from kitchen to bedroom to bathroom and back. My cats are staring at me like I've lost my mind, and it's possible that I have.

There's no way a bajillion dollars' worth of rare books are sitting on my kitchen counter, along with a note that says, "Pick you up at 7 tonight."

It's a prank. It has to be.

For the twentieth time, I grab my phone and begin composing a message to Marcus.

Thank you so much for your insanely generous gifts, but I'm afraid I can't accept them—and I have other plans tonight. Also, are you messing with me?

I erase the text before I can send it, just like I erased the nineteen attempts before it.

Nothing I compose sounds right. I can edit a novel with ruthless precision, suggesting words and phrases that convey the meaning perfectly, but I can't seem to write this text.

I've never been so off-balance. And worst of all, the clock is ticking, getting inevitably closer to seven. In seventeen minutes, Marcus is going to come pick me up, and I still haven't been able to work up the courage to call or text him to make sure that doesn't happen.

It's probably best if I talk to him about this in person, I reason, trying to make myself feel better about my inexplicable cowardice. Maybe if I can see his expression, I'll know what he's after, as opposed to making dumb assumptions. Because none of this—the gifts, the ambiguous notes—makes any sense.

Obviously, I have no intention of going on a date with him—if "pick you up" even means a date. And if it does, what kind of asshole *tells* a woman he's picking her up instead of asking? What if I had other plans? Granted, I didn't, but he can't know that, can he?

Then again, how does he know what my favorite books or flowers are? Or what kind of scarf I wanted? We've never talked about that.

My head is beginning to hurt from overthinking, so I stop by my bed to scoop up Cottonball—who immediately starts purring.

"I know, baby." Cradling him against my chest, I stroke his soft fur. "I haven't cuddled you tonight, and

I'm sorry. Maybe Marcus won't show up. It could all be a massive joke, you know? The books might not even be real but some kind of reproductions—though I have no idea why he'd bother."

Queen Elizabeth lifts her head from my pillow and gives me a narrow-eyed look.

"You *don't* think it's a joke?" I ask over Cottonball's loud purr, and she yawns demonstratively.

"Yeah, okay, maybe it's not that funny, but what else could it be? I told him it's not going to work out between us, and I'm sure he has a million women lined up to date him."

She yawns again and puts her head back on the pillow.

"I know. It's all so confusing, isn't it?" I sigh and sit down on the bed next to her—which Mr. Puffs takes as an invitation to shove Cottonball off my lap. He gets jealous when I interact with his siblings, so I scratch behind his ears, knowing that if I don't, my remaining accessories are in for a world of pain.

Continuing to pet Mr. Puffs, I sneak a glance at my phone.

6:53 p.m.

If this were a date, I'd be freaking out about the fact that I'm still dressed in my ratty old sweatpants and a T-shirt covered with cat hair, but I'm not. I'm really not. Because this is not a date. Even if Marcus shows up at my door as promised, I'm just going to give him back the insanely expensive books and calmly explain that I'm not going anywhere. I will tell him to stop sending me gifts with mocking messages and—oh, who am I kidding?

Ignoring Mr. Puffs's offended yowl, I push him off my lap and rush to the closet, frantically yanking out one outfit after another. I'm not dressing up for Marcus; it's for me, I tell myself. I want to be presentable because it's the civilized thing to do. I'd do it for anyone, even Kendall. Especially Kendall, come to think of it. I'd never hear the end of it if she saw me looking like a hobo.

Of course, as luck would have it, this Saturday is laundry day, and I have next to nothing in my closet. But anything is an upgrade over what I'm currently wearing, so I wriggle into my skinny jeans—so named because I need to be way skinnier to comfortably wear them—and yank on a gray sweater that only has a little bit of cat hair on it.

There. Done. Never mind that I can barely close the button on the jeans or that pulling on the sweater has created static, making my hair look like I've been struck by lightning. I smooth my palms over the madly puffed-up curls, pinch my cheeks to give them a little color, and swipe on a pink lip gloss—just in case.

The doorbell rings as I'm about to put on boots instead of my fuzzy house slippers.

Crap, crap, crap.

I was hoping he wouldn't show.

No, that's a lie. I would've been disappointed if he didn't show—but only because I want to give him a piece of my mind. Who the hell does he think he is?

Getting me those outrageously expensive gifts—that bouquet must've also cost a pretty penny—and ordering me to go on a date with him?

I'm so worked up that I stomp over to the door and yank it open—and only then remember the pink fuzzy slippers I still have on.

"Hi," Marcus murmurs, gazing down at me, and I forget all about my outrage and my slippers, my breath catching at the dark heat in those cool blue eyes.

Somehow, over the past two weeks, I've forgotten how big he is, and how striking his harshly masculine features are. In his intimidating attire of perfectly tailored suit, crisp blue shirt, subtly striped tie, and unbuttoned knee-length coat, he's like some kind of modern-day king, exuding wealth and power—and more than his fair share of potent animal magnetism. I can literally feel my blood rushing faster through my veins, heating up every inch of my skin until the icy gusts of wind outside feel like a balmy summer breeze.

"H-hi," I stutter out, realizing I'm staring up at him with my mouth open. "I mean... hello." The inability to use words that had afflicted me with the text messages hasn't gone away, I note with the small part of my brain that's still functioning. The rest of my mind is blank. I can't recall any of the speeches I prepared as I paced across my room, or why I even prepared them in the first place. All I can think about as I look at him is how those big warm hands had felt on my skin and how those soft masculine lips had nibbled on my ear, sending chills of pleasure down my body.

"Emma." His voice is low and deep, so velvety it's like a massage with a happy ending for my ears. "Kitten, are you ready?"

"Ready?" *Oh God, get it together, Emma! He doesn't mean that sexually!* Unless he does, in which case the answer is yes, a thousand times yes. Maybe other human females don't go into heat, but that's exactly what seems to happen to me when I'm with Marcus. Already, my panties are damp, and it's all I can do to stand still instead of leaning in and rubbing against him like a cat marking her territory.

"To go," he clarifies, glancing down, and I follow his gaze to my slippers—which are still as pink and fuzzy as ever.

With a massive effort of will, I gather my scrambled brains. "Go where? I'm not—"

"To the Greek place we never got a chance to try the other week," he says smoothly. "It's really good, I promise—and not expensive in the least."

"But—"

"It's very casual too," he says. "But you still might want to put on your shoes. Here, those will do." He steps forward, and I instinctively back up, letting him into the apartment and closing the door behind him on autopilot.

Ignoring Mr. Puffs hissing at him, Marcus walks past me and picks up the boots I'd taken out of the closet. Then he returns and kneels in front of me, like an assistant at a shoe store. Clasping my ankle in one large hand, he takes off my slipper and starts fitting my sock-clad foot into the boot.

What remains of my brain short-circuits, the feel of his hard, warm fingers on my ankle as erotic as if he'd started sucking on my toes. Oh God, is that a new fantasy of mine? Because all of a sudden, I can't think of anything I want more than for Marcus to take off my sock and press his lips to my ankle, then trail hot, wet kisses over the top of my foot before—

"Here, give me your other foot," he murmurs, jolting me out of my depraved daydream, and I blink, a hot flush crawling up my neck as I realize that one boot is already on my foot—and that he put it there.

Feeling like a perverted Cinderella, I blurt out, "I can do that," and bend down to intercept him as he reaches for my other foot. Except I miscalculate, and my foot comes up just as I'm lowering my head.

With a startled cry, I pitch forward—only to catch myself on Marcus's broad shoulders. His hands immediately close around my waist, steadying me, and we end up nose to nose, so close that I can feel his warm breath on my lips and smell the faint hint of cool breeze and fresh pine—his aftershave, most likely.

His eyes aren't just blue, I notice dazedly as he pulls me into a kneeling position next to him. His irises have flecks of silver in them, some light enough to be almost white. They're beautiful, and the way his pupils are dilating is mesmerizing me, even as growing arousal quickens my breath and floods my sex with liquid warmth.

"Emma." The soft, deep timbre of his voice vibrates through me, adding to the hypnotic effect as one of his hands leaves my waist to curve around my jaw, the gesture both tender and possessive. Leaning in another inch, he murmurs hoarsely, "Kitten, if you don't want this, tell me now."

Yes, tell him. Only my mouth refuses to cooperate, to form the words needed to stop this insanity. Because I do want this. I want it so badly that I ache. I know there are reasons why this is not a good idea, but for the life of me, I can't remember what they are.

He correctly interprets my silence, and his lips hover next to mine for only a moment longer before pressing against them in a tenderly demanding kiss. His tongue sweeps over the closed seam of my lips, seeking entrance, and I let him in with a soft moan, my eyes closing and my hands fisting in the lapels of his coat as heated pleasure rockets through my body.

Distantly, I hear a pissed-off meow, but it can't penetrate the sensual fog enveloping my brain. The tension is growing in my core, coiling tighter with each skillful caress of his tongue, and my hands slide up his neck to indulge in the feel of his thick, silky hair. My touch seems to please him, and a groan rumbles low in his throat as he pulls me to my feet and maneuvers us both toward the bed, throwing off his coat and jacket on the way.

There are more outraged meows as the cats jump off the bed, clearing the space for us, and then I'm stretched out on my back, with Marcus over me, his lips devouring mine as his hands roam greedily over my clothed body. One big hand ventures underneath my sweater, the palm hot and rough on my bare skin, and I shudder with pleasure as his fingers close over my left breast, kneading it through my bra with firm pressure. His thumb brushes over my peaked nipple, and I arch into his touch, craving more, needing more.

Needing everything.

This must be what it's like to be swept away by passion, I realize dimly, even as my hands yank at the knot of his expensive tie, desperate to get it off him so I can tear off his shirt and feel his bare chest. I've always thought the swept-away bit was just a poetic turn of phrase, a romantic exaggeration. But that's precisely how this feels: like an unstoppable wave, a tsunami of sensation over which I have no control. My entire body is on fire, my nipples taut and aching, my clit throbbing as need coils ever tighter in my core.

I don't know how I manage to get the tie and shirt off him in this state, but I do, and the heat inside me grows into a conflagration as my hands slide across the broad, muscled planes of his chest and back. He's warm and hard all over, his smooth skin roughened only by the sprinkling of coarse hair near his flat nipples and the happy trail running down his ridged stomach. His abs feel like they've been carved from stone, each one delineated so perfectly that I want to slow things down so I can stare at him and drool. But he's already pulling off my sweater and too-tight jeans, along with my socks and the one boot, and all thoughts of slowing down evaporate as he buries his hand in my hair and kisses me again, his tongue sweeping into my mouth with fierce hunger as his free hand slides down my body and delves under my soaked panties.

Yes, oh God, yes, right there. I want to scream the words from the rooftops as he unerringly finds my throbbing clit, but all I can manage is a ragged gasp against his lips, my vocal cords locking up along with every muscle in my body. My eyes squeeze shut, and I arch against him, writhing and panting, my nails digging into his sides as his thumb presses on the swollen bundle of nerves and starts moving in a cruelly teasing circle. I'm close, so very, very close—

"Look at me," he orders, lifting his head, and my eyes snap open, meeting his gaze as his index finger dips lower, smearing the wetness along the rim of my entrance while his thumb continues its exquisite torment of my clit. His eyes are dark and hungry as he says hoarsely, "I want to watch you come."

Yes, oh yes, please. The possessive note in his deep voice adds to the unbearable tension coiling in me, and I hover on the edge for a delicious second before the pressure from his thumb increases and I go over it with a choked scream.

The release is like a bomb going off inside my body, imploding everything in its way. The pleasure pulses violently through my nerve endings, ripples of sensation pounding at every cell. And all the while he watches me, his gaze locked on mine with dark triumph—and his own fiercely growing need.

CHAPTER TWENTY-EIGHT

mma

THE AFTERSHOCKS ARE STILL HAMMERING MY CORE WHEN Marcus reaches up and unhooks my bra, then lowers his head to close his lips around my right nipple as soon as my breasts are bared. The lash of sensation is almost cruel, his hot, wet mouth sucking so strongly that I cry out, gripping his hair in agony-edged pleasure as my eyes squeeze closed once again. But he's relentless, and to my shock, a renewed throbbing starts low in my core, the tension growing again. I've never come twice during sex before, only on my own with my vibrator, but I realize that it's possible with Marcus.

In fact, it's inescapable.

He turns his attention to my other breast, sucking

on my nipple with strong pulls as his hand travels lower, to my soaked underwear. He tugs the panties down my legs; then his fingers return to my folds. Only this time, he doesn't tease. Laving my nipple with his tongue, he penetrates me with one long, thick finger, pushing deep as his thumb presses on my clit.

I combust. There's no other word for it.

Somehow, my first orgasm had only primed me for this, and my entire body spasms with white-hot pleasure as I cry out, bucking underneath him. The wet heat of his mouth on my breast, the feel of his big finger so deep inside me, the heavy weight of him pressing down on my legs—it's all too much and not enough at the same time.

I need more.

I need him in me.

"Yes, you do," he growls, and my eyes fly open to meet his burning gaze.

I must've said the words aloud. Normally, the knowledge would make me flush all over, but I'm too far gone to care—and judging by the tight cast of Marcus's hard features, mocking me is the last thing on his mind.

He's still wearing his pants and belt, and our hands collide as we reach for the buckle at the same time. It would be funny, except I'm so aroused the delay is the worst kind of torture. I feel as if the two orgasms had only whetted my appetite, as if now that I've had a taste, I can't stop until I devour the main dish.

And what a dish it is. My breath stutters to a halt as

he unzips his pants, finally freeing his erection, and pulls a condom out of his pocket. I'd felt that hard bulge pressed against me the other week, and it had definitely seemed impressive, but I still didn't expect *this*.

"Were you ever in porn?"

The words pop out of my mouth before I can think better of it, and this time, I do flush—because I did *not* mean to sound like the semi-virgin that I am. He's undoubtedly used to women with sexual experience as extensive as his own, not twenty-six-year-old cat ladies who've slept with two boyfriends in their entire lives.

His dark eyebrows pull into a frown, but to my relief, he doesn't seem inclined to laugh at me. Instead, he mutters, "No," and finishes putting on the condom. He then moves over me, covering me with his large body. Framing my face with one palm, he claims my lips in another deep, consuming kiss, and at the same time, his knee wedges between my thighs, pushing them apart. The broad head of his cock brushes against my inner thigh, and I feel the blunt, heavy pressure of him at my entrance.

Holy shit, that feels big, even in my hyper-aroused state.

Way too big.

I tear my lips away from his. "Um, Marcus…"

He halts immediately, the tip of his cock less than a quarter inch inside me. Pushing up on one elbow, he asks roughly, "Am I hurting you?"

I swallow, meeting his gaze. "A little."

His jaw flexes. "Do you want me to stop?"

"What? Oh, no. Just… go slow, okay?"

Intense relief flashes in his blue eyes. "You got it," he promises, and then he bends his head and kisses me again. At the same time, his hips start moving back and forth, working himself into me one millimeter at a time. The stretch still burns, but I'm so aroused that I don't mind the slight bite of pain—and the feel of his tongue tangling with mine adds to the slickness easing his way.

At first, I'm grateful for the slow pace, but a minute later, when he's still less than halfway in, I'm ready to claw his back raw.

I need him in me. All the way. Now.

Sinking my teeth into his lower lip, I lift my hips, taking in another couple of inches—and my breath stops in my lungs as he surges into me with a low groan, penetrating me all the way.

Oh, fuck. That is *big.*

I must've said it out loud again because he freezes on top of me and lifts his head. "Did I hurt you?" His voice is strained, every muscle in his large body tense as he holds himself completely still. "Emma, kitten… tell me. Do you want me to stop?"

I manage a small shake of my head. "No. Don't stop." My inner muscles are fluttering in panic, still trying to get used to the overwhelming size of him, but the newly awakened nymphomaniac in me is demanding more.

I want that third orgasm, and I want it now.

He stares at me, his lightly bronzed skin covered with a thin layer of sweat, and I feel the exact moment his self-control snaps. With a low growl, he pulls back and surges into me, thrusting so hard I gasp. But he doesn't stop this time. With his eyes narrowed and his gaze locked on mine, he sets a hard, driving pace.

The fire simmering inside me ignites hotter, each stroke of his massive cock bringing me closer to that delicious edge. Panting, I sink my nails into his sides and match him thrust for thrust, the erotic tension spiking to unbearable levels. I'm about to come, and it feels different, more intense with him inside me. My heart pounds violently, my skin burns, and all of my muscles are so tense I'm trembling. It's like a train is barreling toward me, and I can't stop it, can't slow it down. Each time he bottoms out inside me, his pelvis grinds into my swollen clit, and gasping cries tear from my throat. It's too much, too intense, yet I want more.

"Come with me," he bites out, his face twisting as he hammers mercilessly into me, and the release hits me so hard I scream. My inner muscles clamp on him as pleasure blasts through every nerve ending in my body, and I feel his cock jerk and pulse deep within me as he grinds into me, his eyes screwed shut and his head thrown back with an orgasmic groan.

The aftershocks are like a series of mini earthquakes in my body as he collapses on top of me, then rolls onto his side, holding me anchored against him in a possessive hold as his slowly softening cock slips out of me. Sweat glues our skin together, and our ragged breathing is audible in the silent room as a single thought circles through my mind.

I am so screwed.

$\mathcal{M}$arcus

I TIGHTEN MY HOLD ON EMMA AS SHE SHIFTS, TRYING TO move away. I should let her go, so I can remove the condom and clean up, but I can't bring myself to do so. My heart is pumping like an overworked steam engine, and despite the orgasm-induced relaxation spreading through my muscles, I'm vibrating with a surfeit of adrenaline.

I have never, in all of my life, experienced anything like this—have never lost myself in a woman so completely. From the moment she grabbed on to my shoulders, I was driven by a single primal urge: to get inside her, to claim her and make her mine. I forgot all about my plans for an elaborately staged seduction, how I was going to use what the investigator had uncovered to convince her to give me another shot.

I was going to woo her tonight like a gentleman, but instead, I attacked her with all the finesse of a sex-starved convict, not backing off even when I felt her extreme tightness and knew that I was hurting her.

"Are you all right, kitten?" I murmur, pulling her closer until I'm spooning her from the back, with one hand cradling her breast and the other arm stretched out underneath her neck. Her small, lush body feels so right, so perfect against me. Her ass is deliciously full and round as it rubs against my groin, and the soft globe of her breast fills my palm like it was made for it.

She really does remind me of a kitten, a sweet, warm, cuddly one.

"I'm fine." A visible flush creeps over her bare shoulder, coloring her skin a delicate shade of peach as she tries to scoot away again, mumbling, "I should wash up."

This time, I have no choice but to let her go. Reluctantly, I lift my arm, and she jumps up and off the bed, all wild red curls and pale curves as she beelines for the bathroom. I sit up as well and reach for a tissue from the box on the nightstand. It's just in time too—the condom is already slipping off me. As I ball up the used tissue with the condom inside, I notice two of the cats —the smaller ones—staring at me, their green eyes accusing. Their bigger sibling is, thankfully, nowhere to be seen.

Maybe he got offended that I took his place on the bed?

"What?" I growl at them when they keep staring, then realize I'm talking to fucking *cats*.

Getting up, I zip up my pants and stride over to the bathroom, where I hear a shower running.

"Emma?" I knock. "Can I come in?"

No response.

I take that as a yes and push the door open. Like most people who live alone, she's not used to locking the bathroom door.

Inside, the small room is filled with steam, the mirror all fogged up. Through the semi-transparent blue curtain hanging over her tub, I see the outline of Emma's body under the spray of water, and though I'm still catching my breath from the powerful orgasm I just had, my cock twitches with renewed interest.

Fuck. It was supposed to get better once I've had her.

I hesitate, staring at her for a moment, then remove my shoes and strip off my pants and briefs. Hanging the clothes over the towel rod, I pull aside the curtain. "May I join you?"

She freezes in the middle of pouring body wash into her hand, her eyes rounding in shock. "What?"

"May I join you?" I repeat, my voice roughening as more blood surges to my groin. With the gorgeous spirals of her hair loosely pinned on top of her head and the water sluicing over her smooth, pale skin, she's the most fuckable thing I've ever seen. I'm used to women being shaved or waxed, but she's just neatly trimmed, and the little patch of flame-bright hair between her legs draws my eyes like a beacon.

A natural redhead—not that I've ever doubted it.

Her delectable skin turns a pretty shade of pink as she realizes where I'm looking. "Um… yes." She sounds choked, and when I look up, I see her staring at my rapidly hardening cock. "You can… come in if you want."

Oh, I want. Stepping into the tub, I pull the curtain closed, angle the showerhead so the spray is not blasting us, and take the body wash bottle from her nerveless fingers. "Here, let me."

She blinks up at me, uncomprehending.

"I want to wash you," I explain, pouring the liquid into my palm before setting the bottle down in the corner of the tub. "Turn around."

She obeys, and I spread the lather over her pale shoulders, then run my hands over the soft skin of her back, my heart rate speeding up with growing arousal. She has the sexiest dimples at the base of her spine, where her tiny waist flares into a deliciously full ass. My hands slide down to wash those soft, round globes, and I can't stop myself from squeezing them possessively.

Mine.

This sweet little ass is now mine, as is every other scrumptious part of her.

It's an utterly atavistic thought—fucking a woman

doesn't mean you own her—but I can't squash it. It's a conviction that goes down to the bone.

Emma is now mine. I've staked a claim on her, and I'm not backing off.

The tub we're in is cramped, especially for someone my size, but I manage to kneel behind her as I spread the soap down her legs, my dick stiffening further as her calf muscles flex at my touch. That delicious ass of hers is now closer to my eye level, and my mouth waters with the urge to bite that creamy, supple flesh, to sink my teeth into it as if it were an apple.

"Turn around." My voice is so hoarse with lust I barely recognize it. I don't understand what's happening to me, why I'm feeling this overwhelming need to mark her, to brand her as belonging to me. I've never had the slightest urge to hurt a woman, but something dark in me—something I didn't know was there—likes the idea of marring her pale skin, of seeing signs of my possession on her smooth flesh.

Suppressing the bizarrely sadistic inclination, I wait for her to turn, and when she does, I grip her hips and pull her toward me. Even with my legs folded flat underneath me, I'm too tall—or she's too short—for me to reach my goal. So I lift her leg, hiking it up until she's balancing on her toes, holding on to the tiled wall for support, and then I lean back until her pussy is right over my face.

Her gray eyes are wide as she stares down at me. "What are you—" she starts, but I'm already diving into my feast, lapping at her pink folds like I can't get enough. And I can't. It's like her flavor has been created specifically for me. I need to taste her, to feel her soft, slick flesh under my tongue.

She cries out, her leg tensing in my grip as I get to her clit, and I taste her arousal as more slickness rushes forth to coat her entrance.

She wants me.

Fuck, yes, she wants me.

Forgetting all restraint, I eat her pussy, spurred on by the erotic cries and moans emanating from her throat. She's as sweet as I'd imagined, her flesh silky-soft under my tongue. Her clit is swollen from my previous ministrations, and I suck on it, feeling her thigh quiver with each pull of my lips. More delicious slickness coats my tongue, and I use my free hand to penetrate her with two fingers, pressing my fingertips against the spongy G-spot on her inner wall.

Her cries escalate, her whole body shaking now, and I feel the precise moment when it happens. Her muscles clench on my fingers, and a violent tremor runs through her. I ease up on the sucking in favor of licking her gently as she shudders with the aftershocks, and then I withdraw my fingers, lower her leg, and return to a kneeling position in front of her.

She sways a little, as if weak from her orgasm, and I grip her hips to steady her as I rise to my feet, turning so that she's back under the shower spray. The taste of her is on my lips, and my dick is so stiff it hurts. But I don't have a condom handy, and she might be sore from our first fucking, so I force myself to release her and wrap my fingers around my cock instead.

With her watching me dazedly, I pump my fist up and down, letting my eyes roam over her curvy body.

It takes just a few quick strokes for me to come, marking her pale thigh with thick white ropes of my seed.

CHAPTER THIRTY

mma

My mind is still filled with wool, my thoughts tangled from post-sex endorphins as I stare at my legs, where Marcus's semen is slowly sliding down the front of my left thigh, mixing with the water streaming over me. I feel like I've somehow landed in a porn flick—a particularly long, involved one, with the hottest actor I've ever seen.

Marcus came on me.

On my leg.

While I watched him.

It was so dirty—and so unbelievably hot. Just like the sex dreams I've been having, only better, because this was my fourth orgasm. *Fourth.* I've never come four times in a row, not even with my vibrator. And I was right about his tongue being crazy skilled. *God, is it skilled.* The way he attacked my clit—

"You okay?" he murmurs, and I blink, flushing as I look up.

"What?"

"You okay?" he repeats, thick eyebrows arching, and I realize I completely zoned out, standing there like I'm the only one in the shower.

Like this is one of those dirty dreams of mine, instead of a real-life sexual encounter with the man I was going to send packing as soon as he turned up on my doorstep.

"The books," I blurt out, my mind finally latching on to something other than the fact that I have his seed on me.

That he'd just been *in me*, so deep inside that I still feel tender from his hard possession.

"What about them?" He sounds amused as he picks up the body wash again and pours some on his palm, then proceeds to lather himself all over, his movements as casual as a jock's in a locker room.

"I can't…" I swallow, my eyes falling to the softening column of his sex as he washes it thoroughly. Even like this, he's impressively sized, bigger than either of my two exes. With effort, I force myself to look up. "I can't accept them."

His expression darkens. "Why not? You like books, don't you?"

"Of course. But those are first editions. They must

cost more than my apartment. And the scarf—I can't accept it either. It's too much."

There, I've said it. I feel bizarrely proud of myself— at least until he steps closer, getting under the spray with me, and I recall that I was going to tell him that *before* something like this happened.

The whole point was to chase him away so I wouldn't give in to this dangerous attraction.

He must be thinking the same thing because one corner of his mouth curves up sardonically as he angles the showerhead to have the water hit him more directly. "They're gifts, kitten. You're familiar with the concept, right?"

He's so close now that my nipples are grazing his hair-roughened chest, and my breath catches as he reaches down with that unsettling casualness and wipes the remnants of his seed off my thigh, lightly brushing over my sex in the process.

"There," he says huskily. "All clean now."

Turning, he swiftly rinses the remaining lather off his body and steps out of the shower, leaving me to stand under the spray and gather the tattered shreds of my composure.

———

I HALF-EXPECT MARCUS TO BE GONE WHEN I COME OUT of the bathroom—after all, he got what he wanted—but he's there, sitting on my bed in his business attire, looking as if nothing's happened.

That is, if one ignores the possessive heat in his cool blue eyes as they travel over my short pink robe and the bare legs underneath it.

Holy fuck. Does he want more sex?

With me?

Is this going to be a thing now?

I stop by my closet, eyeing him uncertainly as Mr. Puffs meows from his perch on the top shelf. "So," I start, ignoring the cat, "about the—"

"I told Wilson to move our reservation by an hour." Marcus stands up, his tall, large figure making my studio look even smaller. "We'll make it on time if you don't take too long to get dressed."

I gape at him. "You still want to go out to dinner?"

He frowns. "Why wouldn't I?"

Because you just fucked me ten ways to Sunday without needing to take me anywhere, I want to say, but I choke back the words in time. "No reason," I mumble instead, grabbing a clean pair of panties from the closet before making my way over to the desk, where the jeans, sweater, and bra I'd been wearing are lying neatly folded, with Queen Elizabeth and Cottonball stretched out on top of them.

Marcus must've picked up my clothes from the floor or the bed—or wherever they ended up when he pulled them off me.

By all logic, I should refuse to go to dinner with him. As hot as the sex was, it doesn't change our incompatibility—nor the fact that he's already met the woman he might marry. For now, I can still nip this in the bud, put a stop to the madness before I get badly hurt. That would be the rational thing to do, the smart thing, yet I already know I won't do it.

I want more of Marcus.

I want the madness to continue.

"Give me a sec," I say breathlessly, and shooing the cats off my desk, I grab my clothes and rush back to the bathroom to get dressed.

CHAPTER THIRTY-ONE

*M*arcus

ALL THREE OF HER CATS SEEM DISPLEASED THAT SHE'S leaving with me, with the big one meowing loudly as I lead Emma out of the apartment, my palm resting on her lower back.

On the precise spot where she has those alluring dimples.

Fuck, those little indentations are hot—as is everything about her. I was wrong to think that having her a couple of times would quell this craving. If anything, it's stronger now, as the reality has far surpassed my imagination. Take those sexy dimples at the base of her spine, for example—I'd never fantasized about them, and now I can't wait to stare at them as I take her from behind... fucking her pussy *and* her luscious little ass.

To my shock, my cock stirs again, and I force myself to focus on something other than the filthy things I want to do to her.

Like feeding her some decent Greek food.

That's definitely high on my list of non-filthy activities.

"You've fed them, right?" I ask as I usher her into the back seat of the car. "They'll be okay for tonight?"

She blinks as I climb in beside her and raise the partition between us and Wilson. "The cats? Yes, I fed them as soon as I came home."

Good. That means she won't be able to use that as an excuse not to go to my place after dinner. Because I'm not done with her—not by a long shot.

"So, about those books," she starts again as our car pulls out into traffic. "I meant what I said earlier... I can't accept them. They're far too—"

"They're a gift, Emma, as are the flowers and the scarf." I keep my tone soft but uncompromising. The books are indeed worth more than her apartment, but I have no intention of taking them back. Having gone through the investigator's report, I understand what's behind her fierce self-reliance, and her reaction to the expensive gifts is exactly what I thought it would be.

I suspected she'd see me, if only to return the gifts, and I was right.

"But where did you even get these books?" she asks, frowning. "And how did you know those are my favorite stories?"

I shrug. "You mentioned it on social media at one point." Actually, it was part of her college admissions essay, which the investigator found when he hacked into her college records. I have read and reread it several times over the past two days, along with the short stories she'd composed for her Creative Writing class.

Turns out, Emma is not only an excellent editor but also a brilliant writer. Her words flow in such a way that the simplest sentences become compelling, the very rhythm of her writing telling its own tale. However, it's the content of her stories—and the admissions essay—that had kept me glued to the pages.

There's so much more than meets the eye with my little redhead, so much darkness in her past that I wouldn't have guessed at. If I was fascinated by her before, I'm doubly so now that I've had a glimpse into her mind. A couple of nights to slake my lust won't be enough, I see that now.

I haven't processed what that means yet, but I can no longer deny it.

My obsession with Emma Walsh isn't purely sexual anymore.

"You stalked me on social media?" She sounds appalled.

I make a mental note never to mention the investigator in front of her. "Of course. Isn't that what it's for? Why else do you put your life out there for everyone to see?"

"It's for my friends to see, not strangers." She bites her lip. "This is bad. I'm going to have to review my privacy settings."

"That's a good idea in general," I say, and I mean it. Though it wouldn't keep her safe from me, run-of-the-mill stalkers—or nosy reporters who might come sniffing around her as a result of our relationship—won't be able to access her profile as easily.

She looks out the window, still chewing on her bottom lip, then turns back to look at me again. "Is that how you knew about the scarf? Through my social media? Because I don't remember mentioning that online, ever."

I give her a placid smile. "You might want to check the privacy settings on your Amazon wish list."

She groans and covers her face with her palms. "God, you *are* a stalker."

You have no idea. I've known this about myself—that I'm more ruthless, more determined than most—but until I met her, all my energy had been directed at my career. To succeed, I've done things others might've balked at, and I have zero regrets. I've always been this way, driven and remorseless, and if not for my second-grade teacher, Mr. Bond, encouraging my aptitude for math, I might've chosen to build my fortune in the criminal underworld instead of Wall Street.

It would've been a more logical route to wealth for a kid like me.

Either way, I want Emma the way I once wanted my

first billion: with a single-minded intensity that lets nothing stand in my way. I'm glad she texted me when she did, giving me this opening—because I wouldn't have been able to stay away from her much longer.

"What can I say? I'm a man who goes after what he wants," I say lightly, as if it's all a joke. But from the look Emma gives me when she lowers her hands, I know she's taking my words at face value.

Smart girl.

"Why me?" she demands bluntly. "Why don't you go after this Emmeline? Isn't she like your dream woman?"

"Not at the moment." I haven't spared Emmeline a single thought in the past two days—nor in the past week, come to think of it. We still have our date on the calendar for when she'll be in New York on her business trip, but I can't work up so much as a smidgeon of enthusiasm at the thought.

If anything, the idea of going out to dinner with Emmeline feels like an unpleasant obligation.

"So you haven't seen her since the first night we met?" Emma asks, her gray eyes trained intently on my face, and I shake my head.

"No. I haven't." And I won't, I realize with a peculiar tightness in my chest—not as long as this obsession with Emma continues. Not only do I not have the slightest inclination to do so, but it wouldn't be fair to either of the women.

Emma and I might've just started dating, but I'd

destroy any man who comes near her—which means that for the duration of whatever this is between us, I can't see anyone else either.

A hypocrite is one thing I'm not.

Emma's tense expression eases, but then her eyes narrow. "What about other women? Has your match-maker set you up with anyone else?"

If I were Ashton or most other guys I know, I might've balked at the question—because it sounds a lot like a demand for exclusivity, a serious step so early on in the relationship. But given what I've just decided, I answer calmly, "No. There's no one else."

"Oh." She stares at me. "Okay, then."

"What about you?" I ask, though I already know the answer. "Are you seeing the guy you meant to text the other night?"

An adorable flush covers her freckled cheeks. "Um, no. That is… I might've fibbed about that."

"Did you?" I knew this, of course—her dating status was the first thing my investigator checked on—but I'm enjoying her discomfort too much to let it go. "You mean, you meant to text *me* at three in the morning?"

She glares at me. "It was a mistake, all right? I was talking to my cat, and my finger pressed 'send' acciden-tally. I didn't mean to do it."

"I see." I reach over and pick up her hand. Toying with her delicate fingers, I ask, "Did your cat choose my number and type out that 'hey?'"

More delicious color floods her face, and her hand

curls into a tiny fist in my grip. "Maybe. I'm not sure what happened. Just let it be, okay?"

A dark smile tugs at my lips. "You'd like that, wouldn't you? How about I tell you what happened?" I lean in, my voice deepening as I murmur, "There you were, in the middle of the night, all alone in your bed and unable to sleep. Maybe you'd read a sexy story in the evening... or maybe, just maybe, you'd had a dream." Her hand twitches in my grasp, and my smile grows more wicked. "Ah, yes, it *was* a dream. Was I in it, kitten? What was I doing to you? Fucking you? Licking your sweet pussy? Fingering your tight little asshole? Or maybe all of the above?"

As I speak, her color heightens further, and a visible pulse appears in her neck. "Hush," she hisses, her eyes darting to the partition separating us from Wilson. "He'll hear you."

"Then tell me if I'm right." I bring her hand to my mouth and brush her knuckles back and forth across my lips. "Was I what you were dreaming about that night? Was I—"

"Yes!" She's now flushed all over, her breathing fast and uneven as she yanks her hand away. "You're right. Okay? You're right. Happy now?"

Fuck. Me. Hearing her admit this is like having Viagra injected straight into my cock. I'm so hard it's as if I hadn't had sex in years, instead of mere minutes.

If it weren't for the fact that I promised Emma dinner, I'd tell Wilson to take us to my penthouse, so I could go straight for my dessert.

"Yes," I say hoarsely when I'm able to talk again. "Very happy."

And as she turns to stare out the window, her cheeks bright red, I take deep breaths, trying to cool the raging fire in my blood.

CHAPTER THIRTY-TWO

mma

"OH MY GOD, THIS IS SO GOOD," I MOAN AROUND A mouthful of cheese that was on fire just a few moments ago. I'd never tried halloumi before, and I'd been seriously missing out. Not only was it fun to watch the waiter set flame to the block of cheese as he brought it out, but the result is beyond delicious—rich, salty, a little crispy on the outside, and gooey-melty on the inside.

Probably a million calories in each bite, but so worth it.

"It's one of my favorite things here," Marcus says huskily, his blue eyes intent on my face, and a fresh wave of color washes over me as I realize that my near-orgasmic reaction to the food is turning him on again.

The man is a sex fiend, clearly—and so am I when I'm around him.

Still, after he got that embarrassing confession out of me, we'd somehow managed a normal conversation for the rest of the ride, with me babbling about my job at the bookstore and Marcus attentively listening. I don't know if he was really interested or merely indulging me, but I can't deny that it felt good to have his undivided attention. And I still have it—despite at least two women in this place doing their best to get him to notice them.

I have no idea if they know who he is or if they're just responding to his commanding good looks, but either way, I don't like it.

To his credit, Marcus seems oblivious to their existence—even when the supermodel-hot blonde purposefully drops her purse in front of his chair, so she can bend over and show off her tiny, toned ass in her skimpy dress. *I* gape at her, stunned by her brazenness, but Marcus doesn't so much as spare her a glance. Nor does he look at the gorgeous brunette two tables over, who's already paraded in front of our table twice, flipping her long, straight locks over her shoulder each time and smiling at Marcus like he's Thor reincarnated.

"Do you come here a lot?" I ask, stifling the urge to trip up the brunette when she walks by our table yet again, swaying her slim hips like she's on a catwalk. "To this restaurant, I mean."

He nods, cutting into his own portion of the

halloumi. "It's only a few blocks from my place, so I'm here at least once a month."

That explains it. I bet those two have found out that a billionaire frequents this restaurant, and they're here specifically to meet him. Maybe they've even bribed a waiter to learn about Marcus's reservation.

Why else would the blonde be sitting at a table all by herself? Women—especially gorgeous women—don't go to nice, sit-down restaurants on their own. The brunette, at least, appears to be with a friend—who, come to think of it, is glaring at me as if she'd like to ask the waiter to set *me* on fire.

I look away, the last bite of cheese turning bitter in my mouth as I realize she probably thinks I'm like her friend—a gold digger.

Eenie, meenie, miney, moe, everyone knows your mom's a ho!

I reach for my glass of water with an unsteady hand, the childish taunt ringing in my ears as if it's been minutes instead of years since I've heard it.

"Emma." A large, warm palm covers my free hand. "Are you okay?"

I nod and force a smile to my face. "Yes, of course. Why wouldn't I be?"

"Maybe because you suddenly looked like someone spit in your plate," Marcus says dryly, withdrawing his hand.

"No, I just…" I take a sip of water and set the glass down. "People here know who you are, don't they?"

"Ah." His gaze clears, as if he's solved a mystery.

"Yes, they do—at least the owner and the staff. Is that what's bothering you? You're worried some of them might think you're with me for my money?"

I flinch instinctively. Marcus is either eerily perceptive, or my hang-ups are more obvious than I thought. Unless... "Do *you* think I'm with you for your money?" I blurt, horrified. "Because I promise you, it's not at all what—"

"No, of course not." His jaw flexes. "I don't think that at all."

"Oh, okay." I chew on my lip, studying his closed-off expression. "Are you sure? Because I understand why you'd be concerned, and I can assure you that I would never—"

"I know, kitten." His hard face softening, he reaches across the table to cover my hand again. "I know you would never use me like that."

Use me.

I stare at him, the air in my lungs thickening until it feels like I'm sucking in water.

User. Whore. Sociopath. Manipulative bitch.

"How do you know?" My voice sounds as choked as I feel, all the epithets hurled at my mother playing in my mind on a loop. "What makes you so sure?"

"You." His gaze is steady on my face as his thumb rubs a circle on the inside of my wrist. "The way you are."

"But you don't really know me. We've just met and—"

"I know enough."

I stare at him, the pressure in my lungs intensifying. His trust is both heart-warming and crushing. Because he doesn't know—not really. If he knew the full truth, he wouldn't be so quick to dismiss this possibility.

I certainly wouldn't in his shoes.

Shakily, I withdraw my hand from his hold. "My mother... she was a user," I say, forcing the words past the tightness in my throat. I don't know why I feel compelled to tell him this, but I do.

If he walks away, I want it to be now, before I can fall any deeper under his spell.

His gaze turns inscrutable. "What do you mean by that?"

"I mean that she used people—all people, but especially men who were interested in her." I swallow the growing knot in my throat. "Once, when I was nine, she slept with my science teacher so he wouldn't give me a bad grade on a test. And before you ask—no, she didn't really care about my grades. She just wanted to show a decent report card to her parents—my grandparents—so they'd stop accusing her of neglecting me while she partied all over the city, dragging me from one boyfriend's place to another's whenever she got bored."

Marcus's expression doesn't change, so I plow on, determined to make him understand. "They said she had an antisocial personality disorder, lacked empathy and all that. A sociopath, but not a particularly smart one, you know? Because the smart ones get far in life, and she didn't—though she wasn't hampered by anything like morals and ethics. The only person she cared about was herself, and she did whatever it took to get her way—lying, cheating, stealing… and always, always using people."

"You included?" he asks quietly, and I shrug, though my throat feels even tighter.

"I suppose, though I was too young to be of much use to her. She did like to dress me up and parade me in front of her boyfriends—kind of like a pet. Mostly, though, she ignored me—but that's not the point." I drag in a breath. "Look, Marcus, the reason why I'm telling you this is—"

"You are not like her." His gaze drills into me. "Do you hear me? You are nothing like her."

I stare at him, startled by the intensity in his voice. "I know, but—"

"You are nothing like your mother," he repeats in a softer tone, and something inside me—a cold knot I never knew was there—begins to melt, a warm feeling creeping in.

"Thank you," I say hoarsely, and then I have to look away as our waiter comes by, bringing the main course.

I don't want him or Marcus to see the sheen of tears in my eyes.

arcus

GUILT, STRONG AND UNFAMILIAR, FLAVORS EVERY BITE OF the buttery branzino that is my main course. Emma got herself a Greek salad, and my chest aches as I watch her eat it, her manner unusually subdued.

She opened up to me.

She told me about her painful secret—and it was all I could do to let her carry on as if I was hearing it for the first time.

As if I didn't already know about the whole ugly mess.

She didn't tell me everything, of course—like the fact that her mother was once arrested for prostitution, or that she died in a car crash while being chased by a lover whose bank account she'd emptied earlier that day. But what she told me was enough.

Enough to know that her fear of turning out like her mother—the fear she'd talked about in her college essay—is still there, as much a part of her as her red hair and softly freckled skin.

And I, asshole that I am, used that fear against her, sending her expensive gifts so that she'd have no choice but to see me in person.

In a way, *I* am like her mother—willing to do whatever it takes to get my way.

"I'm sorry," I say quietly when she continues eating without speaking. "Emma, kitten, I'm so sorry you had to go through all that."

My phone vibrates in my pocket, but I ignore it. Work can wait.

She looks up from her plate, blinking. "What? Oh, no, it's fine. My mother wasn't abusive or anything, and in any case, she died in an accident when I was eleven, and my grandparents raised me from that point on. I was just telling you all that in case, you know…" She stops, pretty color spreading over her fair skin.

"In case we get serious?"

Her flush deepens. "I wasn't—"

"It's okay." Fuck, it's more than okay. I like the idea. Love it, in fact.

To my shock, I realize that I *want* her to think about getting serious, to picture us together in the future… because I'm already doing that myself.

Shoving the unsettling thought away, I focus on the

topic at hand. "Emma, listen to me," I say when she resumes eating. "I don't give a flying fuck about your mother. Well, I do—I'd love to go back in time and have you taken away from her long before you were eleven —but I don't care what kind of woman birthed you. That doesn't determine who you are, doesn't change my opinion of you in any way."

She puts down her fork, her lips curving in a faint smile. "You don't think blood will tell?"

"No, I don't." How could I, with parents like mine? I hesitate for a moment, then say bluntly, "My father was killed in prison when I was two—he was there for armed robbery and assault—and my mother was an alcoholic. Not the functional kind, either—a full-on, twenty-four-seven drunk. She died from liver failure when I was eighteen."

I haven't told anyone this in decades; in fact, I've gone to great pains to obscure my past from the media as soon as I had the resources to do so. The only thing my current friends and acquaintances know about my childhood is that I was raised in Staten Island by a single mother, who passed away from a rare liver disease.

No ugliness, no drama, just your run-of-the-mill lower-middle-class upbringing.

For some reason, though, I want Emma to know everything—to understand what kind of man she's dealing with. Because if there's any kernel of truth to the whole "blood will tell" business, mine is far more tainted than hers.

Her eyes widen at my revelations, but to my relief, she looks neither put off nor disgusted. "I'm sorry," she says softly, reaching across the table to lay her small hand on my arm. "That must've been so hard for you, growing up that way. Did you have anyone you could turn to for help? Grandparents? Other family members?"

There's genuine sympathy in her voice, and I know that she, of all people, understands what it's like to grow up essentially on your own, to take care of yourself from a young age.

To know that your mother, the person who's supposed to have your best interests at heart, can't be trusted.

"Neither of my parents came from a close-knit family, but I had a lot of support in school," I answer, figuring she might as well know everything. "My second-grade teacher, Mr. Bond, was particularly instrumental in guiding me through elementary school and beyond. It's thanks to him that I chose to focus on my studies rather than making a quick buck on the streets."

"Oh?"

I smile at the curiosity in her gaze. "Money was tight, as you can imagine, so by the time I was eight, I was doing whatever it took to put food on the table—running errands for the local gangs, peddling weed on the streets, stealing school supplies. It's the latter that got me caught and nearly expelled. Mr. Bond stepped in at the last moment, vouching for me, and then he sat me down and told me about some legitimate ways I could make money—starting with the tutoring of kids whose math skills weren't as good as my own. He also gave me several issues of *Forbes* magazine and told me all about the rich people on the cover, about how they got there and how I could get there too."

A soft smile curves her lips. "And you did, didn't you?"

"I did." I don't try to hide the satisfaction in my voice. "They wrote a feature on me shortly after I made my first billion."

"Wow." Her smile widens, revealing those cute dimples. "Mr. Bond must be so proud of you. Do you still keep in touch with him?"

"I did. Unfortunately, he passed away a few years ago. Pancreatic cancer," I explain, my throat tightening.

I did everything in my power to help him, but neither the world-class doctors I hired nor the experimental treatments I paid for could arrest the deadly disease.

It was the most powerless I'd felt as an adult.

Emma's smile disappears. "I'm sorry. That must've been a terrible loss for you."

"Thank you," I say evenly. "He was a good man."

My only consolation is that his children and grandchildren will never have to struggle financially, thanks to the seventy-million-dollar trust I set up in his name, explaining it to the lawyers as a lottery he'd won shortly before his death.

The waiter comes by to clear our plates and bring

out the dessert menu, and I use the distraction to push away the lingering grief. I've never spoken about this with anyone, but somehow, it felt right to confide in Emma, to have her know the real me, not the sanitized mask I show to the world.

The waiter leaves, and Emma glances at the dessert menu for a second before setting it aside.

I smile wryly. "Let me guess. Not hungry?" Now that I know she's trying to keep her portion of the check to a minimum, I can pretty much predict what she will and won't order.

"I actually had dinner—well, half of it—before I got your latest gift," she says. "Speaking of which—"

"If you don't mind, I'm going to get the baklava," I say, as if I didn't hear her. She's going to try to refuse the books again, and I'm not about to let that happen. "It's amazing here, the best I've ever had."

She blinks. "Of course, go right ahead."

I smile wider and motion to the waiter. "The baklava, please," I tell him when he hurries over. "And bring two plates. We'll share."

"Oh, I'm not going to—" Emma starts, but I hold up my hand as the waiter rushes away.

"It's only fair. I shared your ice cream, so I owe you at least a bite of my dessert," I say with utter seriousness.

"But—"

"No buts. And I'm getting the dessert on my portion of the check. You're not the only one who believes in fairness."

"Oh." Her small white teeth worry her lower lip. "Okay then, I guess I can try a bite."

I conceal a satisfied grin. This might be a small thing, getting her to share my dessert, but it's a step in the right direction. Before long, I intend to be paying for all our meals, as well as anything else she might want or need.

First, though, I have to cure her of her fear of being like her mother, one bite of baklava at a time.

The waiter returns, bringing the dessert. Before she can say anything, I cut a piece and put it on her plate. "Try it," I urge, pushing the plate toward her, and she forks the honey-layered pastry into her mouth.

It doesn't get the orgasmic reaction that the halloumi did, but my cock still hardens as she chews and swallows with a blissful expression on her face.

Fuck. I really have to get her to my place before I attack her in public like the sex maniac I'm turning into.

The baklava is small, so we make quick work of it, and then I motion for the check. Emma grabs it again, and I let her, though it pains me to see her carefully count out the bills for her portion.

In the investigator's report, there was a section on her finances—the miserable state of which makes it even more insane that she's doing this.

Finally, the bill is paid, and I lead her out of the restaurant, my hand resting on the small of her back.

"Where's Wilson?" she asks, looking around for the car. "Or are we taking a cab?" Then her eyes widen, her cheeks flushing as she realizes what she's implied. "Never mind, I forgot you live nearby. I'll just take the subway home and—"

"We're less than four blocks from my place, so I gave Wilson the rest of the evening off," I say, turning to face her. Capturing her small hands in mine, I gaze at her upturned face. "Emma, kitten... I want you to come home with me."

CHAPTER THIRTY-FOUR

mma

I DON'T KNOW WHAT I EXPECTED FROM A BILLIONAIRE'S residence, but Marcus's penthouse in Tribeca is like something from another world—a world I've only seen in glossy magazines and TV shows about the lifestyles of the rich and famous.

Ultra-modern and decorated in shades of gray and white, the place is huge—at least for New York City. Maybe in the South or Midwest, where land is cheap, an apartment this size would be nothing special, but in the heart of Manhattan, it's the equivalent of a fifty-karat diamond. As Marcus guides me around, I see an enormous living room with a sleek spiral staircase in the middle, a movie-theater-like media room, a fully equipped home gym, a dining area with a table big enough for twenty people, and a spacious kitchen with gleaming appliances that wouldn't look out of place on a spaceship.

And a pool.

A forty-foot-long, rectangular swimming pool separated from the rest of the apartment by a thick glass wall and partially shielded from view by eight-foot-tall potted plants with leaves the size of my head.

"Are they real?" I ask in a hushed tone, reaching out to touch one glossy leaf, and Marcus nods, smiling.

"Yes, of course. There's an indoor landscaping company that comes in to take care of them once a week, watering them and so on."

Right, of course. Because that's what wealthy people do: hire professional landscapers to take care of their houseplants.

"Do you have a chef and a housekeeper as well?" I ask, but to my surprise, Marcus shakes his head.

"My butler handles everything, including the cooking and the cleaning. Well, he oversees the cleaning; there's a company that actually does it."

"I see." I sound slightly choked, but I can't help it.

A freaking butler? Am I in *Downton Abbey*?

"Come, let me show you upstairs," Marcus says, and I follow him to the spiral staircase, trying not to look as overwhelmed as I feel. I knew he was rich, of course, but it didn't sink in fully before this.

Everywhere I look are objects that cost more than all of my family's possessions combined. From the abstract paintings on the walls to the sleek sculptures that could've been in a modern-art museum, this penthouse reeks of money. Insane money. The kind of money that makes a joke of my attempts to pretend that because I pay for my meals, we're somehow on equal footing.

God, what am I doing here?

I don't belong in this place any more than a subway rat would.

"This is the library," Marcus says, leading me into the first room off the stairs on the second floor, and I see two lounge chairs in a front of a fireplace and walls lined with books. Some of the bookshelves are covered with what appears to be hermetically sealed glass—they must hold more valuable books, like the signed first editions that he sent me.

Feeling like Belle in *Beauty and the Beast*, I walk over to one of the glass cases and peer inside.

Yep. Hemingway's *The Old Man and the Sea*, the pages yellowed and slightly frayed. I have no doubt that if I opened the cloth-bound cover, I'd see the author's bold scrawl on the title page.

"Have you read all of these?" I ask, looking up when Marcus comes to stand next to me.

"Most, but not all," he says. "Some of the first editions—like the one you're looking at—are just part of my collection. As I started to tell you on our first date, I like books too, both reading and collecting them."

Huh. Maybe we have more in common than I thought. It's always been my dream to have a shelf full of my favorite authors' signed copies. "Is that where you got the first editions you sent me? From your collection?"

He smiles. "Indeed. I'm glad I happened to have your favorites."

I take in a deep breath. "Right. Thank you for that. Unfortunately, I can't—"

"Here, let me show you the rest of the place." Deftly, he shepherds me out of the library and into a guest room bigger than my entire studio. His home office, with five computer monitors and three TVs mounted on the walls, follows, and then we finally step into the master bedroom.

Instantly, my heartbeat picks up speed, my skin prickling with increased awareness of the man beside me. During the tour, I was so overwhelmed by the opulence around me that I almost forgot why I'm here. But now it's all I can think about, my mind flashing to the heated look in Marcus's eyes when he held my hands and asked me to come home with him.

His thoughts must be traveling along the same pathways because his steely fingers loop around my wrist, and when I look up, I find his gaze filled with dark, primal intent. "Emma..." His voice is low and rough as he pulls me to him. "Kitten, I want you."

And as my insides clench on an answering surge of need, his lips crash against mine in a deep, voracious kiss.

CHAPTER THIRTY-FIVE

mma

I WAKE UP SLOWLY AND WITH GREAT RELUCTANCE, NOT wanting to leave the luxuriant warmth of the blanket and the silky softness of the sheets. My limbs feel heavy as I stretch, and my inner thighs are oddly sore, as if I'd done some hardcore yoga. Even my skin is strangely tender, especially in the more intimate—

Oh God. I sit up and look around the unfamiliar bedroom, a burst of adrenaline chasing away the grogginess as I realize where I am and why I'm feeling like this.

I'm in Marcus's bedroom, and he fucked me all night long.

Okay, maybe that last bit is an exaggeration, but that's what it felt like. The man was insatiable, taking me over and over, as if we hadn't had sex just a couple of hours earlier. I've lost count of how many times I'd orgasmed last night. Seven, eight... nine, maybe?

No wonder my sex feels like it's been scraped raw with male whiskers.

Because it has been.

My skin heats at the memory, and I pull up the blanket, realizing I'm sitting there totally naked. Thankfully, I'm alone. Gripping the blanket, I look around for my clothes. I don't see them anywhere, but there is a fluffy pink robe, much like the one I have at home, hanging on the door—and matching fuzzy slippers next to the bed.

I hesitate for a moment, then slide my feet into the slippers and beeline for the robe.

I hate the idea of wearing the same thing as Marcus's other hook-ups, but it's better than prancing around naked.

To my surprise, the robe has a tag attached.

Did he get it just for me, or does he keep a stash for these types of situations?

Either way, I gratefully rip off the tag and put on the robe, wrapping the tie around my waist. Unlike mine, it's long, all the way down to my ankles, and I instantly feel warm and cozy, as if I'm at home cuddling with my cats.

Speaking of which, I have to get back to them soon. They're not used to me being out all night, and I'm sure Mr. Puffs is already on a path of destruction. Plus, if I don't do laundry today, I'll have no underwear for tomorrow.

Marcus is still nowhere to be seen, so I hurry into the adjoining bathroom and take a quick shower, then brush my teeth with a toothbrush I find considerately laid out by the sink, still in its plastic wrapper. There's also a nice, expensive face moisturizer—unscented, just like I prefer—and even a bottle of hair gel that I use to tame the worst of the frizzy explosion on my head.

My host is really acing this whole "having a female guest" thing.

As I do all this, I try not to gape at my surroundings like a peasant. So what if the square whirlpool tub in the corner is deep enough to stand in? Or that the all-glass shower stall is twice the size of my entire bathroom and equipped with five rotating showerheads? None of that impresses me, not even the futuristic-looking toilet with a built-in bidet and a seat that warms my butt.

Oh, who am I kidding? I couldn't be more impressed if the furniture levitated around me. The 0.1 percent really do know how to live.

Shaking my head, I go back into the bedroom to try to find my clothes again.

No luck—though I distinctly remember my jeans and sweater landing on the floor as Marcus yanked them off me. He must've picked them up and put them somewhere, but where? I don't see them in the walk-in closet, where Marcus's suits and shirts hang neatly, sorted by color. Nor are they in any of the drawers in the sleek white chest inside the closet. There are just socks, T-shirts, men's underwear—I close that drawer fast, feeling like a perv—and other foldable items of clothing. Like the rest of the closet, everything in the drawers is arranged with perfect neatness, as if Marie Kondo just blitzed through the place.

Either Marcus has OCD or his butler does.

My boots are also nowhere to be found, but that makes more sense. I left them in the entryway, not wanting to track New York City dirt all over the gleaming floor when we came in.

I stand up on tiptoes to peer into a built-in shelf in the faint hope that Marcus might've stuffed my clothes in there. Nope. Just a box with cufflinks and—

"Emma?"

Heart jumping, I spin around to face Marcus, who's standing in the closet doorway, dark eyebrows arched.

Oh, crap.

I should've realized how this could look.

"Hi. Good morning." I sound breathless—and probably guilty as sin. "So sorry, but my clothes, they weren't there. I swear, I wasn't trying to snoop. It's just that I was looking for my clothes and—"

"It's okay." He steps in, a slow, wicked smile curving his lips. "You can snoop all you want. As for the clothes, I gave them to Geoffrey to be laundered. They should be ready in about an hour."

"Oh." That someone would wash my clothes hadn't even entered my mind. "Okay, thanks."

So much for my plan to make a quick escape this morning.

"Do you have someplace to be?" he inquires, cocking his head, and my cheeks warm as I realize he's dressed in a pair of sweatpants and a soft-looking T-shirt—the first time I'm seeing him in something other than his business attire.

Or naked.

Because I've definitely seen him naked.

Stop thinking about sex, Emma. And stop blushing. "My cats will be upset if I don't come home soon," I say, my face burning despite the admonitions. "And I'm supposed to Skype with my grandparents at 11:30. Speaking of which, do you know what time it is?"

He grins. "Last I checked, it was 11:23."

"What?"

"What can I say? You didn't get that much sleep last night."

Because he kept waking me up by sliding into me, or going down on me, or sucking on my—oh God, here I go again.

"Right, okay." With effort, I focus on something other than the way the soft material of the T-shirt hugs his defined pecs. "Where's my purse? I need to text my grandparents to reschedule."

"Why? You can Skype here. My internet is really fast, and I'll give you privacy."

I blink. "Here? As in, your bedroom?"

"Or library or guest room—wherever you prefer. You might not want to do it downstairs, though. Geoffrey is cooking up a storm for brunch, and the smells will drive you crazy."

He's driving me crazy. Doesn't he realize that if I Skype my grandparents from some place other than my apartment, I'll have to explain where I am?

"No, that's okay, thanks. I'll just—"

"Why not?" He folds his powerful arms across his chest, drawing my attention to the flexing muscles. "Food won't be ready for another half hour, anyway. Geoffrey started cooking late, as I wasn't sure when you'd wake up."

I tear my eyes away from those impressive biceps. "You don't understand. My grandparents are nosy— really nosy—and I don't want to lie to them and claim I'm in some fancy hotel."

"Why would you lie to them?"

I stare at him, dumbfounded. "Well, I'm not going to tell them that we... you know."

"Why not? Are they old-fashioned? Do they expect you to wait until marriage?"

"No, they're actually pretty liberal, but they're my *grandparents*." How dense is he? "If I tell them about you, they'll think it's a big deal and ask a million questions and want to meet you and stuff." *There, spelled out in detail. Now run for the hills, as any sane man would.*

He uncrosses his arms, not looking the least bit concerned. "That's fine. I'm happy to meet them."

"Y-you are?" Is there something wrong with my hearing? Because I'm pretty sure Marcus just told me that he wants to meet my family.

"Yeah, why not? Feel free to introduce me when you talk to them. I'll be in my office, catching up on work. Oh, and the Wi-Fi password is bond$carelli19."

And with that, he walks out of the room—or rather, his ginormous closet.

CHAPTER THIRTY-SIX

mma

I DON'T CALL MY GRANDPARENTS.

Not at 11:30, at least. It takes me several minutes to find my purse in Marcus's huge bedroom—it was sneakily hanging on the back of the door—and when I finally fish out my phone, it's already 11:37 a.m. and I have a worried text from Grandma.

I'm normally never late when it comes to our biweekly Skype sessions.

Ugh. Now I can't *not* explain. If I just text back to reschedule, she'll think something is seriously wrong.

Phone in hand, I look around. The bedroom is as gorgeous as the rest of the penthouse, and there's a nook with a sleek lounge chair where I can Skype. But

I really don't feel comfortable talking to my grandparents next to the bed where Marcus fucked my brains out. *Repeatedly*. It's bad enough I'll be sitting in a borrowed robe.

Library it is, then.

I rush over there and plop my butt into one of the chairs by the fireplace. Then I get my phone on the Wi-Fi, send the videocall request, and wait.

"Emma, sweetheart!" Grandma's rounded face fills the small screen, with Gramps's ear next to her. "What happened? Is everything okay?"

"Yeah, I just woke up late. I'm so sorry. How are you guys doing?"

"Oh, we're great. Already prepping for Thursday," Grandma says, beaming as Gramps moves fully into the camera view. With a start, I realize she's talking about Thanksgiving—which means I'm flying out to Florida this Wednesday, having bought the plane tickets on a mad sale last year.

"Your grandmother's already gotten the turkey," Gramps says as proudly as if it were his achievement. "And she found a new stuffing recipe online." He peers at me, his nose growing as he leans closer to the camera. "Wait a minute. You're not at home."

"Um, no." Crap, I'm so not ready for this. If I'd remembered that Thanksgiving—complete with endless opportunities for interrogation—is this coming week, I definitely wouldn't have done the call here. "I'm at a... friend's place."

Grandma blinks. "Really? Which friend? Kendall or Janie?" She leans closer to the camera as well. "That fireplace looks nice. And are all of those bookshelves?"

"Yep." Sighing, I turn my phone around and move it in a slow semicircle, letting them see the whole room—because they would've badgered me into doing it anyway. "Lots of books here."

"Your friend must really like to read," Gramps says, impressed. "Is that how you met, through your work?"

"So it's *not* Kendall or Janie," Grandma says, stating the obvious.

I turn the phone back to face me. "No, it's someone else." Dammit, why did I let Marcus prod me into this? Short of outright lying, anything I say will make this thing between us sound way more serious than it is. Not that I know what level of seriousness we're at, anyway. It's not a one-night stand, as we'd been on a couple of dates prior to hooking up. A weekend fling, maybe? Casual dating?

It's certainly not the start of a real relationship—not with him dead set on marrying someone like Emmeline.

My grandparents are staring at me expectantly, and I know I need to tell them *something*. Sighing, I pinch the bridge of my nose. "It's no one you know—just a guy I met a couple of weeks ago, okay?"

If this were a movie, the soundtrack would've come to a screeching halt. As is, the silence is deafening, both of them staring at me slack-jawed.

Finally, my grandfather speaks. "A guy?" He sounds incredulous. "As in, a boyfriend?"

I wince. "We're not quite there, Gramps, but yes, someone I'm dating." I hope I don't have to explain the nuances of modern dating to him, because I'm not sure I understand them myself—especially in light of Marcus's bizarre willingness to meet my grandparents.

I could've sworn casual hookups and family don't mix.

"Is that a robe you're wearing?" Grandma asks, peering at my shoulders. "It looks like a robe."

Crap. I was hoping they wouldn't notice. "My clothes are in the laundry," I explain, then realize I just made it sound like Marcus and I are living together. "That is, the clothes I was wearing last night—I don't keep anything else here. Marcus decided to wash them before I woke up, hence the robe."

That's probably TMI—in general, all of this is TMI—but my grandparents clearly don't mind. Gramps is grinning, and Grandma looks positively gleeful as she asks, "Marcus? Is that his name?" At my nod, she presses, "How did you two meet?"

"Oh, just through a… you know, a dating app." Or more precisely, through a mix-up related to a dating app, but that's too long of a story.

"Really?" Grandma leans in. "We didn't know you were doing online dating."

"Yeah, I didn't mention it because it wasn't a big deal. Janie talked me into creating a profile a few months back, but I've only logged on a couple of times."

"Which was clearly enough to meet Marcus and end up at his place. In a robe," Gramps states, his bushy eyebrows twitching with excitement.

I blow out an exasperated breath, wishing for once that my grandparents could be all stodgy and conservative, like most others of their generation. Instead, at nearly eighty years of age, they're as open-minded as any millennial, having embraced the changing mores of the times along with the technology of email, social media, texting, and Skype.

I don't want Gramps to brandish a shotgun or anything, but still, a little bit of Catholic disapproval wouldn't hurt.

"We're just getting to know one another, Gramps. This probably won't go anywhere," I say, but I can tell my warning is falling on deaf ears. My dating life—or lack thereof since college—has been a source of concern for my grandparents, to the point that I was tactfully told during my last Thanksgiving visit that it was perfectly fine to embrace my needs and inclinations, no matter what they might be.

Translation: they thought I might be gay and in the closet.

"So how old is he?" Grandma asks, launching into her patented interrogation mode. "Where is he from? What does he do? How many siblings does he have, and when can we meet him?"

I open my mouth to start answering, but then I

change my mind. "You know what, Grandma?" I say sweetly. "Why don't you meet Marcus right now? He can tell you everything himself."

And getting up, I carry the phone to my host's office.

CHAPTER THIRTY-SEVEN

*M*arcus

"I'M THIRTY-FIVE, AN ONLY CHILD, ORIGINALLY FROM Staten Island, and I run a hedge fund," I say smoothly, propping Emma's phone on my desk while she stands in front of me with an evil little smirk on her rosebud lips. She's clearly expecting me to be discomfited by her grandmother's barrage of questions.

Too bad for her I've honed my skills through dozens of interviews on live TV.

"Really? What kind of hedge fund?" There's a look of keen interest on Ted Walsh's aged face. "I follow CNBC, you know."

I smile at him. "We focus on alpha generation under all market conditions, so it's a mix of everything, from commodities to long-short equity to quant strategies.

Lately, we've also been dabbling in some illiquid investments, including real estate and private equity."

"And how long have you two been dating?" Mary Walsh asks, her gray eyes as bright and clear as her granddaughter's. It's obvious all the finance lingo has gone right over her head, and she couldn't care less about my fund's strategies. "Emma said you met through a dating app?"

I glance over the screen at Emma. She shrugs awkwardly, so I reply, "You could say that." I guess she didn't feel like telling her grandparents the whole messy story. "As to how long we've been together, our first date was earlier this month."

Mary launches into her next set of questions, and I answer with calm patience. Yes, I've lived in New York City all my life except when I was away at school. Where did I go? Cornell for undergrad (finance major) and Wharton for MBA. No, I don't have any family I'm close to, as my parents passed away when I was young. Yes, I own my apartment, and a few other properties as well. No, I have no plans to move out of New York to save on taxes.

For some reason, the interrogation doesn't bother me—nor does the fact that with this call, we've just leapfrogged over months of typical relationship development. Offering to meet Emma's grandparents had been an impulse on my part, but one I can't bring myself to regret. Last night didn't scratch my Emma itch—if anything, it made it stronger—and my fascination with her is growing by the minute. I want to know everything about her, to crawl into her mind and see the world from the inside of her pretty head.

At the very least, I want to meet everyone important to her, so I can figure out how to become one of those people.

Finally, Emma's grandparents seem satisfied that I'm neither a bum nor a serial killer, and we're already saying our goodbyes, with Emma standing next to me, when Mary says, "You're not flying in with our Emma this coming week, are you, Marcus? Because if you are, I'll be sure to make some extra food."

Before I can say a word, Emma is already shaking her head. "Of course not, Grandma. I told you, we've just met, and besides, Marcus's work is crazy busy. Right?" Her eyes cut to me. "You have an insane week at the fund, don't you?"

"Yes." My voice doesn't sound entirely like my own. "Yes, I do. A killer workload all week long."

"We understand." Mary smiles gently. "But if you do manage to get free, you're always welcome at our Thanksgiving table, Marcus. It was a pleasure meeting you."

"Likewise," I say, and give the phone to Emma to disconnect the call.

I had no intention of going to Florida this week—even *I* know that's too big of a step so soon—but for some reason, the knowledge that Emma doesn't want me there stings worse than a Portuguese man-of-war.

CHAPTER THIRTY-EIGHT

mma

MARCUS IS UNUSUALLY QUIET, ALMOST BROODING, AS HE leads me downstairs for brunch. Is he upset with me for allowing the grilling? Because he pretty much asked for it—insisted on it, really. Still, I feel a little bad that I let my grandparents put him through the wringer.

I should've shielded him from the worst of it, like I'd always done with Jim, my college boyfriend.

Oh, well, too late now. And Marcus had held his own the way Jim could never have. He'd spoken to my grandparents respectfully but as an equal, answering their questions without the slightest hint of nervousness or uncertainty. At the same time, he hadn't boasted about his accomplishments, all of his answers factual but revealing little of the extent of his power and wealth. Of course, Gramps and Grandma had been impressed anyway—and why wouldn't they be?

It's not his billions that make Marcus Carelli formidable; it's the steely, indomitable core of the man himself. A few minutes in his company is all it takes to know that he's a force of nature, someone you'd never want to cross.

"You okay?" I ask softly as we approach the dining area with Marcus still not saying a word. The rich, savory aromas emanating from the kitchen are making my stomach growl, but I'm too concerned about his strange mood to think about food. "I'm sorry about my grandparents. They're just—"

"Protective of you." He smiles, and though it doesn't quite reach his eyes, the strange tension between us fades. "They seem like lovely people. Your grandfather reminds me a bit of Mr. Bond."

I beam at him. "Yes, they're great. And Gramps actually *was* a teacher. He taught English and Social Studies for almost forty years before retiring."

Marcus's smile warms. "Really? What about your grandmother?"

"She was a nurse, a really skilled one. I almost never went to the doctor when I was living with them. Grandma can handle anything short of major surgery."

"Mr. Carelli?" A thin man with ramrod-straight posture steps into our path as we approach the table. With a noticeable British accent, he announces, "Your food is ready."

"Excellent, thank you." Marcus glances at me. "Emma, this is Geoffrey, my butler. Geoffrey, this is Emma, my... guest."

I manage a smile despite the sudden acceleration of my pulse. I caught that moment of hesitation before Marcus said "guest," the split second of indecision that must be as rare for him as a lobster dinner is for me. Had he been about to say something else?

My date?

My friend, maybe?

There's no way he was going to say *"my girlfriend."*

"It's a pleasure," Geoffrey says, inclining his head. "Now, please, have a seat. I will bring out the food."

He hurries away, and Marcus leads me to the table —which is set with two straw mats topped with square white plates, sleek modern glasses, and gleaming utensils next to white cloth napkins. In the middle is a carafe of water infused with lemon, mint, and cucumber, and next to it is what looks like fresh-squeezed orange juice, along with a pitcher of dark green liquid.

Marcus pulls out a chair for me, and I sit down, once again feeling overwhelmed. Not only does this brunch seem fancier than at any restaurant, but I'm still wearing a robe. Not that having my own clothes would've helped; I'm pretty sure a single fork here costs more than my entire outfit.

The worst part is that I can't pay for my portion of this meal—unless I offer to cover half of one morning's worth of Geoffrey's salary, along with the cost of the ingredients. And even *I* know that's ridiculous. My best bet is to reciprocate by making Marcus a meal at my place one of these days, but after seeing the way he lives, the idea of asking him over to my tiny studio makes me cringe.

I might as well ask Queen Elizabeth—the monarch, not my cat—to have dinner in a closet.

"Water, orange juice, or green juice?" Marcus asks, and I force a smile to my lips.

"Green juice, please." There's no need for him to know I've never tried the overpriced health elixir before—or that all of this is making me feel like a fish out of water.

Marcus pours the green liquid into my glass, and I take a sip. It's surprisingly good, tart and refreshing instead of bitter. I can taste the Granny Smith apple underneath the grassy flavor of the greens, and I down the rest of the glass in a few long gulps.

"More?" Marcus asks wryly, and I nod, because why not.

It's a delicious way to meet my weekly quota of fruits and vegetables in one morning.

As I'm sipping on the refill, Geoffrey comes out with a silver-domed tray. Setting it on the table, he removes the dome, revealing two plates with a perfectly folded omelet on each, along with two little bowls of cut-up fruit and a basket of fluffy biscuits. The omelets are covered with some kind of creamy orange sauce and topped with a sprig of parsley, and it all smells absolutely scrumptious.

Definitely fancier than any restaurant brunch I've had.

"Shiitake and oyster mushroom omelet with crab and lobster, topped with spicy gorgonzola sauce," Geoffrey announces, putting one plate in front of me and the other in front of Marcus. He then does the same thing with the fruit bowls and puts the biscuit basket between us, adding a pair of tongs for easy grabbing.

"Thank you, Geoffrey. It looks amazing," Marcus says, and I echo his sentiment, barely able to swallow the saliva pooling in my mouth. How is it possible that I was thinking of lobster only a few minutes earlier and now there's a lobster omelet in front of me?

No, scratch that, *a shiitake and oyster mushroom omelet with crab and lobster*—as in, all the foods I love and can rarely afford in one insane dish?

The butler inclines his head and disappears back into the kitchen, and I dig into the omelet, my fork trembling from eagerness. *Holy. Cow.* I nearly orgasm on the spot as the spicy richness of the gorgonzola sauce touches my tongue, followed by the delicious texture of the seafood chunks wrapped in mushroom-flavored egg.

I must've moaned out loud and closed my eyes because when I open them, I find Marcus staring at me like I've just stripped naked. His face is tightly drawn, his eyes burning with savage hunger as his omelet sits untouched in front of him.

"Sorry about that," I mumble, my face turning hot as

I realize I must've looked like I was literally having an orgasm. *Again.* At this rate, he's going to think I have a food fetish. "It's just really, really good."

"One of these days, I'm going to fuck you as I feed you." His voice is a low, dark growl. "I'm going to lay you out on this table, and make a meal of your sweet pussy as you eat."

Oh God. Said pussy clenches on a violent spike of need, flooding with warm slickness in an instant. I can picture exactly what he's saying, and my body's helpless reaction makes me dizzy, a squeezing band around my lungs preventing a full breath.

"Yes, that's right." He leans in, blue eyes glinting as his big hand covers my knee under the table. "I'm going to make a feast of you right here, kitten, and you're going to love every fucking second. I'm going to stuff you so full of me you won't even think of food."

I'm not thinking of food now. I can't—not with my heart thudding in my chest and my entire body burning. I didn't know dirty talk could turn me on like this, that words could fill me with such agonizing need. It's only the knowledge that Geoffrey is here and can walk in on us at any moment that makes me swallow and break eye contact, gulping in shallow breaths to settle the mad thrumming of my pulse.

There are a few beats of silence, moments so thick with tension I can almost taste it in the air. Then Marcus removes his hand from my knee, and I hear the scrape of knife and fork against plate.

"You're right. This *is* delicious." His voice is back to normal, his tone conversational, but I'm not fooled.

As soon as we're done with this meal, we're heading back into the bedroom.

And damn if the thought doesn't make me soaking wet.

CHAPTER THIRTY-NINE

$\mathcal{M}$arcus

"I MEAN IT THIS TIME. I *HAVE* TO GO HOME. IT'S ALREADY past four; my cats must be starving, the poor darlings. Plus, it's laundry day." Evading my outstretched hand, Emma rolls off the bed and sprints for the pile of clothes on the chair in the corner—her clean, neatly folded clothes that Geoffrey brought upstairs while we were eating. Grabbing them, she disappears into the bathroom, and I sit up in bed, biting back a frustrated curse.

It's not that I want to fuck her again—well, I do, my dick having decided I'm fifteen again—it's that I hate the idea of her leaving. That, along with my incessant hunger for her soft curves, is why I've been dragging her back to bed and mercilessly fucking her each time she's tried to go home after brunch.

Damn her cats.

I need her more than they do.

It's borderline pathological, I know, but now that I've got her in my lair, I want to keep her here. The same primitive instincts that demanded I claim her, caveman style, now make me want to chain her to my bed and throw away the key.

Or failing that, handcuff her to me.

In part, it's because I'm still pissed about Florida—both the fact that she's going, and that she doesn't want me there. It means I won't see her from Wednesday until Sunday, and the knowledge eats at me, sharpening my craving until it feels like a blade carving through my guts.

I want her with a violence that scares me, and it doesn't seem to be abating in the least.

If my desire for her were purely sexual, I could've dealt with it. Nobody's ever died of blue balls, as far as I can tell. But I'm starting to want *her*, all of her, not just her delicious little body. Falling asleep with Emma in my arms last night had given me pleasure unlike any other—a feeling of bone-deep contentment, a certainty that all is well in my world.

I can't remember the last time I've felt that way. Maybe I never have. When I was a child, we were always a few days from eviction, one jar of mayo from an empty fridge. I never knew what time my drunk mother would stumble in at night, and what kind of asshole she'd bring with her. Even when I got older and used the earnings from my part-time jobs to smooth over the sharpest edges of our below-the-poverty-line existence, fear of the uncertain future never went away.

It stayed with me as I made my first million, then my first billion.

It's still with me when I close my eyes and fall asleep at night.

Except last night. Last night, I felt safe. Like the small, warm body in my arms was all I needed... all I would ever need.

Like I was home at last.

And now she wants to leave.

Fuck that. I'm not ready to let her go.

"I'm coming with you," I announce when she emerges from the bathroom fully dressed.

And ignoring her wide-eyed look of shock, I get up and walk over to my closet to grab some clothes of my own.

mma

I DON'T UNDERSTAND WHAT'S HAPPENING, WHY I'M IN Marcus's car—with him in the backseat next to me—heading over to my apartment.

"Don't you have work?" I try again. "I thought you Wall Street types worked on the weekends."

He lifts his broad shoulders in a shrug. "It can wait. I'm my own boss."

I give up. Because there's apparently no polite way to ask a man why he's so determined to watch you do laundry and cuddle with your cats. Especially if that man is Marcus. Once he sets his mind on something, there's no stopping him—I've learned that the hard way. And I do mean *hard*.

I'm very sore from all the fucking.

A tendril of heat licks at me at the recollection of how I got that way, and I sneak a glance at the cause of that soreness—who's watching me with a darkly intent stare.

Holy shit. Does he want sex *again*?

Is that why he's not letting me leave his side?

That must be it. I can't imagine why else he'd come to my shoebox studio in Brooklyn instead of staying in his luxurious penthouse. *I* certainly wouldn't leave that place if I were him.

I'm about to inform him that I can't have sex for at least a few hours when my phone dings with an incoming text.

It's from Kendall.

Well? Any more gifts from Mr. Wall Street?

Then a second one: *Did you text him a thank-you like I told you?*

Oh, crap. Kendall has no clue that we're miles beyond thank-you texts, and why would she? I haven't had a free minute to call her since Marcus ambushed me last night with the books, and the sex, and the dinner date, and then more sex, and—

"Who's that?" Marcus asks, and I look up, my face flushing betrayingly.

"No one. I mean, it's just my friend—Kendall, you know? That is, of course you don't know; you've never met her. But she's my best friend from college and—" I stop, realizing I'm babbling. "In any case, she's the one who texted me."

"What about?"

Is he serious?

He certainly looks serious, his thick eyebrows arched expectantly, as if it's a given that I'll answer.

"Just… something random." I'm too flustered to come up with any kind of clever lie. "Like I said, it's nothing."

My phone dings with a third text, and I can't help glancing at the screen.

Ems! Text him. I mean it.

"Nothing? Really? Let me see." And before I can react, Marcus plucks the phone from my grasp, his eyes skimming over the texts with lightning speed.

"No! What are you doing?" I gasp in horror, but it's too late.

A big grin is already spreading over his lean, hard face. "So Kendall knows about me, does she?"

My cheeks burning like Florida asphalt in July, I attempt to snatch the phone back, but he transfers it to his other hand, holding it out of my reach.

"Yes, she does. So what?" I snap, sitting back empty-handed. To get the phone back, I'd have to lean over his lap, and I'm not about to stoop to that indignity. "I didn't sign any kind of NDA."

"NDA?" He's laughing now, white teeth flashing and cheeks bisected by those sexy grooves. "What have you been reading, kitten? *Fifty Shades?*"

My flush impossibly intensifies, and I attempt to grab the phone again—to no avail. He holds me off with one arm, still laughing, and I see his other hand's thumb land on the little phone icon next to Kendall's name.

"Oh my God, you just dialed her. Hang up!" I make another futile grab for the phone. "Marcus, hang up right now!"

He glances at the phone just as Kendall's tinny voice says from the speaker, "Hello? Emma, is that you?"

I expect him to hang up then, or at least hand the phone over to me, but I underestimated his assholeness. Lifting the phone to his ear, he says with a wicked smile, "No, sorry, Kendall. This is Marcus with Emma's phone."

There's a moment of dead silence, during which I try to decide if I should brain him or set him on fire, and then an incredulous: *"What?"*

"Give it to me," I hiss, all but sprawling across his lap to reach the phone, and this time, he lets me have it, mischief dancing in his eyes as I scramble back to my seat, clutching my prize.

"—are you doing with Emma's phone?" Kendall is asking warily as I lift the phone to my ear.

"It's me, hi. Sorry about that. Marcus was just being a dick." I glare at him as I say it, but instead of taking offense, he starts laughing again, his powerful shoulders shaking.

"Are you talking about Marcus *Carelli?*" Kendall sounds as if I've just blasphemed about the Pope in the Vatican. *"The* Marcus Carelli? He's with you right now?"

"Yep." I pointedly turn my back to him. "We're in a car heading to Brooklyn."

"Wait, what? From where? Start from the beginning," Kendall demands, and I grit my teeth, throwing Marcus a fuming look over my shoulder.

He's already stopped laughing, but he's still grinning, the bastard.

"I can't really talk right now," I tell Kendall, looking away lest I smack him with the phone. "I'll call you later, okay?"

"Wait! Just tell me if you two have hooked up."

"Kendall—"

"Just a yes or no, quickly."

"Yes, okay? It's a yes." I hang up and turn to meet Marcus's amused—and not the least bit apologetic —gaze.

My temper boils over. "You had no right to do that. That is *my* phone and *my* friend and—"

"You're right." He catches the hand I'm waving around—the one still clutching the phone. Bringing it to his lips, he kisses the knuckles reverently. "I shouldn't have done it, kitten. I'm sorry. For what it's worth, you're very cute when you're angry. I've thought so from our very first meeting."

"Oh, we're doing clichés now, are we? What's next? You knew I was the one from the moment you laid eyes on me?" To my relief, I still sound pissed, rather than all gooey and melty, like my insides. The traitors have turned to mush at the tender gesture *and* the bullshit compliment.

"No," Marcus says, all traces of amusement gone. "I didn't."

Ouch. I blink and try to smile, as if all meltiness didn't disappear in an instant, my stomach shriveling into a hard ball instead. Obviously, I'm not the one for him—that would be Emmeline or someone like her—but did he have to be so blunt about it? I was using that as an example of a cliché, not fishing for a proposal.

Still, something about my reaction must've given me away because Marcus's face darkens, his hand tightening around mine. "Emma, what I meant was—"

"Just don't do it again." I somehow manage to sound playful, the smile actually appearing on my lips. "This is *my* phone"—I yank my hand out of his hold—"and you don't get to just grab it and look at my messages, no matter how many clichéd compliments you give me afterward."

"What about non-clichéd ones?" he asks huskily, the glimmer of amusement returning to his gaze. I must be a better actress than I thought. "Can I grab it then?"

"No," I say with exaggerated firmness, as if talking to a child or a dog. "My phone is off limits." I make a show of stuffing it into my purse and zipping it up for emphasis.

He sticks out his lower lip in a pout, just like a disappointed toddler would, and I can't help laughing for real, even as some of the melting feeling returns, along with the lingering hurt from his words.

Because in that pout, as comical as he meant it to

be, I see the vulnerable little boy he had been once, and I can't help wishing for the impossible.

Can't help wanting this—us—to be real.

CHAPTER FORTY-ONE

*M*arcus

I GLARE AT THE CAT ON THE BED, AND HE RESPONDS WITH a contemptuous look, the tip of his tail swishing back and forth in a silent threat.

"That's right," my eyes tell him. "I fucked her all night long, and I will do it again and again. You better get used to it. She's mine now."

"I will destroy you," the slitted green gaze replies. "You're going to die a slow and painful death under my paws, just like a mouse. Not that I've ever seen a real mouse, but still. If I ever get my paws on one, it's fucked—and so are you."

"Puffs, get off the clean laundry," Emma says, reappearing from the bathroom, and I watch with grim satisfaction as she shoos the furry creature off the clothes she's folding on the bed—a task I'm helping her with.

She was surprised when I offered, but she shouldn't have been.

There's no way I would pass up a chance to get my hands on her panties.

Speaking of which, she needs new ones. Along with new clothes in general. Almost everything she owns is worn out or of poor quality. My hands practically itch to pick up my phone and place an order at Saks, but I resist the urge. She won't accept clothes from me yet, and I have bigger battles to fight.

Like getting her to come back to my place tonight.

"Here, I got this," she says, grabbing a stack of folded T-shirts from me. She hurries over to the closet and stuffs the clothes inside, then comes back to grab a pile of socks. I let her put away all the folded things while I sort her bras, and before long, we're done with all the laundry.

"Wow, that was quick," Emma says, looking around like she expects a stray sock to jump out at her. "I can't believe we got it done so fast. When I do it alone, it takes me *hours*."

"What can I say? I'm good with my hands," I say with a straight face, and she gives me a dimpled grin.

"You are. Thank you for helping."

"It was my pleasure." I mean it too—and not just because I got to handle her underwear without looking like a pervert. She doesn't have a washer and dryer in her studio, and the laundromat she uses is three long blocks away. I have no idea how she's always dragged her stuff there on her own, but I'm glad I was here to carry the heavy sack for her today.

I'll have to make sure I'm always with her when she does laundry going forward, or better yet, have Geoffrey do it for her.

At my place.

Where I want her to be all the time.

I'm not quite ready to put a label on that desire yet, but it's definitely there, and the more I look around her cramped studio, the stronger it gets.

I don't want her here.

She belongs at home with me.

"Are you hungry?" I ask when she picks up a cat— the mid-sized one, Cottonball—and sits down on the bed to stroke him. "We could grab dinner around here before heading back, or go someplace in Manhattan. Alternatively, if you're not in the mood to eat out, I can ask Geoffrey to prep us something."

She blinks up at me as the smallest cat, Queen Elizabeth, jumps up on the bed and joins her purring brother on Emma's lap. "Heading back? As in, to your place? The two of us?"

"Of course. This bed is too small for us both, don't you think?" Not to mention, overrun with cats—the third of which joins her as I speak. "You can bring an overnight bag if you'd like, so you don't need to wait for Geoffrey to do laundry in the morning. Maybe also leave the cats extra food, so we don't have to come back here tomorrow at all. You can go to work straight from my place on Monday; I'll have Wilson drive you there."

Her eyes widen more with every word coming out of my mouth, and I know—I fucking know—I'm giving away my hand, but it's too late to try to be smooth and subtle. Not that I've ever been able to achieve that with her. When it comes to Emma, my instincts are as primitive as it gets, my need to claim her too powerful to deny.

I want her in my home, at my side, and I can't pretend otherwise.

"I don't think I can..." She swallows. "I can't leave my cats alone for that long." She's petting the furry beasts as she says this, and I again feel a strange stab of jealousy.

I want her touching *me*.

Worrying about *me*.

"Fine," I say tightly, pushing down the irrational desire. "Then you'll come back here tomorrow. I'm sure they'll be fine until then. You've fed them, changed their litter, played with them... What more do they need?"

Three pairs of green eyes narrow at me, as if the cats know what I'm saying, and Emma looks down at them, stroking each one in turn.

"Come here," she says softly, looking up. "Sit next to me."

I frown in confusion but approach the bed.

"Sit." She glances at the spot to the right of her.

I comply gingerly, not wanting to squash a tail or a

paw. I may not like her pets, but I don't want to hurt them.

"Here." She picks up Cottonball and places him on my lap. "Stroke him like this." She demonstrates with her own hand, her short, neatly trimmed nails lightly scratching at the fur as she runs her palm from the top of his head to the start of his tail.

I stare at the cat, unable to believe he hasn't jumped away or scratched me. Instead, he's staring up at me, as if waiting to see what I'll do.

Cautiously, I touch him like Emma showed me, running my hand over his back. The fur is ridiculously soft, and I can feel his animal warmth underneath. It's like having a heating pad on my lap, only an extremely fluffy one.

I try to recall if I've ever held a cat like this, but I'm drawing a blank. Certainly, there were no pets in my childhood—unless I count the stray cats that raided the garbage bins at the apartment complex where we lived when I was six. For a couple of months, I gave them whatever scraps I could find in our kitchen, but then we got evicted, and I never saw the cats again. In any case, they'd been feral, too frightened of people to let me pet them.

Afterward, there was a neighbor's dog—a little one, some kind of mutt. He was friendly, and I'd definitely petted him and played with him a bunch of times. In fact, I liked him so much I asked my mother to get a puppy for my seventh birthday. She laughed and promptly puked into the half-cooked pasta that was supposed to be our dinner, and that was that. I realized soon after what a huge responsibility a puppy would be, requiring food and money we couldn't afford to spare, and I stopped wanting one. I also stopped feeding stray cats.

"He likes you." Emma's dimples appear as she beams at me, and to my shock, I realize the creature on my lap is purring.

Loudly.

His entire body is vibrating with it, his eyes shut in apparent bliss.

Okay, then. I guess I have *not* held a cat before, because this is definitely a memorable experience. I must've petted at least one cat before this—I vaguely recall a skittish Siamese at a friend's house in college—but this is something else entirely.

This animal is *trusting* me.

According to Emma, he likes me.

Carefully, I intensify the pressure, stroking him more firmly, and the purr gets louder, the vibration increasing until I feel like I'm holding a miniature chainsaw. The cat is clearly enjoying what I'm doing, and I can't deny that it feels good to run my palm over his soft fur. Between the purr and the warmth, the sensation is strangely soothing... almost hypnotic. My phone buzzes in my pocket, but I ignore it, strangely reluctant to let work intrude.

"Love."

My head snaps up, my entire body locking up as I stare at Emma. "What did you just say?"

"You asked what more they need," she says quietly, her gray eyes on my face as she continues stroking the two pets on her lap. "And I'm telling you that they need love. Attention. Caring. Same as people."

Right. Of course.

She's talking about the cats, not us.

"So I take it you're not coming home with me," I say with forced lightness, and she shakes her head.

"I want to, but I can't. I'm sorry, Marcus. I can't leave them alone two nights in a row, especially since I'm going to Florida on Wednesday. My landlady is going to look after them, but they'll still be traumatized by my absence." She pauses, then adds hesitantly, "Maybe you can stay here with me?"

"All right." The words escape my mouth before I consciously make the decision. "In that case, I will."

And as the cat on my lap purrs louder, I take my phone from my pocket and text Geoffrey that I won't be home for breakfast.

CHAPTER FORTY-TWO

mma

ALL EVENING LONG, I'VE FELT THE URGE TO PINCH myself to make sure I'm awake, because what are the odds that my billionaire hookup would accompany me to Brooklyn, help me with my laundry, and agree to spend the night in my tiny studio before having a pizza dinner at Papa Mario's with me?

Next to none, I would've said before today.

Yet here we are, stuffed full of pizza, with me doing my best to make my old sheets look semi-decent—and cat hair free—by smoothing them with my palms while Marcus showers in my tiny bathroom before joining me in this very bed.

My phone dings with incoming texts, then starts

ringing, and when I grab it, I'm not the least bit surprised to see that it's Kendall.

"Well?" she bursts out the moment I pick up. "You never called back. What's going on with you and Mr. Billions? Spill. Now."

I glance at the bathroom door, but it's closed and the water is still running.

"I don't have a lot of time," I say in a low voice. "Marcus will come out of the shower any minute, so just listen and don't interrupt, okay?"

"Shower? Where? Holy fuck, Ems!"

"Kendall—"

"Okay, okay, I'll shut up. Go on. Tell me everything."

And so I do, starting with the books he sent me Friday night and concluding with our current situation. The only part I leave out is the conversation with my grandparents, because I don't want Kendall to get the wrong idea.

To her, meeting family is such a big deal she'll be convinced we're about to get married.

"So let me get this straight." My friend sounds like she's on the verge of an aneurism anyway. "The two of you have spent the past twenty-four hours together—literally, the entire twenty-four-hours—and he wants to stay at your place overnight? Like he's actually willing to sleep in your tiny coffin of a bed?"

"It's a regular twin-sized—"

"Whatever. I'm sure *his* bedroom is fit for a modern-day prince."

"Well…"

"Oh my God. I'm so fucking jealous of you right now, you sneaky little bitch. Tell me he at least has a small dick. It *is* small, right? Like all crooked and shriveled up and stuff?"

I fight a hysterical giggle. "No, sorry. He's actually —" I stop, because there's no way I'm going there, not even with Kendall.

"Oh, shut the fuck up! Next you'll be telling me he's already given you half a dozen orgasms."

Well *over* a dozen, but who's counting? I try to think of a suitably discreet answer, but my silence must speak for itself because Kendall lets out a groan and I hear banging sounds in the background.

"You okay?" I ask, concerned.

"Fine." Her voice is weirdly muffled. "Just beating my head against the wall for not listening to Janie and signing up for the dating app with you. Maybe I, too, would now be planning summers in the Hamptons and Christmas vacations in the Alps."

I roll my eyes. "Premature much? We've just started whatever this is. Besides, I'm sure he'll get bored of me soon and proceed with his plan to marry some gorgeous socialite. We're just having fun, like you told me to—and no, before you ask, I'm not going to parlay this into a publishing industry job."

"That's your prerogative, as long as you're parlaying it into multiple orgasms—which it sounds like you are. But seriously, Ems, you are so wrong about his intentions. You haven't played the dating game much, so you might not realize this, but a guy wanting to spend his entire weekend with you *after* he's fucked you? That's rarer than billionaires in Bay Ridge. And staying at your place overnight because you don't want to leave your cats? You might as well expect a proposal next week. He's into you, big time. Mark my words, before long—"

"I have to go," I hiss into the phone, my heartbeat jumping as the sound of running water stops. "He's coming out of the shower. Talk later, okay?"

"You got it. Have fun with Mr. Magic Dick." And on that lewd note, she hangs up, leaving me standing there flushed and flustered.

And hopeful.

Much too hopeful.

So hopeful it's almost a given that I'm going to get badly hurt.

CHAPTER FORTY-THREE

mma

I WAKE WITH A SHIVER AS WARM LIPS TOUCH MY NAPE, their softness contrasting with the scorching heat of mint-scented breath and the roughness of the morning stubble rasping across my skin.

I'm lying on my stomach and Marcus is kissing my neck, I realize groggily, and though I'd love to sink back into sleep, the sensations are too delicious to miss. He's massaging me now as well, his strong hands kneading the muscles of my shoulders, my arms, my back, my butt... Oh, yeah, he's definitely focusing on my glutes, and I had no idea how much those muscles needed tending. His lips follow his hands down my body, trailing over my spine and leaving my skin tingling.

He moves his attention to my legs, and I moan into the pillow, keeping my eyes closed as he massages the soreness out of my inner thighs and hamstrings—areas that badly need it after being overstretched two nights in a row. He had me practically bent in half at one point last night, with my feet resting on his broad shoulders as he pounded into me, his face taut with lust. It was beyond intense, and I came hard, but afterward, I felt even more sore—both inside and out.

I'm seriously going to insist on no sex today, at least of the penetrative variety. Oral is good anytime, as is whatever it is he's doing to me right now. Actually, wait, on second thought—

"Oh fuck," I gasp, my hands gripping the blanket as his tongue dips between my cheeks, toying with my other opening. No one's ever touched me there before, and the sensation is beyond strange, pleasurable yet so dirty that I flush all over. Granted, I showered after sex last night, but it's still wrong that he's licking me there —wrong and perversely hot. I can feel myself getting wet, my clit swelling with arousal, and as his tongue goes deeper, pushing at the tight ring of muscle, his hands grip my buttocks and pull them apart, opening me wide.

"Your asshole is so fucking pretty," he growls, lifting his head, and with a burning wave of mortification, I realize he's looking right into my ass, the *inside* of it. The embarrassment is so intense I feel like I might burst into flames, and at the same time, I'm so turned on my arousal is leaking down my thighs.

"I'm going to fuck your tight little hole. Soon," he promises hoarsely, and before I can react, he lowers his head and pushes his tongue into me, my spread-apart cheeks preventing me from clenching to resist his entry. His tongue penetrates me, thick and slippery and oddly muscular, and as it pushes deep, I feel like I might explode from the shame of it... and the dark, dark pleasure coursing through my body.

There's no pain, but there is a disconcerting full-ness, a feeling of wrongness that only exacerbates the perverse eroticism of it all. Groaning against the pillow, I press my hips into the blanket, desperately needing to rub my throbbing clit on something... anything. Just the slightest pressure would send me over the edge, dissolving this maddening, delicious tension. His tongue is thrusting in and out, fucking me like a cock, and it's too much yet not nearly enough. I'm dying, burning up from the mortifying need, and it's almost a relief when the slippery tongue withdraws and a big, rough finger pushes in instead, using the lubrication left behind.

It's not as thick as his tongue, but it's longer, and I feel the shock of it, the immediate resistance of my body to the intrusion of a foreign object. My insides clench, and even with my cheeks held open, the hard edges of the nail dig into tender tissues, making my nerve endings sing in pain. Except it's not all pain— somehow, it's also pleasure—and I cry out as the tension grows unbearably, all my muscles tightening with coiling need.

"Yes, that's it…" Marcus's voice is a low, dark rasp as the finger curves inside me. "Come for me, kitten." And as he releases my cheeks to pinch my aching clit, I explode, my entire body spasming with the agonizing pleasure of release. It's so intense my vision cuts out for a hazy moment, and when I come to, I hear him groan behind me and feel the hot splash of his seed on my ass.

———

I'M STILL BLUSHING DURING BREAKFAST—PARTIALLY because I can't look at Marcus's mouth without thinking about where his tongue has been. We're standing in my kitchen, eating oatmeal with nuts and berries, and each time Marcus bites into a strawberry and licks the juices off his lips, I feel heat creeping up my cheeks.

It doesn't help that all three of my cats are staring at me with judgey eyes—as they have been all morning.

"What?" I snap at Mr. Puffs when I can't take it anymore, and he swishes his tail and stalks off—leaving his siblings to provide the proper dose of slut shaming.

"They're not used to you having sex in front of them, are they?" Marcus says dryly, and I laugh, realizing I'm not the only one who's feeling the weight of feline judgement this morning.

"They're not," I admit, grinning. "In fact, this may be only their second exposure to human sex—the first being Friday night."

"Good. I'm glad." His voice turns husky as he sets his empty bowl on the counter. "I wouldn't want them traumatized by seeing it done improperly."

I feel another blush coming on, but I raise my eyebrows, determined to play it cool. "Who says it would've been done improperly? I've had good sex before." Or what I *thought* was good sex before I met Marcus, but I'm not about to inflate his ego any further.

It already matches the size of his "magic" appendage.

"Oh, really?" His blue eyes narrow. "Do tell."

I set my bowl down and cross my arms over my chest. "You first." Not that I actually want to know about all the hundreds of beautiful women he's slept with, but I'm not talking about my woefully short sexual history without making him squirm at least a little.

To my surprise, he doesn't laugh off my demand or reply with something cocky. Nor does he look the least bit uncomfortable with the topic. "Since losing my virginity at fifteen, I've had sex with a number of female partners," he says calmly, picking up his coffee. "Mostly in the context of casual relationships, but there have been some one-night stands as well. My most serious relationship to date was in college, where I dated the same girl for two and a half years. We parted ways upon graduation, as I was moving back to New York and she wanted to live in LA. After that, I was too focused on my career to devote much time to dating, so my subsequent relationships were superficial and short-lived, ranging from a couple of weeks to a couple of months." He takes a sip of coffee, then adds, eyes glittering, "And yes, in most cases, the sex was good, though it couldn't have held a candle to this."

My arms drop to my sides, and my heart—which had shrunk into a tiny pincushion from picturing him with other women—lurches into a startled gallop. "It couldn't have?"

"No." He sets his coffee down, his eyes burning into me. "Believe it or not, I don't normally want to fuck five times a day."

"Oh." My throat goes dry as he steps toward me. "I... I see."

"What about you?" He places his hands on the counter on either side of me, caging me with his large body. Holding my gaze, he says softly, "Tell me about your sexcapades, kitten."

I swallow, feeling uncomfortably like captured prey. "Um... there haven't been all that many, really. Just a couple. One boyfriend in college, one in high school. And a bunch more dates that led nowhere. I've never been all that popular."

I cringe internally at how pathetic that sounds, but Marcus's eyes narrow again, his nostrils flaring as he leans in. "And they were good in bed, those two boyfriends of yours?" There's something dark and dangerous in his voice, almost menacing.

If I didn't know better, I would've thought him jealous.

Regardless, I'm tempted to keep up the lie, so I come across as less of a loser. But when I open my mouth, the truth comes out instead. "No, they weren't," I admit, holding his gaze. "Arthur was seventeen and didn't know what he was doing, and Jim... well, Jim was okay, I guess. But it wasn't like this with him. Not like it is with you and me."

Contrary to my expectations, the confession doesn't appease Marcus. If anything, his face darkens further. Dipping his head so that his lips brush my ear, he says in a low, rough voice, "I'm glad you weren't popular, kitten... because if you were, I'd have a lot of fucking Jims and Arthurs to destroy."

And as I'm processing that bizarre declaration, he hoists me up onto the counter and takes my mouth in a deep, darkly possessive kiss.

$\mathcal{M}$arcus

"No, no more. I'm so sore," Emma groans, rolling off the bed when I cup her breast, and I reluctantly let her go, though I could gladly go for round two. Or three—depending on whether coming on her ass this morning counts.

Fuck, no wonder she's begging for mercy. I have zero control around her. And hearing about her ex-boyfriends didn't help. I all but lost it, picturing her with those pimply-faced idiots—which is how we ended up back in bed despite my best intentions.

I was going to be a gentleman and keep my hands off her until tonight.

I really was.

She's wisely decided to remove the temptation by

disappearing into the bathroom, so I get up and get dressed, ignoring the contemptuous stares from the cats. Well, two of the cats; Cottonball seems to have warmed up to me a bit, and *his* green gaze is merely chiding.

Like his siblings, he thinks I'm a sex-crazed beast.

"Come here, buddy," I mutter, sitting down on the one and only chair and patting my knee when Emma takes her sweet time in the bathroom. "I need a distraction so I don't attack your pretty owner again."

The cat eyes me dubiously, then saunters over and jumps onto my lap. I shake my head and start petting him, still amazed that he trusts me to hold him. Aren't animals supposed to be able to tell when people like them? Not that I dislike this particular cat; he seems to be nicer than most.

By the time Emma comes out of the bathroom dressed in her short pink robe, Cottonball is purring loud enough to wake the neighborhood, and I can't deny that I'm enjoying myself. In theory, I should be hating all of this—the cats, the dingy apartment, the lumpy bed that's half a foot too short for me—but instead, I feel good, much too good considering how little sleep I got last night and how much work is likely waiting for me at the office. Normally, I'd spend a good portion of my weekend poring over my analysts' reports and reviewing our biggest positions, but all I've done over the past two days is spend time with Emma... and it's all I want to do. I've barely checked my email today. In fact, this may be the most relaxing Sunday I've had since... well, since grade school.

I started managing money—mine and my classmates' in college—and I haven't been this calm since.

As if on cue, my phone starts buzzing in my pocket. For a moment, I'm tempted to let it go to voicemail, but then my sense of responsibility kicks in. There are billions of dollars and hundreds of employees' jobs on the line. I can't ignore that just because I want to spend the rest of the day with Emma.

Setting the purring cat on the floor, I pull out the phone.

Sure enough, it's Jarrod—who only calls me on the weekends in case of major fuck-ups.

"What?" I bark, my adrenaline already surging.

I don't have a good feeling about this.

My CIO doesn't beat around the bush. "It's bad. The municipals team just called me. Remember that high-risk bond we bought a couple of weeks back? Well, the municipality's capital raise just failed—something about a local politician getting caught with his hand in the cookie jar. It's just hitting the newswires now."

Fuck. I leap to my feet. "How deep in the hole are we?"

"Right now? Three hundred mil, but rumor is, they're going to declare bankruptcy on Monday."

Thus rendering our entire $700 million investment worthless.

Motherfucker. We're about to have our first down month this year—and right before Alpha Zone, too.

"Tell them to liquidate what they can," I order, my mind already scrambling for solutions. "And call an emergency meeting of the PMs—we need actionable short-term ideas."

"On it," Jarrod replies and hangs up.

Emma is now in front of me, a worried frown on her face as she gazes up at me. "What's wrong? Did something happen at your fund?"

I nod, grabbing my coat from the back of the chair. "A trade gone bad. I have to go into the office." I know I sound brusque, but I can't help it.

We're about to lose $700 million, and I almost didn't pick up the phone, too caught up in her spell to think straight. Fuck, what am I talking about? I should've gone over the investment with a fine-toothed comb this Saturday, like I was planning to do before Emma ended up in my bed. My municipals PM is good, but I'm better at seeing the big picture. I might've spotted some red flag regarding the politician, and we could've liquidated yesterday, before the news of the embezzlement hit. But no. I was with my redheaded obsession, and I couldn't tear myself away from her. In one short weekend, I've become so addicted to her that I've lost sight of what matters. Even now, knowing the fund is in trouble, a part of me wants to stay with Emma instead of rushing to the office, to fuck my worries into submission rather than dealing with the fallout of my mistake.

I was wrong. She's not chocolate and Netflix.

She's fucking heroin, and I'm dying for a hit.

"Oh, that sucks, I'm sorry," she says, her gray gaze sympathetic, and even now, I'm tempted to steal a kiss as I step around her on my way out.

"I'll call you later," I say curtly instead and stride out, slamming the door shut before the cats can escape.

I need to put some distance between me and Emma.

I need to detox before I'm in too deep.

CHAPTER FORTY-FIVE

mma

HE'S GONE SO FAST IT'S AS IF I'D IMAGINED HIM HERE. Only the rumpled bedsheets provide evidence of his recent presence—that and the persistent tenderness between my legs. Somehow, we still ended up having sex after breakfast, and now I'm *really* sore.

So, yeah, it's probably for the best that he left so abruptly. Well, not for the best—I feel bad that something went wrong at his fund—but I certainly shouldn't feel abandoned or anything. So what if he didn't kiss me goodbye? We're not boyfriend and girlfriend. He'll probably turn up when he's done at the office, and we'll have a ridiculous amount of sex again.

That is, assuming he still wants me. There's no guarantee of that.

The thought is oddly depressing. Just the possibility of never seeing Marcus again makes my chest feel tight and heavy, like it's being squeezed in a vise.

"He'll be back, right?" I ask Queen Elizabeth, and she gives me the cat equivalent of a shrug—a blank stare, followed by a tiny tail swish.

I sigh and walk over to my desk. I'm imagining this, I'm sure, but for a moment there, it seemed as if Marcus had been upset with me... as if I'd done something wrong. But that's silly. He got bad news from work, that's all. Whatever's going on at his fund has nothing to do with me. The only thing I can think of as far as something *I* could've done is telling him I'm too sore to have even more sex.

Wait a sec.

Is that it?

Did I offend him by refusing his advances?

No, that doesn't seem right. Marcus is too confident, too much of a man to have such a fragile ego. It is, however, feasible that with the possibility of more sex off the table, he didn't see the point in staying.

But no. There was that phone call. He didn't make it up. I saw his face; the news he got really was bad. There might be hundreds of thousands or even millions of dollars on the line—tens of millions, for all I know. It's ridiculous to imagine he'd even be thinking about me during such a critical time; most likely, he seemed short because he was worried about the bad trade.

In any case, he said he'll call later, so I'm sure I'll hear from him tonight. Or if not tonight, tomorrow.

In the meantime, I should use this opportunity to catch up on my editing.

I'm already a weekend behind schedule as is.

CHAPTER FORTY-SIX

*M*arcus

BLEARY-EYED, I SCRUB MY PALM OVER MY FACE AND glance at the clock.

3:05 a.m.

We've been at it for over twelve hours.

Getting up, I toss my disposable coffee cup into the trash and look around the glass-walled conference room. Jarrod and all of my portfolio managers are here, sitting around the long rectangular table surrounded by piles of reports. Like me, they've been going over the investment ideas the analysts have been bringing in, trying to figure out how we can make up a $700 million loss during a holiday-shortened week.

If we're still in the hole come November 30th, we'll lock in this month's underperformance, and it's going to be a permanent black mark on the fund's record—not to mention, a source of embarrassment at the upcoming Alpha Zone conference.

So far, there are a number of promising short-term ideas, but nothing big enough to plug a $700 million hole. And odds are, we're not going to find that gem tonight.

I slap my palm on the table, and everyone snaps to attention.

"Enough," I say. "Everyone, go home. We'll resume this first thing in the morning."

I don't want their judgment compromised by lack of sleep.

It's bad enough I've let my dick do my thinking for me.

"See you back here at seven?" Jarrod says, walking by me, and I nod. It wouldn't hurt to catch up with my CIO before the PMs pile in. He's only twenty-seven, but he has a knack for seeing the big picture, same as I do. One day soon, he's going to strike out on his own, but until then, I've got his clever brain to bounce ideas off of.

Everyone files out of the conference room, and I follow, a tension headache squeezing my temples as I close the door behind us. On the main floor, the analysts are hunched over their computers, crunching numbers and sorting through data, searching for something to bring to their PMs.

I'm tempted to send them home too, but since they don't make the decisions, being clear-headed is less crucial for them. I decide to leave it up to the individual PMs and head out, my headache worsening with every step I take.

It takes less than twenty minutes to get home—traffic is nonexistent at this hour—and as I fall into bed, my thoughts turn to Emma for the fiftieth time this night. She's probably long asleep by now. I can picture her curled up with her cats in her short, narrow bed, her wild red curls spread over the pillow and her lush little body barely covered by the pair of panties and a tank top that she wears in place of pajamas. Even with the headache beating at me, the image tightens my groin and makes warmth curl in my chest.

I'd give anything to hold her right now.

Anything at all.

My hand is already reaching for my phone when I realize what I'm doing. Swearing under my breath, I yank it back, furious with myself. This is the tenth time I've nearly called or texted her tonight, despite my resolution to do an Emma detox.

No seeing her or thinking about her—that's the goal I've set for myself. And that means no calls or texts. I need to be in control of this addiction, to prove to myself that I can go without my fix for at least some time.

That I can function at work and elsewhere even with this obsession.

Squeezing my eyes shut, I try to focus on the investment ideas, so that as I sleep, my brain can process all the information I've crammed into it over the past twelve hours. It's often the best way to do it, to just step back and let the connections form on their own, without forcing the process. Yet as I'm drifting into sleep, it's not debt coverage ratios and volatility hedges that occupy my mind.

It's her.

Emma.

The craving I can't erase.

CHAPTER FORTY-SEVEN

mma

MARCUS DOESN'T CONTACT ME FOR THE REST OF Sunday, but I don't worry about it much. After all, he's probably busy with his emergency. By Monday afternoon, however, I'm checking my phone every five minutes, afraid I somehow missed a call or a text.

There's nothing, though.

Not even a quick "hey."

At dinnertime, my phone finally rings. I grab it eagerly, my pulse jumping in excitement, but it's only Kendall—undoubtedly calling to get all the juicy details about my hookup. Swallowing my disappointment, I start to accept the call, but at the last second, I send it to voicemail instead.

I don't want to discuss Marcus with her—not until I know what's going on between us.

Assuming anything is still going on, that is.

I debate reaching out to him myself, sending a quick text to see how he's doing, but I decide against it. He might get annoyed that I'm bothering him in the middle of his emergency, or worse yet, he might not respond, and then I'll feel *really* awful. In any case, Marcus is not an insecure college freshman who needs to be prodded into contacting a girl he likes. The fact that I haven't heard from him means he doesn't want to talk to me.

It's as simple as that.

I spend Monday night tossing and turning, unable to get comfortable. Even with my cats next to me, my bed feels empty and cold, my blanket too thin to repel the winter chill seeping in through the poorly insulated window. My boss told me a major snowstorm is coming tomorrow night, and it feels like it, with the wind already kicking up and the temperatures starting to plummet.

I hope I can fly out on Wednesday. It would majorly suck if the airline canceled my flight.

I finally drift off to sleep after two, and when my alarm goes off at seven, I immediately reach for my phone.

Still nothing.

No calls, no texts.

My stomach sinks, and the heavy tightness returns to my chest. It's possible that Marcus is still insanely busy at work, but texting something along the lines of "hey, thinking of you" would take less than three seconds. Unless, of course, he's not thinking of me at all—which is looking increasingly likely.

He may have had his fill of sex with me and moved on, in which case I may never hear from him again.

I try not to think about it, but by Tuesday afternoon, I can no longer dismiss the possibility. Maybe with another guy, a two-day disappearance wouldn't have meant much, but Marcus has never played by the rules of modern courtship, complete with all the "keep her guessing" games. From the very beginning, he's been crystal clear about his intentions, going after what he wanted—me in his bed—with the same kind of intensity he must apply to all areas of his life. Daily dates, over-the-top gifts, meeting my grandparents on Skype, spending most of the weekend with me—he all but bulldozed his way into my body and my life. I didn't stand a chance once he set his sights on me... and maybe that's the problem.

Maybe a challenge was what he wanted all along, and since I've ceased to be that, he's moved on to something—or someone—more exciting.

Around four, Kendall calls me again, and I again send her to voicemail. I can imagine how excited and bubbly she'll sound, wanting to hear all about my affair with a billionaire, and I simply don't feel up to dissecting Marcus's actions with her. Maybe it's because I got so little sleep last night, but I feel completely drained, as listless as if I were coming down with the flu.

And maybe I am.

Maybe that's what this squeezing pain in my chest is all about.

"You should go home early," Mr. Smithson advises when I'm done shelving this week's shipment of romance novels. "It's already starting to snow."

"Oh, right. I almost forgot about the storm." I glance outside, where the howling wind is driving the first flurries into twister-like patterns. "I'll have to check on my flight."

My boss grimaces. "It's not looking good, Emma, sorry. They said on the news the airlines have already started announcing cancellations."

Great. Just great. My eyes prickle, and I have to turn away, blinking rapidly to keep the sudden influx of tears at bay. I didn't realize until now how much I've been anticipating this trip—both because I badly miss my grandparents and because I need to get away.

I'm dying to escape from this awful weather... and the growing pain of the realization that I may never see Marcus again.

———

I MAKE IT HOME BEFORE THE WORST OF THE SNOW starts, my neck snug and warm thanks to the scarf Marcus gifted me. I didn't want to put it on this morning, but the wind was too biting to ignore.

Dispirited, I take it off and put it in a shoebox to keep it safe from Mr. Puffs. Then I hang up my coat and give the cats their dinner before trudging to my laptop to check on my flight.

To my relief, my airline has only cancelled tonight's and tomorrow morning's flights so far. They must expect the weather to clear up by tomorrow afternoon.

"Well, that's something," I tell the cats, returning to the kitchen to make my own dinner. "I may be able to make it to Florida, after all." Even to my own ears, however, my voice sounds flat, lacking all hint of excitement.

Because as much as I want to see my grandparents and bask in the Florida sun, I know—deep in my bones, I know—that none of it will chase away the spreading hollowness inside me.

The growing conviction that Marcus and I are done.

CHAPTER FORTY-EIGHT

*M*arcus

By market close on Tuesday, the entire fund is punch-drunk with exhaustion, but we've netted $580 million through a combination of different trades, including a single-day $100 million bet on the Turkish lira. The transportation team has also cashed in on their airline short positions; they've been betting for weeks that the early-to-arrive winter weather would hit those stocks hard, and with the advent of tonight's storm, the rest of the market has finally agreed with them.

All in all, barring any major disasters over the next couple of trading days, we may end up having a decent November. Not a great one, but good enough that we won't have to explain a down month to our investors.

Or to the Alpha Zone attendees—those assholes would've been merciless.

It should feel good, snatching this victory from the jaws of defeat, but all I can think about is that I haven't seen Emma since Sunday. And tomorrow evening, she's leaving for Florida, which means I won't see her for the rest of the week.

For the umpteenth time, I reach for my phone, only to pull back with a herculean effort of will. The craving is still there, stronger than ever, and I know if I give in to it now, there will be no going back.

This obsession will grow until it consumes me.

Not that I'm planning to stay away from Emma much longer. For one thing, I'm not sure I'd be able to, but I also don't want to. As dangerous as my addiction to her is, it's the most exhilarating thing I've felt in years. I've never had this kind of sexual chemistry with a woman, have never wanted—or enjoyed—one so intensely. I want to wake up to her flame-bright curls on my pillow and see her dimpled smile when I come home from work, to bury my cock in her sweet, lush body every night and as many times throughout the day as she'll let me.

I want her, and I'm going to have her—but first, I have to know that I'm stronger than my addiction.

I have to make it through this week without her, to prove to myself that I'm in control.

CHAPTER FORTY-NINE

*E*mma

SINCE MY FLIGHT IS NOT UNTIL 6:25 P.M., I WAS planning to go into work for half a day on Wednesday. However, as I watch the howling fury of the storm through my narrow window, I know it's not happening —and most likely, neither is my flight.

It's already midnight, but I can't sleep, my bed again uncomfortably cold and empty. And lumpy. Why have I never noticed before how lumpy my mattress is? It's nothing like the plush memory-foam expanse of Marcus's king-sized bed. That had been so comfortable, so soft and warm, especially with his big, powerful body wrapped around me—

No. Stop. I squeeze my eyes shut to keep out the memories, but they flood in anyway, adding to the hollow pain in my chest. I miss him. I really, truly miss him. We'd only spent two nights together, but it had felt more like a month, like a dozen dates crammed into one life-altering, amazing weekend. I keep picturing his eyes, his smile, his laugh... the quiet amazement on his face when I put Cottonball on his lap. He'd handled the cat as carefully as a newborn baby, his big hands extraordinarily gentle on his fur. Watching him, I'd felt my heart swell and break a little, a fissure opening to let him in.

God, why had he done this to me? Why go after me so hard, make me think there could be something real between us, only to dump me so cruelly?

I expected it, of course, told myself it was bound to happen, but that doesn't make it hurt any less. If anything, I feel extra stupid. I shouldn't have agreed to see him when he sent me those gifts.

No, scratch that. I shouldn't have agreed to go out with him in the first place. All along, I'd known I was playing with fire, and I did it anyway.

I let him leave a third-degree burn on my heart.

The storm outside now seems more like a hurricane, the wind roaring and the snow piling up by my only window to block out what little light from the street lamps was seeping in. And as I stare into the darkness, my eyes burning with unshed tears, I make myself a promise.

I'm never going to date a man out of my league again.

CHAPTER FIFTY

*M*arcus

THE STORM IS STILL RAGING OUTSIDE WHEN MY ALARM goes off at 5:30 a.m., so I send an email directing everyone at the fund to work from home, and then I get up to do the same. Geoffrey has the day off, but he prepped today's meals in advance, and it takes mere minutes to warm the quiche he made and down it with a cup of coffee before heading into my home office.

As I answer emails and go over research reports, my thoughts turn to Emma again. They said on the news some areas of Queens and Brooklyn have lost power. Could that have happened in her neighborhood? In general, how is she faring in her basement studio? Something like a foot of snow has already fallen, enough to block that just-above-the-ground window in her apartment.

Could she be stuck there in the dark, without electricity and heat?

No, that's ridiculous. She's in Brooklyn, not some shack in the mountains, and it's an early winter storm, not Armageddon. I'm sure she's fine. She's most likely asleep, enjoying an impromptu day off like most of the city. Or if she's awake, she might be packing for her flight to Florida tonight. Speaking of which…

I pull out my phone and check her flight status, like I've been doing every couple of hours since the storm hit.

Still not cancelled.

Fuck.

I'm not planning to see her this week, so I don't know why that bothers me, but it does. Maybe it's because I don't want her to fly in this weather. The snow is supposed to stop by noon, but ice on the planes' wings might be a problem for a while. Not that the airlines will fly if they don't think it's safe, but still.

I don't want her getting on that plane.

I really fucking don't.

Realizing I'm obsessing over her again, I force my attention back to my computer screen and succeed at focusing for another couple of hours. Then I check on her flight again.

Still on. Not even so much as a delay.

Cursing, I get up and head into my home gym. I almost wish her flight number hadn't been in the investigator's report. If I didn't know it, I wouldn't be checking the airline app with the frequency of a schoolgirl refreshing her Instagram feed. Hopefully, a good, hard workout will clear my mind. With the insane workload of the past couple of days, I've been squeezing in quick runs before breakfast, but I haven't lifted weights since Saturday morning, when Emma lay sleeping in my bed.

Fuck, I'm thinking about her again.

With effort, I concentrate on my gym routine, pushing myself to the limit with each set. By the time I'm done, I'm drenched with sweat, my muscles shaking from exhaustion. But I'm still restless, my fingers twitching with the urge to reach for my phone and check on her flight.

And maybe on her.

Just a quick text to make sure she's okay in this storm.

But no. That will seem odd since I haven't contacted her since Sunday. At this point, I owe her an explanation, if not an apology, for my disappearance. Not that I'm going to tell her about the private battle I've been fighting; work will suffice as an excuse. And to further smooth over any ruffled feathers, I'm going to ask her out to dinner that same night, so we can pick up where we left off.

All of this once she returns from Florida, naturally. I have to go at least a week without her, to make sure that I can.

To keep myself from doing something stupid, I dive

into my pool and do three dozen laps. Then I shower and head into my kitchen to grab lunch, noticing as I pass by the window that the snowfall has stopped and the snowplows are out in full force.

That's good. Hopefully, that means they'll restore power to those neighborhoods that lost it soon. Especially if Emma—

Stop. Don't fucking think about her.

Opening the fridge, I take out a tuna salad sandwich and sit down at the bar to eat it. As I chew, I glance at the microwave clock.

11:43 a.m.

Emma is definitely awake by now.

Dammit. I really can't control myself, can I? If I'm going to be spending that much time thinking about her, I might as well be with her.

I pause, a half-eaten sandwich in my hand as I process that thought. Maybe I've been going about it all wrong. Maybe by trying not to think about Emma, I've been ensuring that she's at the forefront of my mind. It's like the classic "white bear" experiment in psych class: If you're told not to think about a white bear for a specific period of time, it's going to be the only thing occupying your thoughts.

Yes, of course, that's it. I should've seen it before.

Emma is my white bear.

By trying to resist my addiction to her, I've been making it infinitely worse.

What I need is the complete opposite approach—to gorge myself on her. Not the way I went about it this weekend, to the point of neglecting my work, but in a more controlled manner. And I know exactly how to make it happen.

I have to get her to move in with me.

The solution is so glaringly obvious I don't know why it hasn't occurred to me earlier. It's pretty much Economics 101. The problem right now is that Emma is a scarce resource. With her living in Brooklyn and not wanting to leave her cats alone for long, I simply can't get enough of her in the limited time we have together. No wonder I dropped the ball at work this past weekend: with her leaving for the trip and refusing to spend two nights in a row at my place, it was all but inevitable that I'd focus on her to the exclusion of everything else.

Because that's how scarcity works.

It makes the scarce item extra desirable... practically irresistible.

Of course, living together is a major commitment—which is probably why I didn't think of this before. Actually, no, I did in a way. My desire for her to be at my place all the time was likely my subconscious proposing this very solution. And the more I think about it, the more I like it.

All the things I want—having her with me every night, seeing her as soon as I get home from work—are going to be so much easier if she's living in my penthouse. And commitment-wise, it's not as big of a deal for me as it is for most people. Partially, it's all the financial logistics that make living together a big step.

A dating couple often has to lease or buy a new place, plus cover the moving expenses for one or both individuals. My penthouse, however, is big enough for a family, much less just the two of us, and I can cover Emma's moving costs with my pocket change. I can also lease another apartment for her if we end up going our separate ways in the future.

The only downside as far as I can see is that the cats will move in too, but it's a small price to pay for such a neat solution.

Yes, that's it, I decide, my heartbeat speeding up with dark anticipation. I'm going to finish my lunch, then call her and apologize for my disappearance. Afterward, as soon as the roads are cleared, I'll have Wilson drive me over to her place, and we'll talk before she leaves for her flight—or maybe we'll do so as I give her a ride to the airport, in case she wants to get there early. The trickiest part will be convincing Emma to get over her financial hang-ups, but I have some ideas in that regard.

If all goes well, by this time next week, she'll be safely ensconced in my lair, and I'll have exactly what I want.

Emma always within reach.

CHAPTER FIFTY-ONE

mma

My phone rings as I'm on the floor, wrestling with the zipper of the suitcase. Thinking it's my grandparents, I grab the phone from the bed without looking and hit "Accept"—only to freeze in disbelief, staring at the name on the screen.

It's Marcus.

He's calling me.

Right now.

"Emma?" His voice is rich and deep, audible even without the loudspeaker being on. "Emma, kitten, can you hear me?"

Jumping to my feet, I end the call. My finger hits the red button on the screen without my conscious decision.

Then, blood drumming in my temples, I stare at the phone in my hand.

Did I hallucinate this, or did it really happen?

The phone rings again, Marcus's name appearing on the screen.

I hit "Decline" again, my heart hammering so fast I can hardly think.

What does he want?

Why call me now, after disappearing for days?

I cried last night. At three a.m., when I still couldn't sleep, I cried because it hurt so much, knowing I'd never hear that voice again. And here he is, calling me "kitten" as if nothing happened.

Unless... unless something did happen.

Ice crystals form in my veins, my stomach twisting with an awful fear as it occurs to me that lack of interest is not the only reason someone might disappear.

What if Marcus was in an accident?

What if he's in the hospital, hurt so badly that he couldn't text or talk?

I'm already pressing the button to call him back when his name pops up for the third time.

"Marcus?" I sound semi-hysterical, but I can't help it. The thought of him injured, his big, strong body broken and covered by blood... "Marcus, are you okay?"

"Me?" To my relief, he seems startled. "Yes, of course. I'm working from home today, and there were no downed power lines in Manhattan. How about you? Do you have power and heat?"

For a moment, I have no idea what he's talking about, but then I recall the storm.

Is he for real right now?

I cried over him last night, and we're talking about the fucking *weather*?

"So you're not hurt?" I clarify, my voice tight. "You weren't in the hospital or jail or otherwise unavoidably detained?"

"No, of course not." There's now a wary note in his tone. "But I did have an insane few days at work. I'll tell you all about it when I see you. Speaking of which—"

"Did you fix it?" I interrupt. "The bad trade, I mean?"

He audibly inhales. "Yes, mostly. Listen, Emma, I'm sorry I—"

"Okay, I'm happy for you. Goodbye." I hang up before my voice can break. I'm shaking from a surfeit of adrenaline, my intense relief that he's all right combining with hurt and growing fury. I wasn't angry at him before—only at myself, for being foolish enough to play with fire—but I am now.

It's one thing to barrel into my life, toy with my emotions, and disappear, another to blithely expect a repeat of the same.

The phone rings again, and I send it to voicemail with a jerky swipe across the screen. My pulse is racing so fast that I'm dizzy, my breathing fast and ragged as I throw the phone on the bed and start to pace.

Why did he call? Why now?

Why reappear just when I've become convinced he never would?

Not that it matters.

Whatever his reasons are, I just can't do this. Maybe other women can handle their lovers blowing hot and cold, but I can't. I'm not cut out for these games. Kendall was right: Marcus is not like the harmless boys I've dated. I've only known him for a short time, and he's already turned me inside out. I've never cried over either of my two boyfriends—nor, come to think of it, any other man.

And that's the crux of it, I realize with a twisting pain.

Marcus isn't like any other man I've known. With my exes, I'd been able to keep a certain distance, to give a portion of myself while holding back the rest. Not with him, though. In just a couple of dates and one mindfuck of a weekend, he'd decimated all of my defenses, bulldozing straight into my heart.

Even knowing that what we had was temporary, I fell for him—and I fell hard.

The realization is like a wrecking ball into my stomach.

I'm in love with him.

With Marcus.

That's why it's hurting so much.

Shaken, I sit down on the bed, letting Cottonball climb into my lap as I stare blankly at my phone.

I'm in love with Marcus. Not the handsome billionaire who gave me more orgasms than I can count, but the man who talked with naked gratitude about his second-grade teacher and answered my grandparents' questions with calm patience and respect.

The man who told me that I'm nothing like my mother before sharing about his own painful past.

My phone dings three times, the screen lighting up with incoming texts.

What do you mean, goodbye?

Did you hang up on me?

Emma, call me back, right now. I can explain.

Each word is like a blade puncturing my lungs, stealing my breath with every blow.

Because I want to call him back.

I want it more than anything.

But if I do—if I give in again—the next time he walks away, I'll be left in pieces.

And there will be a next time... because I'm not Emmeline.

I'm not the perfect wife candidate he needs.

CHAPTER FIFTY-TWO

$\mathcal{M}$arcus

I STARE AT MY PHONE, MY HEART THUDDING WITH mingled chagrin and fury.

She hung up on me.

Cut off my apology with a "goodbye" and hung up.

I call back, in case it was a bad connection, but I get voicemail right away.

Swearing under my breath, I fire off three texts and wait.

Nothing.

No moving dots to tell me she's in the process of responding, nothing to give any indication of her intent.

Drawing on every ounce of my patience, I call again.

Voicemail.

Straight to fucking voicemail.

She's either turned off her phone, or she's rejecting my calls.

The phone in my hand feels like a bomb ready to explode—or maybe that's the ball of fury in my chest. Twice she's done this to me now.

Twice she's tried to make me go away.

And the last time, I went. Like a fucking idiot, I walked away, almost letting her ruin what we have.

Well, not this time.

She's not getting on the plane until she takes back that fucking "goodbye."

———

I'VE COOLED DOWN SLIGHTLY BY THE TIME WILSON GETS me through the freshly plowed streets to Brooklyn. In hindsight, maybe not contacting Emma since Sunday wasn't well done of me. It might've been only three days, but if she feels our connection as intensely as I do, it would've seemed infinitely longer.

I'm still pissed she hung up on me, but I can understand it.

In any case, as the car pulls up to the piles of snow left on the curb by the snowplow, I'm fully prepared to grovel. In addition to explaining just how crazy things were at work, I'm going to offer my most sincere apology and swear never to ghost her again. Not that I did—I just held off on contacting her for a bit—but that's how she must've perceived it.

It's the only explanation for that out-of-nowhere "goodbye."

I'm wearing my waterproof boots, but snow gets in through the leg openings as I wade through the thigh-high piles on the way to Emma's door. Ignoring the icy wetness soaking my feet, I ring the doorbell.

Nothing.

No response.

I give it a couple of minutes, then ring the doorbell again.

Still nothing.

Frustrated, I tromp over to the basement window around the corner. As expected, it's covered with snow, so I bend down and begin brushing it away with my bare hands.

She's not freezing me out this easily.

I won't let her.

"Excuse me. What are you doing?"

Startled by the shrill voice, I look up.

A thin older woman bundled in a puffy jacket is standing a few feet away, her gray-blond perm forming a frizzy halo around her head.

"Well?" she demands with a scowl. "You're trespassing on my property. Explain yourself, or I'll call the police."

She must be Emma's landlady.

I stand up, brushing the snow off my palms on my

coat. "Sorry about that. I'm looking for Emma. She's not answering the door for some reason."

She blinks up at me, her frown disappearing. "You're looking for Emma?"

"Yes. Do you know where she is? I can't reach her."

"Oh, I see." She gives me a thorough once-over, her gaze lingering on my Italian coat as if trying to price it out. "Are you her boyfriend or something?"

I reach deep for my patience. "Yes, we're dating. Do you know why she's not answering the door?"

"Well, of course, dear. She left for the airport extra early—you know, because of all the snow on the roads."

Fuck. "When did she leave?"

"I'm not sure. A half hour ago? Twenty minutes, maybe?" She cocks her head. "How long have you two been dating? I'm looking after her cats, and Emma hasn't mentioned a boyfr—"

"It's new," I interrupt, and hurry back to the car before the woman can launch into an interrogation.

There's no time to waste.

I have a stubborn redhead to catch before she gets on the plane.

———

THE TRAFFIC TO THE AIRPORT IS HORRENDOUS, SO BAD that even Wilson's driving skills can't help. After two and a half hours of inching forward a foot a minute, I finally see the cause of the jam: an accident in the left lane. As soon as we pass it, the traffic starts moving more briskly, but the damage is done.

Emma's flight is due to start boarding in a half hour.

Taking a deep breath to combat my frustration, I try calling her again.

Voicemail. Same as the other five times I've tried it.

I text her again.

Nothing. No response.

Fighting the urge to slam the phone against the window, I check the airline app.

The fucking flight is on time, and the boarding starts in twenty-three minutes.

Even if I were at the airport right now, I'd need longer than that to clear security.

She's going to get on the plane with this huge fucking thing unresolved.

Unless...

Without giving myself a chance to think twice, I call my transportation PM.

"Richard, it's Carelli," I say as soon as he picks up. "I need you to get the CEO of United Airlines to call me right now. It's urgent."

I know the portfolio manager is dying to ask why—airline stocks are his province—but he understands the concept of urgency.

Five minutes later, I have United Airlines' CEO on the phone. Six minutes after that, when I hang up and check the app again, the flight is delayed by an hour—and I've promised to abstain from shorting UAL stock for six months, to spare the CEO from explaining to his board why there's a giant hedge fund betting against them.

The traffic clears further as we approach the airport, and I almost feel bad for holding up the plane by an hour. A half hour might've been plenty. When I enter the airport, however, I'm glad for the extra cushion.

The place is overrun with frantic holiday travelers and pissed-off flyers stranded by the storm. It's so bad that by the time I get through the mile-long security line, First Class and Priority boarding for Emma's flight has already begun.

I begin pushing my way through the crowd massed at the gate, searching for her bright hair.

There. A small, curvy figure toward the front of the Economy Class line. Dressed in a pair of jeans and a white hoodie, she's holding a boarding pass in one hand and the handle of a small, raggedy-looking suitcase in the other.

My pulse picks up, my skin prickling with savage heat.

Fuck, I've missed her so much.

I was an idiot to stay away.

Feeling like a hunter honing in on his prey, I head directly for her. Other people must sense my grim determination, because they get out of my way. She's staring straight ahead, so she doesn't see me until I stop next to her.

And by then, it's too late.

"Emma." I reach out to clasp her wrist just as her gaze jumps to my face, gray eyes wide with shock. "We need to talk."

She's so stunned that she lets me pull her out of the crowd without protest. It's only when we're standing by the empty seats in the corner that she finds her tongue. "What are you doing here?" Her voice is higher-pitched than normal. "How did you get through security?"

I release her wrist to pull a boarding pass out of my pocket. "I bought this on the drive over." It's for a flight to Omaha, the only one that had a seat available today. Stuffing it back in my pocket, I say, "Listen, we need to talk about—"

"No, we don't." She tries to step around me, but I step in front of her, blocking her way.

"Yes, we do."

Her face flushes with angry color. "My flight is boarding—"

"They've just started. You have time."

Apparently realizing that I'm not going to budge, she lets go of her suitcase handle and folds her arms across her chest. "Fine. Talk."

Despite the seriousness of the situation, I almost laugh at the scowl she directs at me. With all those curls puffing up, she really does look ridiculously cute when angry. Adorable, in fact. Of course, she also looks adorable when she smiles, and when she blushes, and when she's lying in my bed, all warm and sleepy and satisfied—fuck, I better focus.

"I'm sorry, Emma," I say as sincerely as I can. "I should've called you earlier. I *was* working around the clock, but that's no excuse. I promise you, it won't happen again." I'm about to stop there, but some demon propels me forward, pulling the words out of my mouth. "The truth of the matter is, I felt like we were getting too deep, too fast, and I seized on the emergency at the fund to put a little distance between us. But that was a mistake. I realize that now. I *want* us to get deeper." I take a breath. "In fact, I was thinking that when you get back from this trip, I'd like you to move in to my place."

Her arms drop to her sides as shock wipes away all other expression on her face. "You *what?*" Her voice is barely above a whisper.

"I want you to move in," I repeat, clasping her small hands in each of mine. "I want you to live with me—you and all three of your cats. I know it seems fast, but I've made a living taking calculated risks, and believe me, this one is worthwhile. If you want to keep your apartment for now, I won't object, but I want you with me every night."

Her hands are icy in my grip as she stares up at me. "Why?"

"Because I want you—and you want me too." Isn't it obvious to her? "The chemistry we have is rare, kitten. So rare that I've never felt it before. I want you all the time, to the point of obsession. I've fought against it, tried to resist, but it's useless. I want you—and I don't want the bridges and tunnels getting in the way of our time together. Move in with me, Emma. It makes so much sense."

Out of the corner of my eye, I see two men in business suits whispering to one another a dozen feet away, and a woman pointing a phone at me from behind them. They've probably recognized me from CNBC or someplace. Normally, I'd get annoyed and step away, but this is too important to get distracted.

"Move in with me," I say again when Emma remains silent, staring up at me in mute shock. "It will be good, you know it. I'll take care of all the moving logistics. All you have to do is say yes." And to remind her of just how good it will be, I curve my palm over her jaw and bend my head to kiss her.

I meant for it to be a light, casual kiss, something befitting the public venue, but the moment our lips touch, a violent hunger takes hold of me. Three days I haven't tasted her, three nights I've stayed away. Forgetting all about the onlookers, I wrap my arm around her waist, hauling her closer, and slide my other hand into her hair, gripping the curls to hold her in place as my tongue sweeps into her mouth. She tastes like bubblegum and luscious heat, like all my dreams wrapped in one sweet little package. My blood is like lava in my veins, and my cock throbs in my jeans, desperate for her slick warmth. I can't get enough of her, will never get enough of her, and for the first time, that doesn't scare me.

I'm going to enjoy her, all of her, for as long as this lasts.

A tiny moan escapes her lips, adding to the dark hunger beating at me, and I deepen the kiss, devouring her, sharing her breath. I can feel her small hands gripping my shoulders, can sense her arousal in the way she arches against me, and—

"Last call. Last call for United Flight 1528 to Orlando. All passengers, please proceed to the gate."

The announcer's strident voice is like a snowball hitting me in the face. Jolted out of the trance, I raise my head and, remembering the onlookers, let go of Emma. She steps back shakily, fingers pressed to her swollen lips.

Breathing heavily, we stare at each other. Then her left hand jerkily gropes in the air, landing on the handle of her suitcase.

"I can't," she says raggedly. "Marcus, I'm sorry, but I can't."

A dark mist veils my vision as a dull ringing starts in my ears. I must've misheard what she said. "What the fuck do you mean, you can't?" My voice is low and tight, a warning in every syllable.

Her face twists, her eyes glittering with painful brightness. "I can't do it. I can't... can't move in with you. I'm sorry, Marcus. What I said earlier, I meant it. It's over. I never want to see you again."

And as I reel from the gut-wrenching blow, she rushes around me, dragging her suitcase to the gate.

———

I DON'T KNOW HOW LONG I SIT AT THE GATE, STARING blindly at the door through which she disappeared. All my life, I've set goals and achieved them, refusing to accept failure as an option. I've gone after what I want with determination and ruthlessness, and it's always yielded results.

Except with Emma.

I've fought for her like I have for no other woman, and nothing.

I've offered her everything, and she's thrown it back in my face.

The pain of the rejection is breathtaking, like someone ripped out my lungs. When she told me to leave after the broken door incident, I'd barely known her, and all I'd been after was sex. It had still smarted, being sent away after those scorching hot kisses, but it had been nothing compared to the devastation I feel now.

I'd been so certain she'd accept my proposal to move in that I'd never considered the alternative, much less that she'd refuse to date me at all.

As the shock of her words recedes, the hurt intensifies, and with it comes anger. Dark and hot, it builds within me, until I feel like it will boil me alive. I want to hurt her, to make her feel some of the pain she's inflicted, and at the same time, I just want her.

I miss her so much I'd kill to hold her one more night.

Squeezing my eyes shut, I inhale deeply, trying to think past the bubbling cauldron of tangled emotions, to analyze this as I would any other investment gone bad.

Why? Why did she do this?

I know I haven't misread her, haven't misjudged her response.

She wants me as much as I want her.

She gave herself to me, only to change her mind and run.

There has to be a reason for her actions, something besides my stupid mistake of staying away. The Emma I know is neither shallow nor fickle, and she's certainly not indifferent to me.

Something happened between Sunday and now, something that spooked her.

Yes, that's it. That feels right. Something happened, something that caused her to do this—and I'm not giving up until I get to the bottom of it.

No, fuck that.

I'm not giving up until I fix it.

I want Emma, and I'm not accepting defeat.

Resolved, I launch to my feet and start walking, pulling out my phone as I do.

"Get the jet ready," I order my pilot. "You have an hour. We're flying to Orlando tonight."

And hanging up, I smile darkly.

If Emma thinks I'll let her go this easily, she doesn't know me at all.

She can run, but she won't get far. I won't let her.

Emma, kitten, you're mine. And I'm coming after you with everything I've got.

SNEAK PEEKS

Thank you for reading! If you would consider leaving a review, it would be greatly appreciated. Marcus & Emma's story continues in *Titan's Addiction*.

If you'd like to be notified when my next book is out, please visit www.annazaires.com and sign up for my newsletter.

Ready for my other sizzling stories and don't mind a bit of darkness? Check out:

- ***The Twist Me Trilogy*** – Nora & Julian's dark, twisted love story
- ***The Capture Me Trilogy*** – Lucas & Yulia's breathtaking enemies-to-lovers romance
- ***The Tormentor Mine Series*** – Peter & Sara's intense captive romance
- ***Darker Than Love*** – an addictive standalone

dark romance between Yan and Mink the assassin, cowritten with Charmaine Pauls

- *The Mia & Korum Trilogy* – an epic sci-fi romance with the ultimate alpha male
- *The Krinar Captive* – Emily & Zaron's captive romance, set just before the Krinar Invasion
- *The Krinar Exposé* – my scorching hot collaboration with Hettie Ivers, featuring Amy & Vair—and their sex club games
- *The Krinar World stories* – Sci-fi romance stories by other authors, set in the Krinar world

Prefer action, fantasy, and sci-fi? Check out these collaborations with my hubby, Dima Zales:

- *The Girl Who Sees* – the thrilling tale of Sasha Urban, a stage illusionist who discovers unexpected secret powers
- *Mind Dimensions* – the action-packed urban fantasy adventures of Darren, who can stop time and read minds
- *Transcendence* – the mind-blowing technothriller featuring venture capitalist Mike Cohen, whose Brainocyte technology will forever change the world
- *The Last Humans* – the futuristic sci-fi/dystopian story of Theo, who lives in a world where nothing is as it seems

- **The Sorcery Code** – the epic fantasy adventures of sorcerer Blaise and his creation, the beautiful and powerful Gala

If you like audiobooks, please visit www.an-nazaires.com to check out this series and our other books in audio.

And now, please turn the page for a little taste of *Darker Than Love* and *The Girl Who Sees*.

EXCERPT FROM DARKER THAN LOVE

Once upon a cold, dark night, a Russian killer stole me
from an alley.
I'm dangerous, but he is lethal.
I escaped once.
He won't let me do it twice.

The revenge is his.
The betrayal is mine.
But so are the lies to protect the ones I love.

We're cut from the same twisted cloth. Both merciless.
Both damaged.
In his embrace, I find hell and heaven, his cruelly
tender touch destroying and uplifting me at once.

They say a cat has nine lives, but an assassin has
just one.
And Yan Ivanov now owns mine.

———

"So, how long have you worked at the bar?" the guy with the skull tattoos—the seemingly kinder one—asks when I remove my winter jacket and we sit down in the living room. With its Soviet-style orange wallpaper and brown drapes, this place looks like it hasn't been renovated since the eighties, but the ratty couch we're sitting on is surprisingly comfortable. Maybe I *will* take him up on his offer to sleep here. That is, if they don't kill me and dump my body in the river before sunrise.

I think my captor was just testing my language skills with that proposal, but I can't be sure.

"Mina?" the man prompts, and I realize I zoned out instead of answering his question. Now that some of the adrenaline is fading, the extreme exhaustion is back, muddling my thoughts and slowing my reactions. I want nothing more than to stretch out on this couch and fall asleep, but I might not wake up if I do.

The Russians might decide that what I heard merits killing me rather than just keeping me captive overnight.

"I've worked there for a couple of years," I answer, my voice shaking. It's easy to sound terrified… because I am.

I'm with two men who may want to kill me, and I'm in no state to defend myself.

The only thing that gives me hope is that they haven't already done so. They could've easily murdered me in the alley; they didn't need to bring me here for that. Of course, there's another possibility, one that every woman must consider.

They might be planning to rape me before killing me, in which case bringing me here makes perfect sense.

The thought makes my stomach churn, the old memories threatening to crowd in, but underneath the fear and disgust is something darker, infinitely more fucked up. The brief sizzle of arousal I'd experienced at the bar was nothing compared to how it had felt when the dangerous stranger caged me against the wall, caressing my face with that cruel gentleness. My body —the weak, ruined body I've spent the past year hating —had come to life with such force, it was as if fire-works had ignited under my skin, liquifying my core and burning away my inhibitions.

Was he able to sense it?

Did he know how badly I wanted him to keep touching me?

I think he did. And more than that, I think he wanted to. His eyes—a hard, gem-like green—had watched me with the dark intensity of a predator, taking in every twitch of my lashes, every hitch of my breath. If we'd been alone, he might've kissed me... or killed me on the spot.

It's hard to tell with him.

"Do you like it? Working at the bar, I mean?" the tattooed man asks, bringing my attention back to him. Now *he* is easy to read. There's unmistakable male interest in the way he looks at me, an obvious gleam in his green eyes.

Wait a sec. *Green eyes?*

"Are you two brothers?" I blurt out, then silently curse myself. I'm so tired I'm not thinking straight. The last thing I need is for these two to imagine I'm gathering information on them, or—

"We are." A smile lights up his broad face, softening his harsh features. "Twins, in fact."

Shit. I did *not* need to know that. The next thing I know, he'll be telling me his—

"I'm Ilya, by the way," he says, extending one big paw toward me. "And my brother's name is Yan."

Oh, fuck. I'm so screwed. They *are* going to kill me. "Nice to meet you," I say weakly, shaking his hand on autopilot. My grip is as limp as my voice, but that's okay. I'm playing a damsel in distress, and the more convincing I am, the better.

Too bad the act is mostly real these days.

Ilya squeezes my hand gingerly, as if afraid of inadvertently crushing my bones, and hope nibbles at me. He wouldn't be so careful with me if they were planning to brutally rape and kill me, would he?

As if reading my thoughts, he gives me another smile, an even kinder one this time, and says gruffly, "I'm sorry about my brother. He's used to seeing enemies around every corner. You *will* walk away from this unharmed, I promise you, malyshka. We need to keep you overnight as a precaution, that's all."

Strangely, I believe him. Or at least I believe that *he*

intends me no harm. The jury is still out on his brother —who chooses that exact moment to walk in, carrying a cup of tea in one hand and two beers in the other.

My breath catches in my throat as he—Yan—sets the drinks on the coffee table in front of us and sits down between me and Ilya, unapologetically wedging himself into the too-small space. Instinctively, I scoot to the side, as far as the couch allows, but that's only about six centimeters, and my leg ends up pressed against his, the heat of his body burning me even through the layers of our clothing.

He's shed the suede winter jacket he was wearing earlier, and is now dressed like he was in the bar, in the stylish dress pants and button-up shirt. Except his sleeves are rolled up, exposing muscular forearms lightly dusted with dark hair.

He's strong, this ruthless captor of mine. Strong and superbly fit, his body a deadly weapon under those perfectly tailored clothes.

"Tea," he says in that smooth, deep voice of his, so different from his brother's rougher tones. "As per the princess's request."

"Thank you," I mumble, reaching for the cup. My hands are visibly shaking, my breathing is shallow, and I'm sweating—and none of it is an act. I can smell the clean, masculine scent of his cologne—something sensual and airy, like pepper and sandalwood—and his nearness unsettles me, making my insides riot with a confusing mixture of fear and desire. Even if he wasn't danger personified, I'd be drawn to his magnetic good looks, but knowing what I know about him—about what he does and what he might do to me—I can't control my helpless response to him.

Even my tiredness recedes, leaving me jittery and high, as if I'd downed two liters of espresso.

I'm acutely aware of his gaze on me as I bring the cup to my lips and take a sip, suppressing a hiss at the scalding temperature of the water. I'm trying not to look at him, to just focus on my tea, but I can't help staring at his hands as he reaches over and grabs a beer, then twists off the cap with a practiced motion. His fingers are long and masculine, and though his nails are neatly groomed, the calluses on the edges of his thumbs belie the elegance of his appearance.

This is a man used to doing things with his hands.

Terrible, violent things.

A normal woman would be repulsed by the thought, but my heart hammers faster, and an aching pulse starts between my legs, my underwear dampening with liquid heat. The darkness in him calls to me, making me feel alive in a way I've never experienced before.

It's as if like recognizes like, the wrongness in me craving the same in him.

Ilya picks up the remaining bottle, his hands thick and rough, with a few tattoos on the back. There's no pretense in him, no attempt to hide what he is behind an elegant mask. "To new friends," he says, clinking his bottle against his brother's and then, more gently, against my cup of tea. I risk a glance at him, but catch Yan's hard green gaze instead.

I quickly look away, but not before a betraying flush crawls up my neck and covers my face. "To new friends," I repeat, staring into my cup as if I might see my fate written in the tea leaves. I'm not sure I want Yan to know about the effect he has on me—though he probably already does.

I'm not exactly at the top of my game tonight.

"Yes, to new friends," Yan murmurs, his large hand landing on my knee and squeezing it lightly.

Startled, I look over at him and see him tipping back the beer, his strong throat working as he swallows. It's a strangely sensual sight, and my insides clench as he lowers the bottle and meets my gaze, his eyes darkly intent as the hand on my knee moves a couple of inches up my thigh, closer to where I'm wet and aching.

Oh God.

He knows.

He definitely knows.

"Ilya," he says quietly, still holding my gaze. "Make us a couple of sandwiches, will you? I think Mina here is hungry."

"She is?" Ilya sounds confused as he stands up, and I look up to find him frowning at us—specifically, at my thigh, where Yan's hand is resting so possessively. Slowly, tension permeates his big body, his hands flexing at his sides as his gaze swings to his brother's face.

"I don't think she's hungry," he bites out, his voice low and hard. His eyes cut to me. "Are you, Mina?"

I swallow thickly, unsure of what the right answer is. If I'm reading this right, Yan has just staked some sort of an exclusive claim on me, one that I would reinforce if I admitted to this made-up hunger.

Is that what I want?

To send away the brother who's been nice to me, so I could be alone with the man who proposed dumping my body in the river?

"A... a sandwich would be nice." The words don't seem to belong to me, yet it's my voice saying them, even as my brain scrambles to figure out the implications. "That is, if it wouldn't be too much trouble."

Ilya's mouth thins. "Fine. I'll see what we have in the fridge."

And turning around, he stalks off, leaving me on the couch with his brother.

———

Go to www.annazaires.com to order your copy of *Darker Than Love* today!

EXCERPT FROM THE GIRL WHO SEES BY DIMA ZALES

I'm an illusionist, not a psychic.

Going on TV is supposed to advance my career, but things go wrong.

Like vampires and zombies kind of wrong.

My name is Sasha Urban, and this is how I learned what I am.

————

"I'm not a psychic," I say to the makeup girl. "What I'm about to do is mentalism."

"Like that dreamy guy on the TV show?" The makeup girl adds another dash of foundation to my cheekbones. "I always wanted to do his makeup. Can you also hypnotize and read people?"

I take a deep, calming breath. It doesn't help much. The tiny dressing room smells like hairspray went to war with nail polish remover, won, and took some fumes prisoner.

"Not exactly," I say when I have my anxiety and subsequent irritation under control. Even with Valium in my blood, the knowledge of what's about to come keeps me on the edge of sanity. "A mentalist is a type of stage magician whose illusions deal with the mind. If it were up to me, I'd just go by 'mental illu-sionist.'"

"That's not a very good name." She blinds me with her lamp and carefully examines my eyebrows.

I mentally cringe; the last time she looked at me this way, I ended up getting tortured with tweezers.

She must like what she sees now, though, because she turns the light away from my face. "'Mental illu-sionist' sounds like a psychotic magician," she continues.

"That's why I simply call myself an illusionist." I smile and prepare for the makeup to fall off, like a mask, but it stays put. "Are you almost done?"

"Let's see," she says, waving over a camera guy.

The guy makes me stand up, and the lights on his camera come on.

"This is it." The makeup girl points at the nearby LCD screen, where I have avoided looking until now because it's playing the ongoing show—the source of my panic.

The camera guy does whatever he needs to do, and

the anxiety-inducing show is gone from the screen, replaced by an image of our tiny room.

The girl on the screen vaguely resembles me. The heels make my usual five feet, six inches seem much taller, as does the dark leather outfit I'm wearing. Without heavy makeup, my face is symmetric enough, but my sharp cheekbones put me closer to handsome than pretty—an effect my strong chin enhances. The makeup, however, softens my features, bringing out the blue color of my eyes and highlighting the contrast with my black hair.

The makeup girl went overboard with it—you'd think I'm about to step into a shampoo commercial. I'm not a big fan of long hair, but I keep it that way because when I had it short, people used to mistake me for a teenage boy.

That's a mistake no one would make tonight.

"I like it," I say. "Let's be done. Please."

The TV guy switches the screen back to the live feed of the show. I can't help but glance there, and my already high blood pressure spikes.

The makeup girl looks me up and down and wrinkles her nose minutely. "You insist on that outfit, right?"

The really cool (in my opinion) borderline-dominatrix getup I've donned today is a means to add mystique to my onstage persona. Jean Eugène Robert-Houdin, the famous nineteenth-century French conjuror who inspired Houdini's stage name, once said, "A magician is an actor playing the part of a magician." When I saw Criss

Angel on TV, back in elementary school, my opinion of what a magician should look like was formed, and I'm not too proud to admit that I see influences of his goth rock star look in my own outfit, especially the leather jacket.

"How marvelous," says a familiar voice with a sexy British accent. "You didn't look like this at the restaurant."

Pivoting on my high heels, I come face to face with Darian, the man I met two weeks ago at the restaurant where I do table-to-table magic—and where I'd impressed him enough to make this unimaginable opportunity a reality.

A senior producer on the popular *Evening with Kacie* show, Darian Rutledge is a lean, sharply dressed man who reminds me of a hybrid between a butler and James Bond. Despite his senior role at the studio and the frown lines that crisscross his forehead, I'd estimate his age to be late twenties—though that could be wishful thinking, given that I'm only twenty-four. Not that he's traditionally handsome or anything, but he does have a certain appeal. For one thing, with his strong nose, he's the rare guy who can pull off a goatee.

"I wear Doc Martens at the restaurant," I tell him. The extra inches of my footwear lift me to his eye level, and I can't help but get lost in those green depths. "The makeup was forced on me," I finish awkwardly.

He smiles and hands me a glass he's been holding. "And the result is lovely. Cheers." He then looks at the makeup girl and the camera guy. "I'd like to speak with

Sasha in private." His tone is polite, yet it carries an unmistakable air of imperiousness.

The staff bolt out of the room. Darian must be an even bigger shot than I thought.

On autopilot, I take a gulp of the drink he handed to me and wince at the bitterness.

"That's a Sea Breeze." He gives me a megaton smile. "The barman must've gone heavy on the grapefruit juice."

I take a polite second sip and put the drink on the vanity behind me, worried that the combination of vodka and Valium might make me woozier than I already am. I have no idea why Darian wants to speak to me alone; anxiety has already turned my brain to mush.

Darian regards me in silence for a moment, then pulls out a phone from his tight jeans' pocket. "There's a bit of unpleasantness we must discuss," he says, swiping across the screen of the phone before handing it to me.

I take the phone from him, gripping it tight so it doesn't slip out of my sweaty palms.

On the phone is a video.

I watch it in stunned silence, a wave of dread washing over me despite the medication.

The video reveals my secret—the hidden method behind the impossible feat I'm about to perform on *Evening with Kacie*.

I'm so screwed.

"Why are you showing me this?" I manage to say after I regain control of my paralyzed vocal cords.

Darian gently takes the phone back from my shaking hands. "You know that thing you went on about at the restaurant? How you're just pretending to be a psychic and that it's all tricks?"

"Right." I frown in confusion. "I never said I do anything for real. If this is about exposing me as a fraud—"

"You misunderstand." Darian grabs my discarded drink and takes a long, yet somehow elegant sip. "I have no intention of showing that video to anyone. Quite the contrary."

I blink at him, my brain clearly overheated from the adrenaline and lack of sleep.

"I know that as a magician, you don't like your methods known." His smile turns oddly predatory.

"Right," I say, wondering if he's about to make a blackmail-style indecent proposal. If he did, I would reject it, of course—but on principle, not because doing something indecent with a guy like Darian is unthinkable.

When you haven't gotten any for as long as I haven't, all sorts of crazy scenarios swirl through your head on a regular basis.

Darian's green gaze turns distant, as though he's trying to look through the nearby wall all the way into the horizon. "I know what you're planning on saying after the big reveal," he says, focusing back on me. In an eerie parody of my voice, he enunciates, "'I'm not a prophet. I use my five senses, principles of deception, and showmanship to create the illusion of being one.'"

My eyebrows rise so high my heavy makeup is in danger of chipping. He didn't approximate what I was about to say—he nailed it word for word, even copying the intonation I've practiced.

"Oh, don't look so surprised." He places the now-empty glass back on the vanity dresser. "You said that exact thing at the restaurant."

I nod, still in shock. Did I actually tell him this before? I don't remember, but I must have. Otherwise, how would he know?

"I paraphrased something another mentalist says," I blurt out. "Is this about giving him credit?"

"Not at all," Darian says. "I simply want you to omit that nonsense."

"Oh." I stare at him. "Why?"

Darian leans against the vanity and crosses his legs at the ankles. "What fun is it to have a fake psychic on the show? Nobody wants to see a fake."

"So you want me to act like a fraud? Pretend to be for real?" Between the stage fright, the video, and now this unreasonable demand, I'm just about ready to turn tail and run, even if I end up regretting it for the rest of my life.

He must sense that I'm about to lose it, because the predatory edge leaves his smile. "No, Sasha." His tone is exaggeratedly patient, as though he's talking to a small child. "I just want you to not say anything. Don't claim to be a psychic, but don't deny it either. Just avoid that topic altogether. Surely you can be comfortable with that."

"And if I'm not, you would show people the video? Reveal my method?"

The very idea outrages me. I might not want people to think I'm a psychic, but like most magicians, I work hard on the secret methods for my illusions, and I intend to take them to my grave—or write a book for magicians only, to be published posthumously.

"I'm sure it wouldn't come to that." Darian takes a step toward me, and the bergamot scent of his cologne teases my flaring nostrils. "We want the same thing, you and I. We want people to be enthralled by you. Just don't make any claims one way or another—that's all I ask."

I take a step back, his proximity too much for my already shaky state of mind. "Fine. You have a deal." I swallow thickly. "You never show the video, and I don't make any claims."

"There's one more thing, actually," he says, and I wonder if the indecent proposal is about to drop.

"What?" I dampen my lips nervously, then notice him looking and realize I'm just making an inappropriate pass at me that much more likely.

"How did you know what card my escort was thinking of?" he asks.

I smile, finally back in my element. He must be talking about my signature Queen of Hearts effect—the one that blew away everyone at his table. "That will cost you something extra."

He arches an eyebrow in silent query.

"I want the video," I say. "Email it to me, and I'll give you a hint."

Darian nods and swipes a few times on his phone.

"Done," he says. "Do you have it?"

I take out my own phone and wince. It's Sunday night, right before the biggest opportunity of my life, yet I have four messages from my boss.

Deciding to find out what the manipulative bastard wants later, I go into my personal email and verify that I have the video from Darian.

"Got it," I say. "Now about the Queen of Hearts thing... If you're as observant and clever as I think you are, you'll be able to guess my method tonight. Before the main event, I'm going to perform that same effect for Kacie."

"You sneaky minx." His green eyes fill with mirth. "So you're not going to tell me?"

"A magician must always be at least one step ahead of her audience." I give him the aloof smile I've perfected over the years. "Do we have a deal or not?"

"Fine. You win." He gracefully sits on the swivel chair where I went through my eyebrow torture. "Now, tell me, why did you look so spooked when I first came in?"

I hesitate, then decide it will do no harm to admit the truth. "It's because of that." I point at the screen where the live feed from the show is still rolling. At that precise moment, the camera pans to the large studio audience, all clapping at some nonsense the hostess said.

Darian looks amused. "Kacie? I didn't think that Muppet could frighten anyone."

"Not her." I wipe my damp palms on my leather jacket and learn that it's not the most absorbent of surfaces. "I'm afraid of speaking in front of people."

"You are? But you said you want to be a TV magician, and you perform at the restaurant all the time."

"The biggest audience at the restaurant is three or four people at a dinner table," I say. "In that studio over there, it's about a hundred. The fear kicks in after the numbers get into the teens."

Darian's amusement seems to deepen. "What about the millions of people who'll be watching you at home? Are you not worried about them?"

"I'm more worried about the studio audience, and yes, I understand the irony." I do my best not to get defensive. "For my own TV show, I'd do street magic with a small camera crew—that wouldn't trigger my fear too much."

Fear is actually an understatement. My attitude toward public speaking confirms the many studies showing that this particular phobia tends to be more pervasive than the fear of death. Certainly, I'd rather be eaten by a shark than have to appear in front of a big crowd.

After Darian called me about this opportunity, I learned how big the show's studio audience is, and I couldn't sleep for three days straight—which is why I feel like a Guantanamo Bay detainee on her way to enhanced interrogation. It's even worse than when I pulled a string of all-nighters for my stupid day job, and at the time, I thought it was the most stressful event of my life.

My roommate Ariel didn't give me her Valium lightly; it took a ton of persuasion on my part, and she only gave in when she could no longer bear to look at my miserable face.

Darian distracts me from my thoughts by fiddling with his phone again.

"This should inspire you," he says as soothing piano chords ring out of the tinny phone speaker. "It's a song about a man in a similar situation to yours."

It takes me a few moments to recognize the tune. Given that I last heard it when I was little, I up my estimate of Darian's age by an extra few years. The song is "Lose Yourself," from the *8 Mile* movie, where Eminem's character gets a chance to be a rapper. I guess my situation is similar enough, this being my big shot at what I want the most.

Unexpectedly, Darian begins to rap along with Eminem, and I fight an undignified giggle as some of the tension leaves my body. Do all British rappers sound as proper as the Queen?

"Now there's that smile," Darian says, unaware or uncaring that my grin is at his expense. "Keep it up."

He grabs the remote and turns up the volume on the TV in time for me to hear Kacie say, "Our hearts go out to the victims of the earthquake in Mexico. To donate to the Red Cross, please call the number at the bottom of the screen. And now, a quick commercial—"

"Sasha?" A man pops his head into the dressing room. "We need you on stage."

"Break a leg," Darian says and blows me an air kiss.

"In these shoes, I just might." I mime catching the kiss, throwing it on the floor, and stabbing it with my stiletto.

Darian's laugh grows distant as my guide and I leave the room, heading down a dark corridor. As we approach our destination, our steps seem to get louder, echoing in tune with my accelerating heartbeat. Finally, I see a light and hear the roar of the crowd.

This is how people going to face a firing squad must feel. If I weren't medicated, I'd probably bolt, my dreams be damned. As is, the guide has to grab my arm and drag me toward the light.

Apparently, the commercial break will soon be over.

"Go take a seat on the couch next to Kacie," someone whispers loudly into my ear. "And breathe."

My legs seem to grow heavier, each step a monumental effort of will. Hyperventilating, I step onto the platform where the couch is located and take tiny steps, trying to ignore the studio audience.

My dread is so extreme that time flows strangely; one moment I'm still walking, the next I'm standing by the couch.

I'm glad Kacie has her nose in a tablet. I'm not ready

to exchange pleasantries when I have to do something as difficult as sitting down.

Knees shaking, I lower myself onto the couch like a fakir onto a bed of nails (which is not a feat of supernatural pain resistance, by the way, but the application of scientific principles of pressure).

Time distortion must've happened again, because the music signifying the commercial break comes to an abrupt close, and Kacie looks up from her tablet, her overly full lips stretching into a smile.

The pounding of my pulse is so loud in my ears I can't hear her greeting.

This is it.

I'm about to have a panic attack on national TV.

Go to www.dimazales.com to order your copy of *The Girl Who Sees* today!

ABOUT THE AUTHOR

Anna Zaires is a *New York Times, USA Today,* and #1 international bestselling author of sci-fi romance and contemporary dark erotic romance. She fell in love with books at the age of five, when her grandmother taught her to read. Since then, she has always lived partially in a fantasy world where the only limits were those of her imagination. Currently residing in Florida, Anna is happily married to Dima Zales (a science fiction and fantasy author) and closely collaborates with him on all their works.

To learn more, please visit www.annazaires.com.

Made in the USA
Monee, IL
14 July 2020

36517061R10197